**The lights began to flash and an alarm sounded,
so loud that I instinctively clamped my hands over my ears.**

"What's happening?" I yelled.

Rogan's gaze darted around the room.

And then I heard something else. A metallic, computer-generated voice that seemed to come from every direction.

"*Sixty...*" it announced. "*Fifty-nine...fifty-eight...fifty-seven...*"

Rogan began struggling hard against his chain. "Kira, throw me that key. Right now! Do it!"

"Why? What's happening?"

"It's the countdown!"

Okay, I'd figured out that much all by myself. If I hadn't been scared out of my mind, I'd have taken the time to roll my eyes at him.

"Which means what?"

He craned his neck to look wildly around the empty room as the lights continued to flash, plunging us into darkness and light like a strobe light in a dance club. "We've wasted too much time."

"*Fifty-two...fifty-one...fifty...*"

"What happens when it gets to zero?"

He stared across the room at me, his gaze panicked. "When it gets to zero, *we die.* Do you understand? If you don't throw me that key, in less than fifty seconds we're both going to die!"

COUNT DOWN

MICHELLE ROWEN

Refreshed version, newly revised by author

WITHDRAWN

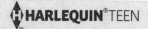

Recycling programs
for this product may
not exist in your area.

ISBN-13: 978-0-373-21090-9

COUNTDOWN

This is the revised text of a work first published as COUNTDOWN under the
pseudonym Michelle Maddox by Dorchester Publishing Co., Inc., in 2008.

HARLEQUIN®TEEN

™ www.HarlequinTEEN.com

Printed in U.S.A.

COUNT DOWN

LEVEL

1

IT'S CALLED NYCTOPHOBIA. I LOOKED IT UP once. It's the official term for an abnormal and persistent fear of the dark. I've had it ever since my parents and sister were murdered during an in-home burglary while I hid under my bed.

In the dark I couldn't see anything; all I could hear was the screaming.

And then the silence.

So, yeah. I've been scared like hell of the dark ever since. Go figure.

Unfortunately, that's where I found myself when I opened my eyes. Frankly, I didn't remember closing them. I'd been in the mall, I remembered that much. I'd just lifted a new pair of shoes—my old pair was worn out since all I do is walk everywhere in the city, day in and day out. This pair was nice. Red. With strong laces that, if necessary, could double as a weapon.

The streets were tough sometimes. Especially at night. *Especially* in the dark.

Like right now.

But this wasn't the street, I knew that much. I was inside. Somewhere.

Choking panic began to flood my body. I knew freaking out wouldn't help, but sometimes you can't stop yourself—or reason with yourself—when you're in the process of freaking out.

I felt a pinch at my right wrist and reached over with my other hand, trying to feel my way through the inky blackness. It was a metal cuff. Attached to a chain. Attached to the smooth, cold metal wall behind me.

What the hell is going on?

Had I been caught shoplifting? Was this prison? I wracked my brain to try to remember being arrested, but came up blank. No, I'd grabbed the shoes, shoved them under my coat, and left the store to go into the half-abandoned mall where I'd put them on and thrown my old ones in a garbage can. And then…*then* what happened?

I remembered wanting to grab some food. I'd had two bucks to my name, so I'd figured I could buy a small order of French fries at one of the few restaurants that were still open. That would last me a day before my stomach would start complaining again.

Had I even made it to the food court?

I couldn't have. I was still hungry. Starving. My body felt as if it was eating itself, but that was a bit of an exaggeration, I guess. Yesterday I'd had an entire meal. Ordered off the menu even, and then tried to skip out before the bill came. The owner of the diner had caught me, reprimanded me, and I'd figured that that was it—he'd call the cops.

Instead, he'd taken pity on me and made me wash dishes.

It was a humbling experience, but I'd had a lot of those since my family died.

In the end, I appreciated his kindness. Washing dishes was a whole lot better than getting arrested.

Okay, breathe, Kira, I told myself. And I did. I took a deep breath in through my nose and let it out through my mouth. My heart thudded hard in my ears.

Why couldn't I remember what had happened after I'd taken the shoes? Damn it. And where was I?

I seriously had to calm down. This wasn't helping.

I took another breath in and out and forced myself to listen. For anything. There had to be something other than this total silence that told me absolutely nothing helpful.

And then I heard...*something.* I pushed my fears out of the way as best I could and strained my ears.

Breathing. I could hear soft breathing.

Someone else is in the room.

This realization did not ease my mind. Just the opposite. The thought that somebody was in the darkness with me scared me enough that I almost started to cry.

But I was tough now. At least that's what I tried to tell myself every morning when I woke up to face another day. This shouldn't be any different.

"H-h-hello?" *Stuttering does not help the situation,* I thought. "Who's there?"

The breathing hitched. I heard something heavy shift against the floor about fifteen feet away.

Then the something spoke. "Wh...what the hell?"

A guy's voice. His words were gruff and raspy as if he'd just woken from a deep sleep.

"Who are you?" I ventured again.

Why did I sound so weak? I hated that.

He cleared his throat and groaned. "Shit."

Well, he did seem to have a fine command of the English language.

I strained to see something, but there was only black. "Tell me who you are."

There was a pause, and then another groan. It actually sounded like a moan of pain as I heard him shift position again.

I frowned. "Hey, are you okay?"

He snorted. "Fantastic. I'm just fantastic, thanks for asking. And you?"

Sarcasm. Yeah, I recognized that.

"I've been better, actually."

Chains rattled. Not mine, so that meant that this guy was also restrained. But why?

"I'm Rogan," he said after a moment. "So pleased to meet you."

"Where are we?"

"I tell you my name and you don't reciprocate? Didn't your mother teach you any manners?"

"My mother's dead."

That shut him up. Momentarily. "Sorry to hear that."

"It was a long time ago."

"Doesn't make it any easier."

Very true. Two years. Felt like forever—yet, at the same time, it felt like only yesterday. "My name's Kira."

"Well, Kira, where we are is anyone's guess."

I pressed back against the hard wall.

We could be anywhere, and there wasn't a damn thing to give me a clue where that was. Except for the main drags, the city was so vacant that we could be in any one of dozens of abandoned warehouses or factories. And nobody would ever find us.

I'd heard about kids who'd vanished from the streets never to be seen again. I was sure they weren't stories with happy endings.

"What's the last thing you remember?" I asked. "Who brought you here? Are you chained, too?"

"I don't know who brought me here. And, yeah, I'm locked up real tight."

"Who would do this?" My voice caught on the words.

"Try to relax."

"I'm relaxed."

"Doesn't sound like it to me."

I banged the back of my head lightly against the metal wall and hugged my knees in close to my chest. "You sound relaxed enough for the both of us."

"What can I say? So far this is a lot better than where I was scheduled to go in a few days."

"Oh? And where's that?"

He was silent for a moment. "You really want to know?"

Not really. I didn't care. "Sure."

There was another lengthy pause. "Saradone."

My blood ran cold. Saradone was the maximum security prison just outside the city limits. Only the worst criminals were sent there; some for life, most for death. Horrible people who'd done horrible things. Luckily, they didn't put girls who stole shoes there...yet.

He laughed at my answering silence. "Guess you've heard of it."

I was in the same room with somebody bound for Saradone—so that meant he was dangerous. Criminally dangerous. Panic returned to swirl through me, constricting my chest, my breath.

Both of us were chained. What was this? What was going on?

A cold trickle of sweat slid down my back.

"Why were you going there?" I tried to make the question sound flippant, as if I was making conversation about the weather.

"My days at St. Augustine's end in a couple days when I turn eighteen."

St. Augustine's. That name I also knew. It was a juvenile detention hall located on the west side of the city. If I ever got arrested, that might be where I ended up.

I'd heard that it was hell.

I hesitated to ask, but couldn't help myself. "What were you at St. Augustine's for?"

"Murder," he answered simply.

"Oh." My stomach churned as I tested the chains again. They were too strong. I wasn't going anywhere. "Was it self-defense?"

"No." There was a sharp edge to his voice now. "But what do you care?"

"I don't."

But I did. Of course, I did. I cared because I was trapped in this room with an admitted murderer—stuck in the dark with him, just as I'd been when my family was murdered.

Maybe I was just having a really bad dream. Maybe I'd fallen and hit my head in the mall and was passed out cold in front of the understaffed burger place in the food court. Maybe some gorgeous rich kid would find me. He'd fall instantly in love with me, kiss me like Prince Charming did with Snow

White, wake me from my deep sleep, and we'd ride away into the sunset, away from my past and into a bright, exciting future, just the two of us.

I blinked against the darkness.

No, I was awake. Definitely awake.

Too bad.

"You're quiet all of a sudden," Rogan said. "Don't want to talk anymore?"

"Not particularly."

"Why not? Because you're scared of me now?"

Pretty much, but I wasn't going to let him know that if I could help it.

"No. Mostly because I've decided that you don't know anything that can help me."

"Doesn't mean you have to be rude."

"Rude?" I felt a flare of anger and then settled back, trying to remain calm. My ass hurt from sitting on the hard metal floor so I shifted to cross my legs. "Yeah, I'm so rude. Sorry about that. I guess you've been treated so nice at St. Augustine's that my behavior's a real shocker. Besides, sounds to me like you deserve rude. Or worse."

He was silent so long that I felt even more uncomfortable than I had been to start with.

"And are you so innocent if you're here with me right now?" His words were clipped, sounding as if I'd struck a nerve. "What did you say your name was...Kerry?"

"*Kira,*" I corrected. What a dick this guy was. "I'm not innocent, but I know I won't end up at Saradone."

"Don't be so sure."

I guess I could thank this jerk for keeping my mind off my

fear of the dark. He was getting me angry enough that fear had moved a couple notches down the list.

I chewed my bottom lip. "I haven't murdered anybody."

"Not yet."

"Not ever."

"Yeah, we'll see about that."

"What's that supposed to mean?"

"They've got you now. They'll make you do whatever they want you to do, and don't kid yourself. You'll do it."

"They? Who are *they?*"

Rogan went silent.

My heart pounded in my ears. "You can't just say something like that and not say anything else. Who are they?"

"The ones who put you here. Who put *me* here."

"I thought you said you didn't know who put you here?"

"I have an idea."

"Want to share?"

"Maybe not. You're not all that nice." It sounded as if he was smiling now. Was he mocking me?

"I'm not all that nice?" I repeated.

"Is this a surprise to you? Do you normally charm the pants off the boys you meet? Because you're failing big-time with me."

"Who put us in here?" I said it flatly. I wanted him to realize I wasn't joking around. If he didn't tell me, then I was going to scream and keep screaming until they—whoever *they* were—dragged me out of there.

"They gave me a choice," he said after a moment. "Go to prison for the rest of my life, or come with them and play their sick little game. At least here I might have a chance. A small one, but a chance. As soon as I agreed, they knocked me out.

And then I woke up a few minutes ago to have this fascinating discussion with you. And…and I think they did something to me when I was unconscious. To my shoulder. I'm hurt pretty badly, but I'm not sure how. Or why. Probably to slow me down." He snorted. "Playing fair isn't exactly their style."

"I didn't agree to this." I pulled at the chain until my wrist felt raw. "I want to leave."

"I'm sure they'll let you. Just like that. Sure."

"You said they gave you a choice. Why didn't they give me one?"

"I have no idea." He paused. "You said your mother was dead?"

"Yeah."

"And the rest of your family?"

"All dead." My voice broke as I said it.

Silence again. "So you're on your own."

"When I have to be." He didn't deserve more of an answer than that.

I'd been on my own for the past two years, since I was fourteen. Before that, I was safe and relatively happy and free to do what I wanted with the love of my family to support me. But once they were gone, I had nothing.

The courts had wanted to put me into foster care, but I'd run instead. A friend of mine had gone into foster care a few years ago, and I never heard from her again. Not even an email.

"Why would they pick you," Rogan said, but it sounded more like he was talking to himself than to me, "other than the fact that you have no family? What did you do?"

I hissed out a sigh of exasperation. "At the risk of sounding like I'm repeating myself, who are *they?*"

"You haven't murdered before…so that's out. Are you…" He paused and then laughed softly. "Of course. You're a thief, aren't you?"

I let the darkness answer the question for me.

"A female thief without a family. Perfect." He let out a long, shuddery breath. "Well, thief-girl, I have to admit that I'm not feeling so great over here. Whatever they did to me…I don't think they'll have to worry about me finishing off my sentence. An eye for an eye and all that."

I licked my dry lips. "You think you're dying."

"Feels like it."

"Why do you sound so calm?"

"Because I'm not an idiot. There's no escape. We're both going to die."

"Shut up. There's a way out, I know there is."

Just as I said it, light flooded the room, blinding me. Ironic. Didn't these people believe in happy mediums?

I rubbed my eyes, which had started to water at the unexpected light. I blinked at the room as my vision slowly came into focus.

I sat against the wall in an entirely silver room. Floors, ceiling, walls, all made from smooth, cold metal. I'd never seen anything like it. The silver metal band that circled my wrist was attached to a silver chain secured to the wall. It was all very bland, very clinical, clean and pristine.

Almost all.

My gaze moved to the other side of the room and locked with that of the most dangerous-looking boy I'd ever seen in my life.

He stared back at me with a half smirk. His hair, plastered

across his forehead, was dark and unkempt. He wore a shirt that might have once been white but was now torn and dirty.

A dark and angry red stain near his left shoulder stood out as the only color in the room. No, scratch that. His eyes. They were blue-green—the color of a tropical ocean and surprisingly jarring in their intensity.

There was a scar on his face that ran from the top of his left eye down to his cheek like an angry exclamation point. It was still reddish, as if it had healed recently. It didn't do much to take away from his looks—which were incredible. Clean him up and I'd have to guess he'd be painfully handsome.

He wore faded jeans, also stained and dirty, and scuffed black boots with untied laces. A silver shackle led from his right wrist to the chain to the wall behind him.

Despite the good looks beneath the grime, he *looked* like a murderer. Like trouble. Like nobody I wanted to be trapped in a room with now or anytime soon. I was almost sorry that the lights had come on.

"You're prettier than I expected," he said, keeping me locked in his oddly hypnotic gaze.

I swallowed. It was exactly what I was thinking about him, too. "Well, you have been stuck in juvie for a while."

He smiled. His teeth were white and straight, which struck me as odd for a confessed killer. Though, I suppose it was a bit of a cliché to expect him to have broken, rotting teeth—especially at his age.

"True. Sorry I look like hell." His smile widened. "They didn't even let me have a shower before they knocked me out and dragged my ass here."

"Forget it."

His gaze slid down the rest of me, black tank top, khaki

cargo pants and my new red shoes. My face warmed at his bla-
tant appraisal, until I saw his eyes move away from my body
and toward my side. He frowned. I looked to the floor on my
right and gasped.

There was a key lying there, only an arm's reach away.

2

"TRY IT," ROGAN PROMPTED.

I was way ahead of him. I'd already grabbed the key and found the small keyhole on my shackle, my heart drumming loud in my ears.

I frowned when it didn't fit. I tried again. Why didn't it fit?

I looked over at Rogan, who stared at me with a deep frown.

Something sparkled next to him, and I pointed at it. Another key. He grabbed it and tried his lock.

Nothing.

I heard a whirring and looked up toward the sound. At the top of the far wall to the left near the ceiling, a small shutter had opened and what looked like a security camera—only more modern, very sleek and silver—emerged.

"What is that?" I asked.

He looked up at it grimly. "Must be show time."

I clenched the key so tightly that I knew it would leave an impression on my fingertips. "Why would they be recording us?"

"Because they like to watch."

"Watch what?" I snapped. "Can you stop being so damn vague and just tell me what's going on?"

But he wasn't looking at me, he was looking at my key. "I'm going to take a guess here that your key fits my lock and my key fits your lock."

I frowned. "How do you know that?"

"I didn't say I *know.* I said I *guess.*" The nearly eighteen-year-old murderer smirked at me again. "Try to pay attention, would you?"

I gritted my teeth. "I don't like you."

"My heart is breaking. Now, why don't you be a good girl and throw that key over here so I can test my theory?"

"Screw you."

He shrugged and then grimaced as if the wound on his shoulder caused him massive pain. "We can do that, too, if you like, but I'll need to be unchained first. Then again, we can bring the chains with us if you're into that sort of thing."

I gave him the look I always gave to guys who tried to pick me up. The losers and the freaks who thought sex was a sport and I was just somebody to score with. In the circles I'd hung out in lately, boys like that were the norm rather than the exception. All the good ones seemed to have left the city long ago. And you know what? With some of them, I played it as good as I could. I knew that I wasn't ugly—that despite living on the streets a little more than I'd like, I'd developed a good body and a nice face that boys—and men—seemed to find attractive. I played them, and then I took their wallets when they weren't looking.

So sue me. But not one of them had gotten in my pants yet.

This boy didn't have a wallet as far as I could see. He had nothing I wanted. Nothing except that key.

I shifted my position into something a little more alluring. Chest out. Stomach sucked in. I raised an eyebrow and forced a smile to my lips. "Why don't you throw me your key first?"

Not too much. Let's not be obvious here, okay?

He studied me. I still wasn't letting him have what he wanted, but the vibe I was giving off was much more...*friendly*. I mean, the guy had been in a detention hall I'd heard was worse than anything I could imagine—and with his record, I doubted he'd been in a coed wing. He had to be horny as hell by now, right? I could work with that. He should be putty in my hands.

Dirty, murdering putty. With nice eyes and—I hated to admit it—a sexy smile. An unusual combination, to say the least.

He licked his lips. "Oh, you're good. If I didn't feel like my arm was about to fall off, you might have me, but pain *does* help me focus. Your key. Throw it to me. *Then* I'll throw you mine."

My fake smile slipped. "And when I throw you my key, how do I know you'll give me mine?"

"You'll just have to trust me."

"Give me one good reason why I should."

He stared at me and then laughed that short, humorless laugh. "I'm coming up blank here."

"Then I guess we're both out of luck."

"I guess so." An unpleasant smile twisted his mouth, then he closed his eyes, and pain shadowed his face.

Damn. I didn't want to feel sympathy for this guy. He was a

murderer, just like the bastard who had killed my family. But if that blood was any indication, he was seriously wounded.

Then again, how did I know for sure? Maybe it was a trick. Maybe he was acting like he was hurt. After all, that camera had just appeared out of nowhere. What had he said a minute ago? *Show time?*

The camera whirred again as it changed direction to point at Rogan.

He pried his eyes open and looked up at it.

Then he gave it the finger.

Suddenly the lights began to flash, and an alarm sounded, so loud that I instinctively clamped my hands over my ears.

"What's happening?" I yelled.

Rogan's gaze darted around the room.

And then I heard something else. A metallic, computer-generated voice that seemed to come from every direction.

"60..." it announced. *"59...58...57..."*

Rogan began struggling hard against his chain. "Kira, throw me that key. Right now! Do it!"

"Why? What's happening?"

"It's the countdown!"

Okay, I'd figured out that much all by myself. If I hadn't been scared out of my mind, I'd have taken the time to roll my eyes at him.

"Which means what?"

He craned his neck to look wildly around the empty room as the lights continued to flash, plunging us into darkness and light like a strobe light in a dance club. "We've wasted too much time."

"52...51...50..."

"What happens when it gets to zero?"

He stared across the room at me, his gaze panicked. "When it gets to zero, *we die*. Do you understand? If you don't throw me that key, in less than fifty seconds we're both going to die!"

My stomach dropped. "What do you mean, die? How do you know that?"

"There's no time to explain. I know you don't trust me, but, please. Just do what I say so we can live."

I stared at him. No. I couldn't do it. I couldn't trust him. If I threw him the key, he'd unlock himself and leave me here. He was a murderer. He'd admitted it. He'd told me that there was no reason he could give me to trust him. And I *didn't* trust him. I didn't trust anyone but myself.

"Come on!" he yelled.

"35…34…33…"

I stared blindly around at the metal-walled room. Who would want to kill us? It didn't make any sense. None of this made any sense.

Rogan swore so loudly it hurt my ears over the alarm and countdown.

"Fine!" he yelled. "Take it! You go first."

He threw his key at me, and it landed by my feet. Without thinking twice I grabbed it and worked it into my lock. The shackles popped open and I scrambled to stand up.

Just as my bindings unlocked, a door to my left swung open into more darkness. I eyed it before I took a step toward it.

"Wait—" Rogan held a hand out to me. "What about our deal?"

I hesitated. He was a murderer bound for maximum security prison the second he turned eighteen. I should leave him here, wherever *here* was.

"19…18…17…"

"Forget it. Leave me. Whatever." He slumped against the wall and looked away, his chest heaving with each labored breath. He wasn't going to beg.

He'd given up just like that?

He thought he was going to die—honestly, truly die—when the countdown ended. I'd seen it in his eyes. You couldn't fake that. Whether it was true or not didn't matter. He *believed* it.

I swore under my breath and ran back to grab my key off the ground. I sank down beside him and worked the key into his lock. It snapped open. I quickly got to my feet and turned to go, glancing over my shoulder at him. He was struggling to get to his feet. It was the shoulder wound—it slowed him down. He could barely walk.

"10...9...8..."

I turned back and grabbed him around the waist, practically pulling him through the room with me. He leaned heavily against me.

"4...3...2...1."

We were through the door on the last count and it slammed shut behind us with a deafening, metallic crunch that shook the ground.

Rogan groaned and collapsed to his knees. I frowned and reached toward him to touch his shoulder to find it was knotted with tension.

"You're seriously hurt."

He blinked at me. "You thought I was faking?"

"I wasn't sure."

"Thanks for the help."

I was about to say "anytime," which would have been the typical response, but I stopped myself. There was no "anytime" with Rogan. This was it. We'd escaped the room and I was so out of there.

However, I still wasn't sure where we were.

We'd entered another room. This one didn't look much more interesting than the first one, but I could see the outline of a door with no handle. I walked to it and kicked it as hard as I could.

"Let me out of here!" I yelled. My voice echoed against the metal walls.

"That's not going to do anything," Rogan said.

"We'll see about that." I kicked the door again. And again. I finally stopped when my leg started to hurt and the door didn't look any worse for wear. I hadn't even made a dent.

Panting and sweating buckets, I turned toward Rogan and thrust a finger in his direction. "Start talking. I want to know everything you know."

He blinked at me, holding one hand against his wound. "You came back for me."

"Yeah. I did. Don't make me regret my decision."

"I thought you'd leave me to die."

"You still think we would have died if we stayed in there."

He nodded. "The grinding noise was the ceiling slamming down on the floor. I'm just guessing that might have killed us on contact."

I stared at him blankly.

"How do you—?"

Before I could finish, I was interrupted.

"Congratulations, Rogan and Kira, on successfully completing level one of Countdown."

The disembodied voice came through unseen speakers, just as the countdown had. It was almost as if the voice was inside my head. I couldn't pinpoint the exact direction, and the sound of it physically hurt, like something literally being pushed into my brain.

Unlike the countdown, which had had a metallic sound that had betrayed it as a computer-generated voice, this one sounded very human. Very male. And very smug.

"You son of a bitch," Rogan growled. "Let us out of here!"

"Level one—" the speaker continued as if he hadn't heard Rogan's comment or was choosing to ignore it *"—was to test your abilities of reason and compatibility. You have won the chance to continue on to level two, and due to your performance thus far, we have teamed you as partners."*

My heart slammed. "I don't know what you're talking about. I didn't sign up for anything like—"

Suddenly, what felt like a bolt of lightning ripped through my brain. White-hot pain tore through me, and I screamed, clamping my hands on either side of my head as I fell to the ground.

Out of the corner of my eye I saw Rogan do the same.

The pain vanished as quickly as it had come, and I stared around the room, numb and in shock.

"Wh-what—?" I managed.

The voice continued as if nothing out of the ordinary had happened. *"Your implants have been activated and tuned to each other's frequency. Kindly keep in mind that you are playing as a team and to separate more than ninety feet from your partner will lead to immediate disqualification."*

I scrambled to my feet and stumbled over to brace myself against the cold metal wall.

"I want to know what is happening," I demanded, my voice

hoarse. "I want to be let out of here immediately or I'm calling the police!"

It was an empty threat. The police wouldn't give a crap what happened to somebody like me. I didn't even have ID. They'd probably throw me in St. Augustine's for causing a disturbance.

I was on my own.

Rogan was struggling to get up from the floor as I moved toward the door and kicked it again, knowing it wouldn't help but feeling the desperate need to do something—to do anything! "Come on! Come on, you bastards. Let me out of here!"

I saw a flash of light out of the corner of my eye and turned around slowly. The lights in the room dimmed and a holo-screen appeared out of nowhere, showing an overhead view of the city.

The only time I'd seen anything like it was when I'd snuck in to see an old sci-fi movie at the only theater in the city that was still open. I hadn't thought technology like this existed in real life. Could it be real?

Obviously it was, because I was looking right at it.

I walked around the screen, trying to see where it was projected from, but there was nothing. I touched it, and the image flickered and morphed as if I'd dipped my finger into a shallow pool of water. It was partially transparent, and I could see Rogan on the other side.

He looked at me and shook his head. "It begins."

"What begins? What *is* this?"

On the map a round, white glow appeared at an intersection that was otherwise unmarked.

"Level one has been completed successfully." The disembodied voice sounded enthusiastic. There was a creepy singsong qual-

ity to the words. *"There are six levels to* Countdown. *Complete them all without suffering disqualification or elimination and you will be considered the winner. Your next challenge is to reach the marker you see on the map by the time the clock runs out. If you are not successful, you will be eliminated. Do not delay. You have thirty minutes to complete this level. Your time starts now."*

The map faded into the image of a ticking clock. Then that also disappeared, leaving me staring directly at Rogan. The lights came up, and a draft of cool air brushed my bare arms.

I turned to see that the door I'd been kicking had slid open. Beyond it was the outdoors. The city. Familiar territory.

"Kira!" Rogan called after me.

But I barely heard him. I was too busy running.

LEVEL
2

3

THE BEEPING BEGAN WHEN I'D RUN ALMOST A block. It was soft at first but grew steadily in volume and speed with every step I took.

I decided to ignore it for now.

I'd escaped. And the more distance I could put between me and whatever *that* had been was distance well traveled.

I looked around at the gray street and the gray buildings that reached high into the sky. Not another person to be seen.

Yeah. Welcome to my city.

Twenty-five years ago it had been a thriving and successful place of business—one of the most prosperous cities in the whole country. In fact, the whole world had been on an upswing then. Technology was increasing. The economy was thriving. Things were good. And just when everybody was feeling all positive about the future, the Great Plague swept across the world, and in a matter of weeks, sixty percent of human life was wiped out. Dead and gone, just like that.

Those who survived continued on—I mean, what choice did they have? The world kept turning. They rebuilt, they had children, but everything was different. The city swiftly became a sad and empty shell of what it used to be as many people chose to move away from the more dangerous urban landscapes, full of gangs and scavengers and illness, in order to risk living off the land instead, as people had done hundreds of years ago. The Plague was gone, but other illnesses ran rampant and killed off tons of people every year. City or country, either way there were no guarantees that life would be easy. Living in the city was all I'd ever known—my father was a scientist who taught classes at the university, so we'd never lived anywhere else.

Still, I couldn't imagine living here when the city was crammed with people. It was still busy over in the village, a ten square block neighborhood where almost everyone who remained had congregated in a sort of mini-city. But the rest of the streets and neighborhoods were close to deserted, like this one apparently was.

However, another city had been built—one with money, jobs, opportunities…and closed borders. It was called the Colony—a shiny, beautiful, environmentally controlled domed paradise that everyone aspired to get to.

You could live a healthy and prosperous life in the Colony. A life with a future. A life with a chance for happiness.

There's this secret shuttle that will take you on the first leg of your journey. But to get on board, you need to know the right people, have the right kind of money, get the right entrance data, including a special scannable ID implant, and have a whole lot of luck. Even with sixty percent of the population no longer breathing, there were still at least two-and-a-half billion people looking for a ticket to a better life. That would be a pretty damn big shuttle. And a really big city.

The Colony was the only place of its kind, at least on this continent.

And it was my dream to get there. Somehow. Someday.

"Kira! Stop!" It sounded as if Rogan was catching up, but I didn't look. I didn't need more problems in my life, and that boy was one big problem from head to foot.

"Kira!" Rogan shouted again. I looked over my shoulder. He was running after me. Well, actually it was more like a speedy shuffle. He was injured, possibly dying, and yet he was still trying to catch up to me.

I ignored the rush of empathy that thought triggered.

Why was he chasing after me?

It was the pain that clued me in. The stabbing pain through my head that stopped me dead in my tracks. The beeping was so loud now, I couldn't think, couldn't concentrate. I fell to my knees and pressed my hands hard against my ears to block out the deafeningly loud beeping—like an endless train roaring over the tracks—but it wasn't going to do any good.

The noise had to be coming from *inside* my head. Nothing I did could block it out. And it was getting faster. And faster. I looked to my far left. Rogan had stopped running and was holding his head.

And then I remembered what the voice told us.

Your implants have been activated and tuned to each other's frequency.

And what else? I racked my tortured brain.

To separate more than ninety feet from your partner will lead to immediate disqualification.

I crawled over the rough pavement toward Rogan. The beeping decreased the closer I got to him, as did the pain. He lay on his side, only his moving chest showing that he was still breathing.

"Rogan—" I grabbed his shoulder.

He blinked his eyes open and looked at me. "That hurt."

"Tell me about it."

He frowned. "You run really fast for a girl."

"Faster than you."

"I have an excuse. I'm mortally wounded."

"So you keep promising." I let out a long sigh, but it wasn't from relief, it was from frustration. "This 'disqualification and elimination' that voice was talking about in there—he means death, doesn't he?"

His throat worked as he swallowed, and he propped himself up on one elbow. "Smart girl."

"If I was that smart I wouldn't be here, would I?"

"True."

I looked him over thoroughly now that we were outside. The light wasn't all that great. The sky was overcast. It seemed to always be overcast these days. Something to do with global warming and pollution levels. I never paid much attention to the news feeds. All I knew was I hadn't gotten a good suntan in ages.

At the moment, Rogan looked barely strong enough to hurt a fly, but there was still an undeniable aura of danger surrounding him. Something in those pretty ocean-colored eyes made me think that I shouldn't turn my back on him if I could help it. I couldn't trust him. Not now. Not ever.

I would never trust a murderer.

But apparently we were partners. That is, if I didn't want my head to explode.

"I'm not going to beg," I said softly. "But you're going to tell me everything you know about this...this *Countdown*."

He nodded and tried to get to his feet. He failed. I stood and offered him a hand. He took it, and I helped him up. He didn't let go of me immediately. His hand was as dirty as the rest of him, but firm with long fingers that wrapped warmly around mine.

I let go first, pulling my hand back before it was too late. Before *it* happened.

I'd had just about as much pain as I could deal with for one day.

It had been like this since I'd turned thirteen, this weird, freakish thing inside of me. If I touched somebody skin to skin and focused on them for too long...sometimes it hurt. My *brain* hurt, that is. And then I'd get these bizarre flashes zipping through my mind like electrical charges. Not flashes so much as...feelings.

Not *my* feelings, either. *Their* feelings.

I didn't know what it meant, and I'd never told anyone about it. All I knew was that it hurt. And, call me crazy, but I liked to avoid pain whenever possible.

Whenever it happened, I got a horrible headache that lasted for hours. The scummier the person that I touched, the longer the pain lasted.

The last person I wanted to touch was somebody like Rogan.

His expression shadowed as if my actions had somehow hurt his feelings, and he stuffed his hands into the pockets of his torn, dirty jeans.

"I'll tell you everything I know," he said. "But we need to move."

"There are twenty minutes remaining in this level of Countdown," the voice said from out of nowhere.

When I didn't immediately start walking, Rogan raised an eyebrow at me.

"Let's get going," he said. "I'm not in good enough shape to keep running. Better make it a brisk stagger, so we need to move *now.*"

"Okay, yeah. Then let's go." I frowned and tried to recall the map. Damn. I should have paid more attention. Fingers of panic dug deep into my stomach.

As if he'd read my thoughts, he forced a grin. "Don't worry, kid. I know where we're headed."

I scowled at him. "I'm no kid, I'm sixteen. And the name's *Kira.*"

His grin widened a fraction. "No nicknames. Got it."

I studied him for a moment longer. That scar across his left eye. I wondered how he'd gotten it. Probably at St. Augustine's, in a scuffle with another loser. Or maybe his victim had attempted to fight back before he'd mercilessly snuffed out his or her life.

Scumbag.

He caught me staring at his face and turned away so I could see only the good side. "Let's get going, *Kira.*"

Vain, was he?

We walked. Slower than I would have liked, but it was fast enough to keep some of my panic at bay. With every step, I felt the clock ticking down the seconds we had left. What if we didn't make it in time? Would they really kill us? Just like that?

I was finding it easier and easier to believe.

"Countdown," Rogan began as we trudged along, "is just

what it sounds like. A series of challenges with a set time frame and a win-or-lose outcome. It's a game."

I glanced at him and kept walking. My heart pounded in my ears. "I didn't agree to play any game."

"You didn't have to. *Countdown* plays to the fringes of society over a top-secret televised network. That's what makes it so appealing to the Subscribers."

"Subscribers?"

"Bored rich people who haven't headed to the Colony yet and want to be entertained by a modern Roman Colosseum. Death matches. There are a few other twisted games on the network to hold their interest. This is only one on the list."

My gut started to churn with disgust. "How is this even allowed? It's illegal."

"I know that. You know that. But, like I said, it's a secret. Even if it wasn't, do you really think cops would give a damn about what happens to criminals, no matter how young those criminals might be? Makes their jobs easier in the long run, doesn't it? Subscribers are fitted with cranium implants so they can watch in their heads. It's like virtual reality, only they're just watching, not participating. Safer that way." His expression soured. "Bunch of rich cowards who get off on violence."

"How do you know all this?"

He didn't look directly at me. "I just know. The players used to be older prisoners recruited from Saradone, but recently it seems like the Subscribers prefer younger meat. I knew a couple kids who disappeared one night a month ago. The rumor was they were offered the chance to play the game."

"Why would they agree to something like this?" I hadn't been given a choice.

He shrugged. "At least with the game there's a possibility

you can win. A fresh-faced eighteen-year-old transferring to a prison like that—no matter what his crimes are…" His jaw tightened, and he finally offered me a sidelong glance. "His days are numbered."

"That's how they got you. You didn't want to go to Saradone if there was a way to avoid it."

"Basically."

I shook my head. "It doesn't make any sense."

"It doesn't have to. The bottom line is that it exists. And we're right in the middle of it now." He eyed me. "I don't get *you,* though."

"Right back at you."

"No, I don't understand why you were recruited. You weren't in detention. You haven't been arrested. You're into low-end crime, and you have no family, but still. Only sixteen…" His brows drew together. "You're too young. Too soft."

"There's nothing soft about me."

His lips twitched. "I don't know about that."

"Keep walking." I put one foot in front of the other. "You're sure you know where we're going?"

He nodded. "Yeah, it's not far from here."

This was insane. All of it. "So, if we finish—how many levels again?"

"Six."

"If we finish six levels like the voice said, we'll win. What does that mean?"

"Freedom. Money. I don't know what else. It depends on the player, I think."

"And if we mess up—"

"No freedom, no money and a bullet in the brain. That's if we're lucky."

My stomach lurched. "Who would want to watch this?"

"You'd be surprised. A subscription to the Network isn't cheap, and it's based on how much they watch. And the cranium implant that gets them access has to be surgically implanted. It's not easy to do. The Subscribers expect to get their money's worth. Maybe that's why they had you join the cast. I don't think *Countdown* has had a female contestant before."

That wasn't terribly comforting. "Lucky me. Maybe they think we'll be a good team."

He glanced at me. "Maybe we will."

"Don't bet on it." I looked away. "Are we almost there?"

He nodded. "I think so."

"You *think* so? I thought you were sure where we were going?"

"I've been out of commission for a while. Things change. Do you know this neighborhood?"

"No."

I took a good look around. Gray on gray. No trees, no parked cars. Even the street signs were broken off the poles on the corner ahead. Nothing was familiar.

Something flew out from behind a corner ahead of us. A silver ball. It floated in midair and headed straight for us at lightning fast speed. I ducked so it wouldn't hit me, but it stopped three feet in front of my face and bobbed at eye level.

A flying digicam. Yet another thing I'd never seen before in real life. It reflected me in the black iris of its lens.

The voice spoke again in my head.

"Level two for Rogan and Kira is well under way. Let's take a moment to get to know these two contestants...."

It was an implant. That was what the voice said earlier, didn't it? They'd put one of the implants in my head. I reached into the tangle of my dark brown hair and felt around until I found the stitches over a two inch cut in my scalp. The area surrounding it was numb. They'd put the implant in my head. That's why I'd been unconscious in the metal room. I'd been recovering from surgery.

Outrage swelled inside me.

We didn't have time for this. I attempted to get past the digicam, but it blocked my way.

"Kira Jordan, sixteen years old, was left an orphan two years ago after her family was brutally murdered. But don't let her sob story or good looks fool you—she's made her way in the world by becoming a street thief and pickpocket who would steal from her own grandmother if she still had one. And she isn't afraid of using her body to get exactly what she wants. This girl's as cold as ice."

I felt the color drain from my face, and I glanced at Rogan.

"That's not true," I said.

His expression was guarded, but there was an edge of curiosity in his gaze. "All of it or most of it?"

"Most."

The camera then whirred over to block Rogan's path.

"Rogan Ellis, seventeen years old, is guilty of nine counts of first-degree murder in what is now known as the Dormitory Murders. After a one-night rampage that left nine female university students dead and dismembered, he was sent to St. Augustine's Detention Hall for dangerous youths until his eighteenth birthday, when he was to be transferred to Saradone Maximum Security Prison to serve a life sentence with no chance for parole."

Rogan glanced at me with an unfamiliar expression playing across his face, but I'd gone cold and silent.

"That's not true, either," he said, his voice suddenly void of emotion.

"All of it or most of it?" I asked shakily.

"Most."

Nine girls. Dead and dismembered.

I felt ill. I could have dropped to my knees on the cold, hard pavement and thrown up, but there was nothing in my stomach. It was one thing to imagine what he was guilty of, but another to have it sent across the airwaves directly into my brain.

He was horrible. He was a monster, like the man who'd murdered my family.

And if I didn't stay with him I was going to die.

The thought made me feel even sicker.

Maybe they're lying, a small voice in my mind insisted. *Why would you believe what they say? They totally exaggerated who you are. Maybe he didn't do it.*

Why would I even think that? Because he had nice eyes? Because he was vaguely charming and injured, and I wanted to make it out of this alive—and to do that, I needed him?

Yeah, something like that.

"Tell us, Rogan Ellis, do you feel any remorse for what you've done? And how do you feel your sociopathic tendencies will serve you in Countdown, *especially now that you're teamed with Kira—a girl who lost her own family to a brutal murder?"*

I tried to catch his eye, but he wouldn't look at me, instead staring daggers at the camera, refusing to answer any of the "get to know you" questions the voice was asking on behalf of the audience.

"Ten minutes now remain in this level of Countdown.*"*

The time update was like a slap in the face.

I grabbed Rogan's shirt again. "We have to get going. Now."

The camera moved to block our way, and I swatted it with the back of my hand.

"We're not far," Rogan said.

"We better not be."

"You didn't tell me your family was murdered."

"Forget it."

His brow furrowed as we hurried along the road. "Kira, what they said about me…"

"Let's get one thing straight. I don't care who you are or what you did. I just want to live. And if it means that I have to put up with a piece of garbage like you, then that's exactly what I'll do."

"I understand."

"And one more thing—" I squeezed his shoulder hard, under the collar of his shirt just above his wound, and he let out a gasp of pain "—you try anything or you even look at me funny? I swear to God I'll kill you myself."

He knocked my hand away, his gaze fierce. "Sounds fair enough."

I wiped a drop of his blood off my hand and ignored the mild flash of pain in my head. I'd touched him. Touched his skin. I'd concentrated as best as I could considering the situation I currently found myself in—

And I'd tried to feel something, some feeling. Some clue to help me.

There wasn't time to get much more than a headache and a jumble of confusion.

All I knew for sure was that there was more to Rogan's

story. Much more. But right now there was no time to figure it out.

If we didn't hurry, in less than ten minutes, we were going
to die.

4

"HOW MUCH FARTHER?" I TOOK A QUICK LOOK over my shoulder to see that Rogan was about twenty feet behind me. I ran fast. Currently, he didn't. Since I couldn't let him lag too far behind—thanks to the brain implants from hell—it was becoming a problem.

His already strained face creased into a deeper frown. He stopped walking and looked around the gray, deserted street.

"We should almost be there" was his final proclamation, but he sounded uncertain.

"We better be," I muttered. "Which way?"

"Take a left at the next intersection."

I took the left along the street up ahead. None of it looked familiar to me. The area was desolate; there was no one around—unless you counted the spherical silver digicam whizzing around that I already hated enough to fantasize about smashing into a million little pieces.

I'd taken a swipe at it a minute ago when it got too close. The thing was faster than it looked—and it looked pretty damn fast.

This whole situation was so bizarre I just couldn't wrap my head around the fact that it was actually happening to me. But it was. If my heart wasn't pounding so hard that it hurt and if I hadn't already experienced enough stress and pain to fill up five lifetimes, I would have sworn that I was dreaming.

Rogan cursed.

I looked back at him with alarm. "What now?"

He scanned the dead-end alley we'd just walked into. "It's not supposed to be like this."

"Like what?" I didn't try to hide the hard edge of panic in my voice. "And hurry up, because we're almost out of time."

As if in reply, the voice in my head announced, *"There are two minutes remaining in this level of* Countdown.*"*

Rogan brought a hand up to his wound and swayed on his feet. I ran to his side to support him before he keeled over.

"Did you hear that?" I asked.

"I heard it."

"So?"

"I could have sworn this was the right turn. I know this neighborhood. At least, I *used* to know it. It's been a while, though. Things change." His dark brows drew together.

I was now bracing his full weight against me to keep him from toppling over. "Yeah, you're a whole lot of help."

"I guess we won't be winning the grand prize, will we? Knocked out at level two. It's embarrassing." He said it so wryly that I knew he was joking.

Joking. At a time like this? He was even crazier than he looked.

He was also very pale, and there was a sheen of perspiration on his grimy face. My hand was pressed to his chest to hold him steady, and his heart beat erratically. I pulled at his shirt to take a quick peek at the wound underneath. It looked raw and open, as if it had been inflicted with a sharp object like a big butcher's knife. Definitely not from a gun. I'd seen bullet wounds up close and personal before—the image seared into my brain forever, along with my father's glazed, unseeing eyes.

Blood oozed steadily out of Rogan's shoulder.

"You're a mess," I informed him.

"Tell me something I don't know."

"You stink, too."

"Again, well aware. Like I said, they didn't give me a few hours at the spa before locking me up in that room so I could smell like a flower for you."

My throat thickened with panic. "You really think this is where we should be? Are you sure?"

"I was. But there aren't any doors. There's nothing. And if we'd reached the finish line, you'd think there'd be some sort of sign." His words finally betrayed a sharp edge of strain.

"I'm going to let go of you now," I said.

"Thanks for the warning."

He eased back against the concrete wall behind him, and I stepped away to stand in the middle of the alley. I turned around slowly, trying hard to ignore the ticking that was potentially counting down the last seconds of my life.

"I used to watch TV shows like this," I said. "Not *exactly* like this one, of course, but they have the races and the puzzles to solve. Usually at this early level of a game, it's still fairly easy. Or at least, not insanely impossible to figure out." I glared at the camera hovering in the air four feet from my face.

"You don't know the people who set this game up. It's all about the losing, not the winning, for them."

"I'm just saying that it can't be the end. Not yet. What's the fun in eliminating contestants in level two?"

I scanned the alley. Two brick walls. One concrete wall, gray and unyielding, behind Rogan's hunched-over frame. I looked up. A sliver of slate-gray sky showed above the thirty-story buildings that surrounded us like cold, emotionless sentries.

"What did you think we were running toward?" I asked. "What did you see on that map?"

He looked around. "It was an office. I remember it from before I got sent away. I could have sworn it was right here."

"One minute remains in this level of Countdown."

"59...58...57..."

There was a Dumpster to the side of us, full to overflowing. Strange, considering that the neighborhood was deserted. A rotting apple core lay to the side of it, the fruit turning brown. No flies, though. It didn't seem as if anyone or anything lived here anymore, but that piece of fruit didn't seem as old as it should have, considering the surroundings.

"What kind of office was it?" I asked.

"What?"

"What kind of office?" I repeated, loud enough to be heard over the countdown.

"It was a...a doctor's office. A psychiatrist."

"Let me guess, *your* doctor?"

Rogan's expression shadowed. "I had a few appointments there, yeah."

"Obviously he wasn't very good at what he did if you went psycho, anyway."

He glowered at me.

A doctor's office. Right here. But now it was gone? Was

Rogan tripping out, or was he remembering something important?

I sure hoped it was something important. We didn't have time to be wrong.

I went toward that Dumpster and jumped in.

"What are you doing?" Rogan demanded.

"Trying very hard not to die."

I plunged my hands into muck and filth. Rotting food, discarded boxes, plastic bags filled with rancid garbage. Living on the streets had given me a necessary talent for Dumpster diving. You could find some really good stuff if you had the time and motivation to go searching.

Currently I didn't have the time, but I sure as hell had the motivation.

I didn't know what I was looking for. Even when I found it, I still wasn't sure.

"24…23…22…"

It was a bell attached to a sign that read: *Please ring bell and the receptionist will be right with you.*

Okay, it was something.

I held my breath and rang the bell.

Nothing happened for a moment, and what little hope I had started to fade, but then I heard something. A heavy, metallic sound.

"Kira. Look." Rogan pointed at the ground.

I looked over the edge of the Dumpster to see that a door in the ground had slid open. I hadn't even noticed the edges of it before.

"10…9…8…"

I launched myself out of the garbage like somebody possessed and grabbed Rogan's arm. There was a flight of stairs leading down. I pulled him with me, and we quickly descended into the semidarkness below.

"3...2...1..."

The door above us slammed shut with the force of a guillotine. When nothing else happened, I quickly continued down to the bottom of the stairs. A short hallway led into a white room.

Rogan met my gaze. "I don't feel dead yet. Should we be celebrating?"

I thought about that as I tried to bring my breathing back down to a normal pace. "If we're dead, then death wasn't nearly as bad as I thought it would be."

"Congratulations, Rogan and Kira, on successfully completing level two of Countdown."

I rubbed my temples, finally allowing myself a measure of relief. "Is he going to say that every time? Because that's going to get old really fast."

Another camera appeared and whipped past my face. I watched my eyes narrow in the shiny surface. By no stretch of the imagination did I look happy. My dark brown hair was matted and tangled, and my long bangs were slicked against my forehead. My jaw was clenched tightly, and my dark eyes flashed with anger. I hated that digicam. Hated it more than I remembered hating anything for a very long time.

"You shouldn't look directly at it," Rogan advised, touching my arm with the hand that wasn't clasped to his injured shoulder.

I shrugged away from him. "Why not?"

"You don't want to give the Subscribers more than their money's worth. They *want* you to look at them that way. It gets them off to see you suffer." He pulled me away so that

I wasn't staring right into the lens anymore. "How did you know to ring the bell?"

I finally looked at him. "Lucky guess."

"Yes," a voice said. "Very lucky indeed."

I turned to see that a door had opened and a man had entered the white room. He was tall and skinny, with short black hair and a trimmed goatee. He wore wire-framed glasses and a white doctor's coat and he held a clipboard.

"Who are you?" I forced myself not to step backward. He was the first live person I'd seen other than Rogan since this nightmare had begun.

He stopped walking. "My name is Jonathan. I'm your liaison to *Countdown*."

"What does that mean?"

He didn't answer me. Instead, his gaze flicked to Rogan. "You're injured."

"I'm surprised you didn't know that already, being our liaison and all." Sarcasm mixed with the pain in Rogan's voice.

"It's worse than I thought it would be." Jonathan let out a long sigh and shook his head. "We will have to wait a moment first."

I looked around the room. He wasn't moving, just staring straight ahead.

"What are we waiting for?" I asked.

Jonathan held up a finger. "One moment."

Every muscle in my body was tense and ready to run, but instead I waited, standing silently in place. After a couple of minutes, a small door in the wall to my right opened up, and the silver ball camera left the room. The door closed behind it.

"What happened?" I said.

"*Countdown* is now on an official break," Jonathan explained. "We have a little time to prep you for your next level."

"I won't last another level," Rogan said.

Jonathan nodded. "I know. I've been monitoring your vitals."

He left the room briefly and returned with a white box.

"Sit," he instructed, and Rogan sat down in a white chair next to him.

I swear, everything in the entire room was white and scrubbed immaculately clean. It felt like a hospital—or, at least, the kind I'd once seen in an old movie.

Jonathan pushed away the material that covered Rogan's wound. Then with no sound from the murderer other than a pained groan, Jonathan cleaned the wound and sprayed it with some sort of colorless substance. The skin around the cut turned a sick shade of green.

"Ah," Jonathan breathed, peering closer. "The knife they used on you was tipped with calcine poison."

"That would explain why I feel like my insides are melting," Rogan grumbled. "Because they are."

"What's happening?" I demanded again. My fists were clenched so tightly at my sides that my fingernails dug painfully into the palms of my hands. Instead of relaxing, I let it happen. The pain helped me stay focused.

"What does it look like?" Jonathan asked, glancing up at me.

"Why are you helping him?"

"Kira," Rogan growled. "Didn't you hear the part about my insides melting?"

"But—"

"I can't play this damn game if I have melting insides. Do you get that?"

"Of course I get that. But why is he helping you? Doesn't he work for the damn game?"

"I do." Jonathan nodded. "But that doesn't mean I always agree with their idea of entertainment."

With a syringe, he injected a blue-colored solution into Rogan's shoulder. Rogan clenched his jaw. "That should be enough antidote to halt the damage and hopefully reverse it. You're not going to feel great, but you'll feel a lot better than you have." He peered at the now clean wound. "The antidote will also help the wound knit rapidly. You shouldn't require any stitches."

"Thanks." Rogan pulled away from Jonathan the moment he was finished.

He seemed oddly at ease with the man—as if they'd already met.

Jonathan closed the box. "Are you well, young lady?"

"Am I *well?*" I repeated. "No, I am not well. I want out of this game right now."

"That's not possible. But you're doing fine so far. I anticipate that you will last several more levels." He looked away.

My breath hitched. Could I fight him to escape from this place? If I had to? "I don't belong here."

"None of us belong here, Kira," he said wearily. "Sometimes we need to do the best with what we're given."

"I would have to disagree with you there," Rogan said.

Jonathan looked at him sharply. "Time has a tendency to change many things, Rogan."

"Not as many as you might think. But time does have a way of making things a lot clearer."

"If you say so."

Rogan glowered at him. "I do."

I watched their exchange with growing certainty. "Do you two know each other?"

Rogan flicked a glance at me. "No."

Like hell they didn't. I wasn't that blind. Before I could ask any more questions, he turned to Jonathan.

"Are you going to get in trouble for fixing me?"

Jonathan didn't answer the question. "We need to talk about level three."

"I'd rather have a long nap in a comfortable bed," Rogan said with a humorless snort.

"I'm sure you would. And you're partially in luck. Since the broadcast is on a break, you've just entered a mandatory rest period."

Rogan's throat worked as he swallowed. "That's not necessary."

"I thought you said you wanted a nap?"

"On my own terms, yeah."

Jonathan pressed a button on the wall and another holo-screen appeared in the middle of the room. The image of an average-looking man flickered into focus. "This is Bernard Jones. He is forty years old, has been married for fifteen years, and has one child. He makes his living as an accountant. He has dreams of moving to the Colony with his family and opening a restaurant there."

My heart jumped into my throat. Another mention of the Colony. I was starting to believe it really existed—somewhere. Sometimes I wondered if it might just be a rumor.

"Sounds like a fun guy," I said, trying to shield my interest in the secret city. "So, what are we supposed to do, get him to do our taxes?"

"No. To successfully complete level three you are required to assassinate him."

My mouth dropped open. "*Assassinate* him?"

"That's right. There will be no weapons provided for this level. You will have to use whatever means are available to locate and eliminate this target. You will be informed on your timeline once the level begins. That's all I can tell you. I wish you good luck."

Rogan was frowning. "Jonathan, there has to be some way out of this. You have to let me speak to—" He broke off and yelled, clutching his head. The next moment he crumpled to the ground, unconscious.

I watched him fall and then raised my horrified gaze to Jonathan.

"I'm very sorry," he said.

I opened my mouth to say something, I wasn't even sure what; but before I got out a word, the lightning-fast pain ripped through my brain and everything went black.

LEVEL

5

I OPENED MY EYES SLOWLY AND BLINKED UNTIL everything came back into focus. Along with my vision, my anger returned in full force.

I absolutely hated the idea of somebody out there with their finger on a little button that could cause me pain like that. However, I did like the idea of finding whoever was in charge of that little button and giving their groin a nice, sharp introduction to my knee.

My head hurt. Badly. But at least I still seemed to be in one piece.

I glanced around and realized I was somewhere more populated. Not another empty, clinical room. I could hear voices. There was a faint sound of clothes swishing and rubbing together as a few people passed, nearby but out of sight.

There was a heavy weight pressing on my shoulder, and I slowly realized that it was Rogan—specifically his head. He was still out cold and currently using me as a pillow. We were both sprawled against a wall like a couple of homeless people. Pretty accurate, really. But this wasn't the street. Linoleum tile felt smooth and cool against my hands. We were inside. Somewhere.

I know this place.

And then it dawned on me.

We were in the mall a few blocks north of the village. One of my main haunts. The same place I'd been when this nightmare first began—when I'd stolen my new pair of shoes. I looked down at my feet to see that the bright red sneakers were still there.

I jostled him. "Rogan."

He didn't wake up.

I moved my hand to the back of my head and took a moment to feel the incision mark. Then I felt for the same thing on Rogan. His dark hair slid through my fingers.

Strange. I felt not one but *two* incision marks on his scalp. Why were there two?

He appeared so innocent while asleep—and very nearly handsome. His eyelids fluttered, and I wondered what he was dreaming about. I looked closely at the scar on his face, and traced the line with the tip of my finger.

"Are you really as much of an evil bastard as they say you are?"

I glanced around the hallway. No one was within spitting distance, and as far as I could see, neither were the flying digicams. I wasn't sure how long this fleeting moment of privacy would last.

I felt at his throat for his steady pulse, warm and alive beneath my touch. Then I slowly trailed down to his collarbone and under the edge of his ripped T-shirt to press my hand against his chest. Skin to skin. And I opened myself up to whatever it was I could do.

I didn't think I was psychic or anything. But then, it couldn't be my imagination. The pain made it real. Before, on the street, I hadn't sensed anything from Rogan but a jumbled mass of...something.

Something.

I needed to know if I could do it again. If I could figure it out, get more this time. If I could get some sort of sense of just how bad Rogan Ellis really was and how much I should hate his guts.

All I knew for sure was that bad guys had this bad vibe that was impossible to ignore when I did this, like a cold blanket of darkness that sucked the warmth right out of me.

I didn't know what this strange ability of mine actually was. What it meant. But I needed it to work.

I closed my eyes and tried to concentrate.

Then I suddenly found my hand in his as he pulled it away from his chest. "Hey—I'm out for a few minutes and you suddenly can't keep your hands off me?"

I scowled at him. "Hardly."

A glimmer of amusement lit up his ocean-green eyes. "Then what were you doing?"

"Just making sure you weren't dead. FYI...you're not."

He gave a humorless laugh and glanced around wearily. "Where are we now?"

"We're in the mall."

"The mall," he repeated with a frown. "Why are we in the mall?"

I reached back to feel my incision again. "We need to get these implants out."

Rogan grabbed my wrist. "Don't do that."

"Why not?"

"You can't tamper with it or it will kill us."

"Who told you that?"

"Nobody. But it makes sense, doesn't it?" He rose to his feet and held out a hand to help me up. I ignored it and got up on my own.

"You have two incisions. Does that mean you have two implants?"

He raised an eyebrow. "Do I?"

I nodded, surprised at his calm reaction to such a strange— to me, anyway—observation.

He reached around to the back of his head to feel. "Maybe they made a mistake when they were digging around. Put it in the wrong spot."

"Maybe." My gaze traveled to his wound. "What Jonathan did to you back there. That antidote. How do you feel now?"

He gingerly touched his shoulder. "It worked. I feel stronger already. It doesn't even hurt much anymore."

I couldn't figure it out. "Why did he do that? Seems kind of risky for him to help somebody he doesn't even know. Just another contestant."

"Don't know." A grim smile tugged at the corner of his mouth. "Must be my charm. I've always been able to win people over. Make them do whatever I want."

"Yeah, sure," I said. "It's working so well with me so far." I glanced around again. I could see the main mall from where we were, but they'd tucked us down a hallway that was roped off for maintenance. I looked at Rogan. He wasn't hunched over anymore, and I got a better sense of his height. He was tall—I'd guess a couple inches over six feet. Also, even with all that dirt and grime he was…well, I had to admit that he was far from ugly. I wondered what he might look like all cleaned up.

Like a cleaned-up mass murderer, probably.

I was fooling myself if I thought there was more to this guy. Wouldn't matter if he was the most gorgeous boy in the universe. What he'd done made him hideous.

He seemed to flinch at my appraisal. "You don't seem to like what you see."

That wasn't entirely true, unfortunately. But it was better for both of us if he believed that. "*Should* I like you, Rogan?"

He gave another half laugh that sounded pained. "Absolutely not."

"Then I guess we're in agreement." I turned my back to him and tried to focus. The mall. I hung out here all the time and so did a good friend of mine. "Come on. I think I know someone who might be able to help us. Got to find him before that camera catches up to us."

Before I got too far, his hand on my shoulder stopped me. "What are you talking about?"

"I know a guy, he's like a computer genius. At least that's what he's always telling me. If I find him, he might be able to help us get rid of the implants—disarm them, remove them, whatever—and we can end this once and for all."

"You think it's that easy?"

"I think it could be." I tried to pull away from him.

His grip on my arm increased. "You touch these implants, and unless you have the right tools, they'll explode. Turn your brain to goo that'll drip out your ears while you finish dying. Is that what you want?"

I grimaced at the thought. "You sound pretty certain. I guess I didn't get the manual when I woke up on the do's and don't's of implant ownership. Did they give you a quick course in juvie?"

He glared at my sarcastic tone. "People talk."

I turned away again. "Doesn't mean I have to listen."

Without waiting to find out if he was or wasn't going to follow me, I made my way out of the hallway and into the mall. Finally, I was somewhere I knew. It felt good, like I'd been returned home. It gave me some sense of control in this crazy situation.

Pre-Plague, this had been one of the largest malls on the east coast. Over a thousand stores in a complex that spanned blocks and blocks. Now there were about thirty stores still open. Three places to eat in the food court. Some old people said that it had an eerie, ghost town kind of feeling for them, just like the entire city now did. It didn't seem that strange to me since I'd never known any other way. It was a good place to hang out indoors, and that was all I cared about.

I glanced over my shoulder. Rogan trudged after me. Just looking at him made me realize that we'd better make this quick. We didn't have too much time before we got kicked out. Security wasn't all that tight, but torn, dirty and bloodied clothes did not represent your average mall shopper. Luckily I knew where I was headed.

The food court. My friend Oliver hung out there a lot. If he wasn't there, then he was at his other main haunt, some basement in the city where he disappeared for days at a time to play networked games with other geeks. I meant that term fondly.

I actually let out a small whimper of relief when I saw him sitting in his usual spot, tapping away on his laptop, an extra-large soda in front of him on the table. There were about ten other people in the large food court, scattered around at different tables. A clock hung from the ceiling in the center of the court. The glass on it had been broken months ago but hadn't been fixed yet. It still worked, though. It was just after five o'clock.

I walked right up to Oliver and stood in front of him. He didn't immediately look up from his screen.

"Oliver," I said.

He finally glanced at me, and his eyes widened. "Kira, hey. I've been looking all over for you. You totally disappeared yesterday."

Yesterday? How long had I been unconscious before I woke up in that room? How long had I been unconscious before this *level?*

I let out a shaky breath. "I need your help. Badly."

He raised his eyebrows. "You look serious."

"You have no idea."

"Are you in some sort of trouble?"

Rogan's hand curled around my arm. "Kira, this isn't a good idea."

Oliver's gaze shifted to him, and his eyes widened again. "New friend?"

I looked at Rogan and then back at Oliver. Rogan outweighed the shorter, scrawnier kid by at least fifty pounds of muscle.

"Uh, this is Rogan Ellis." I gulped. "We both need your help."

"Rogan Ellis…" Oliver's eyes widened even more at hearing the name. I guess I was the only one who hadn't heard of his crimes before today. "Kira, do you have any idea who this guy is?"

"Yes, but you have to listen to me…" I trailed off. I suddenly felt something. A strange sensation like we were being watched.

I glanced over my shoulder and was positive I saw a silver digicam slide behind the far corner.

"We can't involve your friend in this," Rogan whispered only loud enough for me to hear. "Unless you want to get him killed."

Oliver's knuckles were white, and he gripped the edge of the table. "Look, I don't know what's going on, Kira, but if you need my help, you know I'd do anything for you. But him—" His voice caught a little with fear. "I don't want him anywhere near me."

Oliver had a crush on me. Thankfully, he'd never acted on it, but it was always there, an undeniable presence in the room with us. And I'd admit it, I took it as a compliment. It was nice to feel wanted. I was banking on that crush to make him want to help us. To help *me*. But the last thing I wanted to do was to put him in danger.

And that was exactly what I was doing by even talking to him.

Damn. Rogan was right.

"Where do you want to go?" He closed his laptop and stood up from the table.

"You know what?" I swallowed and shook my head. "Never mind."

He moved a step toward me. "Kira, you look really stressed. Tell me what's wrong."

I took a step back and felt Rogan behind me. "This was a mistake."

He eyed Rogan with a mix of fear and hate. "Is it him? Is he forcing you to do something?"

"None of your business what I'm doing," Rogan growled.

Oliver's jaw tensed, and he turned his glare from Rogan to me again. "I can help you. You just have to come with me."

"Help her? Yeah, you look so tough." Rogan snorted. "You think you can save her from me?"

I really wanted him to shut up and not make this worse than it already was.

"If I have to." Oliver gave me another confused look. "Is he hurting you?"

I shook my head. I had to back away. I couldn't get Oliver involved in this. It had been a mistake to approach him. "No...Rogan and me...we're together."

"Together?"

I nodded. It was better to hurt him now if it would keep him safe in the long run. "I just wanted you to know so you... so you stop bothering me."

He put a hand to his chest. "I'm bothering you?"

"Just leave me alone, Oliver."

He blinked. "He's a murderer, Kira. Don't you know that?"

I gave him a blank look and turned my back to him. "Maybe I don't care."

Wow, what a huge lie that was.

"Kira—"

"Don't follow us," Rogan snarled at him.

"Or what?"

"Or you'll regret it. Trust me on that."

I didn't look back as I left the food court with Rogan at my side. I never should have gone there in the first place. Oliver must hate me. I hadn't wanted to hurt him. He had nothing to do with the mess I'd somehow gotten myself into.

Tears of frustration slid down my cheeks. "You didn't have to be such a dick to him."

"I did what I had to do."

I brushed my tears away before Rogan could see I was crying.

Two men in security uniforms approached us.

"We're going to have to ask you to leave the premises," one said. He had a hand on the gun at his side. "Now."

Rogan's lips twitched. "My, how times have changed. How do you know I wasn't about to do some shopping with my daddy's gold card?"

One of the guards eyed his dirty clothes and the bloodstain on his shoulder and then glanced at me. "Is this boy bothering you, young lady?"

They didn't seem to recognize Rogan like Oliver had.

Tell them! my mind screamed. *Tell them everything. They can help you.*

I caught a flash of silver out of the corner of my eye. The digicam.

"The level's already begun, hasn't it?" I asked Rogan quietly.

"Yeah, it has."

I knew then, without a shadow of a doubt, if I told the security guards what was going on, I would be severely and painfully punished. And the guards themselves would probably not walk out of here alive.

"He's with me, actually." The words felt thick and unnatural leaving my mouth.

The other guard grabbed my arm. "Then you'll both have to go."

"Fine. We'll go." I wrenched away from him.

We cleared the food court and headed down a mostly abandoned hallway toward the exit. More tears burned my eyes, but I forced them back. Crying wouldn't solve a damn thing.

"What are they doing to us?" I asked after a moment, mostly to myself. "How could anyone find this entertaining?"

"You'd be surprised. Some people are sick."

Yeah, he should know. "Why did they even put us here in the mall? Just to mess with our minds?"

"Something like that." Rogan's arm tightened around my waist then, as if he was trying to comfort me. Weird. A moment later, as if he realized what he'd done, he pulled away from me and crossed his arms over his chest. "Do you remember what Jonathan told us this level is all about?"

I tried to think back through the thick storm cloud of memories. "The accountant."

He nodded. "Take a look."

I looked in the direction he pointed to see the man who had been featured on the holoscreen. Bernard Jones. I recognized his balding head and bland features. He emerged from an electronics shop with a bag of purchases, then turned left and started walking toward the same exit we were headed for.

I heard the whir as a camera moved behind us. It was moving behind things to stay hidden from any regular people.

Rogan's attention was fixed on the man. "We've got to follow him."

"He's got a wife. And a kid."

"Yeah, you're right. And we can't let him leave our sight."

"There are ten minutes remaining in this level of Countdown.*"*

I turned to meet Rogan's gaze.

"You know what we're supposed to do," he said, his jaw tensing. "And we have ten minutes to do it."

To successfully complete level three you are required to assassinate him, Jonathan's instructions echoed in my mind.

I shook my head. "No. It's not going to happen."

"Do you want us to die?"

I blinked at him as a sick churning steadily grew in my gut. "I don't want us to die. But I also don't want to kill a man I've never met before. Somebody who doesn't deserve it or even see it coming. There's no way."

"Come on." He grabbed my hand and pulled me along with him. "We can't let him get away."

"You can't kill him."

"It's him or us."

"I don't care."

"We'll see if you're still thinking that way in a few minutes."

"I'm not capable of murder. I'm not like you."

Rogan let go of my hand but kept walking. He didn't look at me. "You don't know what I'm capable of. You don't know me."

"I don't want to know a sick bastard like you." I pressed my lips together to keep from saying anything more. That had sounded crueler than I'd wanted it to.

That earned me a sharp look. "We're running out of choices. Get that through your pretty head. There are no choices. We do what they tell us to or we die."

"Maybe I don't care. My family was murdered. I'd never do that to another person's family. I'd rather die first."

"I'm not in the mood to argue with you, Kira. We don't have the time."

I watched as Bernard Jones exited the mall through the swinging doors.

"So you're going to follow him and then what?"

"And then I'm going to kill him." He raised an eyebrow. "But then again, I am a sick murdering bastard, right?"

"So it's that simple for you?"

His fists clenched at his sides. "You're acting as if I have a choice."

"There's always a choice."

"Not for me," he said grimly. "Not anymore."

And with that he stalked out of the entrance to follow his prey. I raced to keep up with him.

Kill or be killed.

There had to be another way. And I needed to figure it out. Fast.

6

BERNARD JONES WALKED DOWN THE SIDEWALK
outside of the mall completely oblivious to the fact that he
was being stalked.

"Where'd the camera go?" I looked around the area, gray
and bland, and noticed that we were alone again.

"It's around, I'm sure."

"You seem to know a lot about how this game works."

He raised a dark eyebrow. "Do I?"

I narrowed my eyes at him. "Yeah. You do. Who are you,
Rogan? Who are you really?"

"I'm nobody." He flinched and looked away from me, but
not before I saw a hint of pain slide through his gaze. "You're
imagining things."

Was that a moment of vulnerability? It was enough to un-
balance me again. "I—I'm not imagining anything. I swear
I'm going to figure out what your real story is."

"Sure. Good luck with that." His gaze returned to mine, but
this time it was more guarded. "You think you can figure out
what makes me tick other than the countdown in my head?"

"Don't make fun of me."

"But you make it so easy." He gave me a sideways glance, a bit of humor returning to his eyes. "Do you give all the guys in your life such a hard time?"

"There are no guys in my life."

"What about your boyfriend, Oliver?"

I made a face. "He's not my boyfriend."

"And what the announcer said about you using your body to get whatever you want?" His gaze slid down the length of me.

I ignored the sudden heat in my cheeks. "It's not true. And even if it was, it wouldn't get me what I want right now."

"Which is?"

"To get out of this game."

"So, that's all you want? To get out of this game?"

"Yes."

"And then what?"

Bernard slipped behind a corner of a crumbling building ahead.

"Then I want to figure out how to get into the Colony," I said.

He smiled thinly. "Everybody wants to get into the Colony. What's so great about that place, anyway?"

"It's not here. It's a place where somebody can make a fresh start and have a chance at a better life." I crossed my arms as I trudged along. I didn't want to reveal too much of myself to Rogan, considering how little I knew about him. It made me uncomfortable. "What about you? If you don't want to go to the Colony, what do you want?"

"Revenge." He said it so quickly that it surprised me.

"Against who?"

He smiled cruelly, showing his perfect white teeth. "Against everyone who's screwed me over. Trust me, it's a long list."

His cold words chilled me. "I'll try my best to stay off it."

"Good idea."

"There are seven minutes left in this level of Countdown," the disembodied voice announced.

Rogan's shoulders tensed, and he picked up his pace.

"Wait." Panic welled in my chest. "There has to be another way."

He met my gaze, and I could see his was strained. "I have a theory. This guy…this Bernard Jones…he's a plant, a paid actor. Something. Maybe he's not as innocent as you think. Maybe he knows what's going on, and this is just another test."

"Why would you think that?"

He shook his head. "I'm not positive. But, the game…they don't bring in outsiders. They don't target civilians who have nothing to do with *Countdown* in the first place, it's just not their style."

"You keep talking about the game like you know all about it. *How?*"

"You're going to have to take my word for it, Kira. Just listen to me. If they start bringing in unassuming civilians, then they run the risk of being exposed. The last thing the Subscribers want is to have their friends and family learn their dirty little secret—that they pay money to see torture and murder on live TV."

It made sense. Even though the cops might not care what happened to criminals, they'd definitely care what happened to the regular civilian. The city might be a mess, but it wasn't total chaos.

"So, you think all we need to do is confront him? Get him to admit who he really is?"

He nodded. "That's my theory. I'm hoping like hell I'm right."

Before I could say anything else, Rogan stopped walking and shouted, "Bernard Jones!"

The man halted and turned around. We were currently in the middle of a city parking lot that was totally abandoned. No cars. Nobody was even in the pay booth. Dusk had begun to creep in and the shadows grew longer in front of us.

Even from a distance I could see Bernard's wariness as he saw the teenage boy who'd called out his name.

"What do you want?" he asked.

"Just to talk," Rogan said.

"Who are you?"

"I'm Rogan. This is Kira. We need some help."

He shook his head. "Not from me, you don't."

I looked back in the direction of the mall, but it was blocked by other buildings. This part of the city was vacant.

No witnesses.

No witnesses except for the cameras, that is. Two of them approached from behind us, parting and moving to either side of the parking lot.

Multi-view. How convenient.

"Who are you, Bernard?" Rogan asked.

"Wh-what do you mean?"

"I mean, who are you? Who sent you here? Tell me what you know."

Bernard shook his head. "I don't have any idea what you're talking about."

There was a sharp, discarded piece of metal on the ground,

and Rogan snatched it up. He moved closer. "You have very little time. Tell us who you really are."

"There are five minutes remaining in this level of Countdown."

Bernard's eyes widened, but he said nothing to give any indication that he was a game plant.

Oh, God, I thought. *He is just a civilian.*

"Rogan, what are you doing?" My heart was pounding painfully against my ribs.

He didn't look at me. "I already told you. I'm doing what I have to do."

I shook my head. "You can't. Please. My family—"

"What happened to your family has nothing to do with this." He glanced over his shoulder at me and met my gaze. "I'm sorry, Kira. There's no other choice. Not if we want to live."

His eyes held a look of despair, which quickly closed off to cold blankness. Then he tore his gaze from mine and stalked toward Bernard.

Bernard froze as Rogan approached, weapon in hand.

Why wasn't Bernard running? We didn't have him cornered.

"You're Bernard Jones," he said.

"Yes. I already said I was. I don't know what this is about. I—I don't want any trouble."

"Neither did I."

The man blinked nervously. "Listen, you can have my money. All of it. Just don't hurt me."

"Money doesn't do me any good anymore."

I'd approached on Rogan's left side, and I touched his arm, which felt every bit as hard as that metal bar would.

"Rogan…" He was going to kill this man in cold blood.

I could see the icy determination in his eyes. I felt as helpless as I had the night my family was killed, when all I could do was hide in the dark and wait for the horrible silence to finally come, the silence that meant it was all over.

"Please!" Bernard's voice shook as he eyed the shiny weapon. "I have a family who needs me."

"Do I look like I care?" Rogan's voice caught on the last word.

"I recognize you," Bernard babbled. "You...you're Rogan Ellis. You killed people. Girls. Killed them brutally. Some while they were asleep in their beds. I remember seeing it on the news."

A tremor went through Rogan at his words. "Do you believe everything you see on the news?"

"You're going to kill me, too, aren't you? *Aren't you?*" He fell to his knees and shielded his face with his hands.

"Rogan, please don't do this," I begged. I didn't understand why this man was giving up so easily, without a fight. Without any physical resistance at all. "Please!"

Rogan's chest heaved in and out. Then he raised the piece of metal above his head as if he would bring it down in a death blow.

But...something stopped him. Slowly he lowered the weapon back down to his side.

He looked at me, his brows drawn tightly together over haunted eyes. "Do *you* believe everything you see on the news, too?"

My breath caught. "I don't watch the news. But, no. I make my own decisions. And you...I—I don't believe you're a bad person—no matter what they say. I *don't*. You're better than this. I know you are."

I meant every single word. Somehow, I just hadn't realized it before this moment.

His hands were shaking. "I can't do it, Kira. I can't do it. I can't kill an innocent man. Even to save us. We're going to lose."

The deadly piece of metal fell from his grip.

"There are four minutes remaining in this level of Countdown."

I pulled Rogan to me and hugged him tight. "It's okay. This isn't losing. If you'd done it, *that* would be losing to me."

Bernard was fumbling around in his pockets. He let go of his shopping bag, and it hit the cement with a thud. Pieces of paper and old tissues fell out of his jacket pockets.

What was he looking for? His wallet? His ID? A piece of gum?

Then he pulled out a gun and raised it up to Rogan's head.

When he smiled, there was something unnatural about it. "Other contestants have taken me out in less than ten minutes."

Rogan tensed and swore under his breath as he let go of me, shoving me behind him. "I knew it."

"You are supposed to be a remorseless murderer. I expected that you would have no problem at all with this level. She—" he nodded at me "—was the wild card. She's not a murderer. It would have been interesting to see if she tried to stop you, but she didn't."

"I did," I said as confusion slid through me over this unexpected turn of events. "I didn't want him to kill you."

He shrugged. "You didn't put up much of a fight. He would have killed me, and you would not have stopped him. Unfortunately, Rogan Ellis is a coward. The Subscribers will be horribly disappointed. According to a recent poll, they had very high expectations that you would survive this level."

Rogan eyed the gun. "Ask me if I give a shit what the Subscribers think."

Bernard smiled that strange, steady smile. "It is fine. The Subscribers will be sated when I eliminate both of you for failing to complete the level successfully." He moved the gun toward me. "Perhaps I will start with you, Kira Jordan."

Rogan put an arm in front of me. "What are you?"

I frowned at his choice of words: *What,* instead of *who.*

Bernard's head swiveled toward him. "I am highly surprised you don't already know the answer to that, Rogan Ellis. I am an Ellipsis Cyber Drone, model number 6.1."

What kind of an answer was that? What did that even mean?

"An *Ellipsis* Cyber Drone?" Rogan's eyebrows shot up. "But—but how?"

"There have been many advancements made in artificial intelligence in recent years, Rogan Ellis," Bernard said evenly. "I am only one of them."

"What does that mean?" I asked, breathless, my hands raised in front of me, shaking. This was too much to understand— my head spun with confusion and frustration.

"He's a robot," Rogan growled without taking his eyes off Bernard. "With a very advanced artificial intelligence program. I knew there was something wrong, but I guess I just don't trust my instincts anymore. Of course they wouldn't make us kill a civilian."

"Three minutes remain in this level of Countdown.*"*

Bernard's fake smile slipped back to reveal more of his bright white teeth. "Rogan Ellis, a murderer scheduled to be transferred to Saradone Maximum Security Prison in three days, could not bring himself to kill an Ellipsis Cyber Drone. For that, both of you shall be eliminated from the game."

A cold line of perspiration slid down my spine.

The robot smirked, and suddenly I could see what he truly was. Before I'd been too much in shock to see that this guy didn't look human after all. He was too shiny, too seamless. His eyes reflected no inner personality. His voice had a slight metallic tininess to it that reminded me of the computer countdown in my head.

"Rogan Ellis, willing to risk his life to compete on *Countdown* rather than go to prison. Did you fear it? Did you have nightmares of what might happen to you there? My database tells me that the scar on your face is from a fight with two of your roommates at St. Augustine's. They wanted to kill you. Instead, you killed one of them with your bare hands. You are a killer."

"You're right," Rogan growled, before flicking a look at me. "I am a killer. Don't doubt it. And I'd kill that son of a bitch again if I got the chance."

"Self-defense," I whispered, my throat tight. "It's different."

"Didn't feel different to me."

"There are two minutes remaining in this level of Countdown."

"You know what, robot?" Rogan said with zero emotion in his voice. "I still have two minutes left to reduce you to a pile of tin cans. You can't kill us until *after* the level's done, right? So, we still have time."

The robot nodded with a firm jerk of his head. "This is true. I cannot kill you yet."

He lowered the gun and pulled the trigger.

I fell to the ground, screaming and clutching my leg where the bullet had ripped into my upper right thigh.

"Kira!" Rogan roared.

"However," the robot continued. "I can still entertain the Subscribers as we wait for the level to come to its conclusion." He chambered another round. "Rogan Ellis, I would have believed that you would appreciate watching another young girl writhing around in agony before her inevitable death. Why do you look so unhappy?"

I could barely hear him. My leg was on fire, and it was all I could do to wrestle through the pain. For a moment, my vision went completely white. I couldn't hear anything except the countdown, now at one minute.

One minute until there would be no more pain.

"59...58...57..."

Rogan rushed Bernard and grabbed his arms, wrestling him to the ground. The gun skittered across the pavement, coming to rest an arm's reach away from me.

"Son of a bitch!" Rogan snarled as he pounded his fist into the robot's face. Through my blurred vision I saw a glimmer of metal show beneath the artificial skin.

With a metallic roar, Bernard flipped Rogan onto his back, effortlessly pinning him to the ground. A viselike metal grip fastened around his neck.

"Do not fear, Rogan," the robot said in an eerily calm voice. "It will all be over soon. You failed. You failed Kira Jordan and you failed yourself."

"30...29...28..."

I reached out and wrapped my hand around the gun, and then staggered up on my left leg, doing my best to ignore the searing pain in my right leg. Nausea nearly forced me back down to the ground. Swaying unsteadily, I somehow managed to stay upright. Bernard looked up at me from where he had

Rogan pressed against the hard ground. I could see the robot underneath the skin. Just multicolored wires and smooth silver metal like the cameras that spun around the area taking in every angle of the scene. His skin must have been plastic. Just plastic.

All of it was fake.

I'd been ready to die to protect somebody who didn't even exist.

"10...9...8..."

I raised the gun and pulled the trigger over and over until it was empty. I hoped it would be enough.

It was. It blew Bernard's robot head clean off his body.

I dropped the gun, collapsed back to the ground, and let the pain wash over me. Rogan crawled to my side.

"Kira." There was a red mark around his neck where the robot had almost choked him to death. "Are you okay?"

His hand clamped down on my thigh, attempting to slow the bleeding.

I tried to speak but found that I couldn't form any words.

What I wanted to say was: *Okay? Do I look okay to you?*

Just before I passed out, I heard the voice in my head:

"*Congratulations, Rogan and Kira, on successfully completing level three of* Countdown."

7

IT WAS DARK THAT NIGHT. SO DARK.

"Mom?...Dad?" I said, too softly for anyone to actually hear me. I'd gone to bed early, mad that I couldn't get something—new jeans, a new purse...didn't matter anymore. Didn't matter then.

My bedroom door was closed. Locked. I didn't want to talk to anybody. Not even my friends who were sending me text messages. I ignored the soft vibrating sound my new phone made every few minutes.

It was after midnight on a school night. I remember I had a big test the next day that I hadn't studied for. Math, I think. Or Neo-Geography. I didn't care what happened—if I passed or failed. I actually couldn't think of one thing in this stupid, boring city I really cared about.

The creaking sound in the hallway of somebody moving around startled me. I heard heavy boots and the scrape of something metallic, which immediately told me—through both my gut instinct and my actual senses—it wasn't either of my parents. It also wasn't my older sister returning from a late date and sneaking back in the house so she wouldn't get in trouble for breaking the new citywide curfew of eleven o'clock. She'd gotten back from the movie theater hours earlier.

It was somebody else.

Somebody bad.

For a moment I thought it might just be my imagination. My overwrought, overworked brain always came up with the worst-case scenario. My mom said I should be a writer since I always made up such crazy, overly dramatic stories.

All I knew for sure, as I lay in my bed that night with the sheets pulled up to my nose, listening to the footsteps outside my door, was that I had this sense. A sense of impending doom.

Something was wrong. Horribly wrong.

I could hear my father's footsteps as he moved into the hallway to investigate the noises. I heard shouting.

There were gunshots—two gunshots—and then a heavy thump as my father's body hit the floor.

Then I heard the screams as my mother…and then my sister—oh, God, both of them—as they were confronted by the intruder. More shots rang out. My whole body shook as I tumbled off the side of my bed and crawled underneath it, tears streaming down my cheeks. My whole world narrowed in on that moment. Those three minutes felt like three years.

When all was silent, when my family was dead, I heard my door rattle as the murderer tried to get into my room. My door was locked, but he would have had no problem busting it open.

I'm going to die, *was all I could think. And I was afraid. So afraid.*

But suddenly there came the sound of police sirens, and the intruder fled, without another sound, without a word, into the night. He was never caught.

I hadn't even said good-night to my family. And then they were gone forever.

Ever since that night, the inky black of darkness just reminded me

*of how close to death I'd come. How powerless I was. Darkness, any
darkness, felt like hands clutching at my throat, holding me down.*

"No… No…please. Not again."

"Kira, it's okay. You're going to be okay. Open your eyes.
It's okay. I'm with you."

A warm touch brushed away my tears and stroked the hair
back from my face.

My eyes shot open. The first thing that came fully into
focus was Rogan. He sat on the edge of the bed I was lying
in. He looked like hell, still dirty and bloody and a total mess,
but the sight of him managed to chase away the last traces of
my nightmare.

He frowned. "What's that?"

"What do you mean?" My voice sounded croaky.

"That thing on your face."

I reached up. "What is it?"

"I think it's…yes, it's definitely a smile."

I let out a long breath and rolled my eyes. "Obviously a total
mistake. There's no reason for me to be smiling right now. Is
my leg still attached?"

He glanced down the length of my body and then looked
back up at me with half a grin on his face.

"For now." The grin faded. "You were having a bad dream."

"I can't imagine why I would be. We've been having so
much fun." I tried to look around but didn't see anything other
than a bland room with a small window that only looked out
to another building. "Where are we now?"

"They brought us to a medical station. I guess you getting
shot wasn't in the script."

"There's a script?"

He shrugged. "Who knows?" His gaze met mine, and I

noticed for the first time since I woke up how anguished it was. "I was worried about you."

"That makes two of us."

"Don't joke." He brought his hand back up to stroke my face gently. "Seriously, though. I'm really glad you're okay."

For a moment, he didn't move his hand away, and I didn't push it away. But then he blinked and dropped his arm to his side.

I bit my bottom lip. "So, uh, now what?"

"So now we're waiting for somebody to check your leg and release us, I guess. They took the bullet out already and patched you up. They gave you some pain meds, which is probably the reason you were out so long."

"How long?"

"Nearly eighteen hours."

I raised my eyebrows. "Eighteen hours?"

He nodded. I lifted the white sheets to look down at myself. My clothes were gone, and I was now wearing a white, scratchy hospital gown. My right thigh had been bandaged.

I looked up at him. "You've been here the whole time? With me?"

He nodded. "They said I should wait outside, but I refused. I thought they'd beat the crap out of me for giving them attitude, but they didn't. Don't know why. They let me sit in here with you after they were finished with your leg."

"For eighteen hours? You've been sitting next to me the whole time?"

"I dozed for a bit myself, but otherwise…yeah." He looked away. "I was here."

I felt my cheeks heat up. He'd been watching me sleep. That should totally creep me out, but instead it made me feel… I don't know. It made me feel *secure* for some reason. Like he was looking out for me. Making sure nobody hurt me.

Which didn't make a damn bit of sense.

Why would a murderer want to be my guardian angel? Why did being around him fill me with anything but fear? Why did I trust him not to hurt me when I was completely helpless?

Because I didn't totally believe he was guilty, that's why. I'd seen no indication at all that he was cruel or heartless— someone capable of killing and dismembering nine girls. While he'd admitted he'd killed his roommate in self-defense, he hadn't been able to bring himself to kill Bernard when he thought he was just an innocent civilian.

He didn't do it.

The clear and sudden revelation helped to push the rest of my doubts away.

Which was probably why I found myself placing my hands on either side of his face and drawing him closer to me. I slid a hand down and over his chest to feel his heart pounding hard and fast.

"Kira, what are you doing?" Our lips were so close. His breath was so warm.

But then he tensed and pulled back. The look on his face held such confusion and awkwardness that it almost made me laugh.

I'd nearly kissed him.

Then it hit me with crystal-clear clarity.

Oh, my God. *I'd nearly kissed him.*

It was the pain drugs. Yeah. Had to be the pain drugs. They were totally tripping me out and making me do things I would never normally do in a million years.

Not like this. Not here. And not with somebody like Rogan

Ellis, who would only make my life even more complicated than it already was.

I bit my bottom lip. "Can I ask you a question?"

He eyed me as if I might do something else utterly unexpected—either kiss him or kill him. "Of course."

"When we were out there with that robot thing...you asked if I believed everything I saw on the news."

His mouth formed a thin line. "Yeah."

"What did you mean?"

"Nothing. I was stalling for time. Didn't work. He shot you anyhow." He crossed his arms. "You said no, right? That you didn't believe everything the news says."

"That's right. I don't. And I don't watch the news to begin with, haven't for ages." I reached up and grabbed his shirt to force him to look at me. "I'm going to ask you something and I want you to tell me the truth. You hear me? The *truth*." I sounded surprisingly strong for somebody stuck on her back with a bullet just pulled from her leg.

"What?"

"Did you do it?"

His eyes narrowed. "Do *what*?"

"What they said you did."

His jaw clenched and he looked away. "I'm going to check on what's taking them so long."

I grabbed a tighter hold of his shirt. If he was getting up, then he was taking me with him. "Those nine girls. Did you murder them like they said you did? Damn it, Rogan. Tell me the truth."

He searched my face. "Why are you asking me this? Everyone just assumes I'm guilty as sin. Why wouldn't you?"

"Because they're the scumbags that plucked me out of my

normal life and are trying to kill me in their stupid game. Why would I believe *anything* they tell me?"

He was silent for a long time, and then said, "I'm a very bad person, Kira."

I clutched his hand tightly, just in case he was thinking about trying to get away from me again. "Just being a bad person doesn't necessarily mean that you did what they said."

He looked away.

"Just tell me. It's simple, really. You either did it or you didn't."

He shook his head. "Nothing's simple. Nothing in my life has ever been simple."

"Did you kill those girls?"

"No, I didn't." He met my gaze again—his tortured. Haunted. He'd been through hell even before entering this game. For someone who was still a teenager, his eyes held a lifetime of pain and misery.

Rogan wasn't lying to me. He was innocent of those horrible crimes. I'd bet my life on it. In fact, I think I already had.

"You believe me," he said very softly.

I nodded, my throat tight. "I believe you. But why would they say that if it isn't true? Why would you let them?"

His brows drew tightly together. "It's complicated."

My gaze softened, and I touched his face, tracing my index finger gently along his scar. "So, you were locked up for something you didn't even do?"

He swallowed hard and entwined his fingers with mine. "I told you already. I'm a very bad person. If you knew the truth about me, you wouldn't be looking at me like that. You'd hate me. And you'd sure as hell not want to be this close to me."

"You killed your roommate, but it was in self-defense. I can't hold that against you. You had no choice."

He shook his head. "No, I'm not talking about that. It's something else. Something worse."

My stomach twisted. "Tell me. Rogan. I promise I won't hate you."

Our eyes locked, and I was certain he was going to answer me. But then the door on my right opened and Jonathan walked in. Two men dressed all in white accompanied him, but they stayed by the door while he approached my bed.

"You're awake," Jonathan said, adjusting his wire-frame glasses.

I glared at him. "You're observant."

His smile held no warmth. "I've been instructed to tell you that your next level will lead to a contestant reward. Should you complete it successfully, you'll receive something very special."

We both gave him a blank look.

He cleared his throat. "Rogan, would you mind giving Kira and me a few moments alone?"

Rogan's expression tensed. "I'd rather stay here."

Jonathan's smile grew. "To protect her from me?"

"Maybe."

"Trust me, that won't be necessary." He paused. "I really would prefer you leave of your own free will, Rogan. If not, then there are other methods I can use to remove you from the room."

The silent, white-clad men stood at the doorway with their arms crossed.

"It's okay." I touched his arm to find that it was tensely corded muscle.

He met my gaze and nodded once. With a last look at Jonathan, one edged in violence, he finally let go of my hand and left the room.

The two men also left, closing the door behind them, leaving Jonathan and me alone.

"Who *are* you?" I asked after a heavy, silent moment had gone by.

"We already met earlier. Jonathan, remember?"

I rolled my eyes. "I remember everything that's happened to me. Vividly. Consider it burned into my brain forever. But that doesn't explain anything."

The smile continued to play on his lips, which I found annoying. To say the least.

"What's so funny?" I demanded.

"You are, Kira."

"Is that so?" I straightened up in the bed, my fists curled tightly at my sides.

"I mean it as a compliment." The smile faded around the edges, and I noticed that it had never reached his eyes. They were dead serious. "Most normal girls would not have lasted as long as you have in this game. When you were chosen to play, I had my doubts, but they've dissipated with each passing level."

"What do you mean by normal girls?"

He spread his hands. "We've had only males play, until now. Men and boys who were accustomed to a life of struggle and violence, whom no one would miss should they be...unsuccessful. Some rise to the challenge and others crumple under the pressure to perform, or face the consequences of failure. We've never had a female competitor before."

"Why was I the lucky chosen one? I'm sure there are a lot

of women in prison who would have jumped at the chance to come on this Reality TV show from hell."

Jonathan cocked his head. "Is that what you think this is? A Reality TV show?"

"Isn't it?"

"This may bear a passing resemblance to the television programs available decades ago, but that was then and this is now. Nothing on the Network is like those innocent survival games."

I glared at him. "Yeah, Rogan was telling me something about elimination meaning death. And that robot guy put a bullet in my leg to prove it."

He glanced at the white sheet that covered me from my chest down. "How is your leg? May I see?"

Was he evading this discussion? I needed more information. "No, you may not."

He hissed out a long breath. "I know you don't trust me, Kira—"

"Oh, *should* I trust you? As far as I can tell you're just one of the bastards who put me and Rogan in this situation in the first place."

"You include Rogan. Have you come to be concerned for his safety as well as your own in such a short time?"

I slunk down in the bed. "That's none of your business."

"It is curious to me how a vibrant young girl like yourself would so quickly come to care for someone like Rogan. You are aware of the reason he was sent to juvenile detention, aren't you? Why he was on his way to prison once he legally becomes an adult?"

I frowned at him. "Crimes that I'd never forgive anyone for."

"Yes, given your history, and what happened to your family, I can see that. But you seem to like him, anyway. Why is that, if I might ask?"

"Because he's innocent," I said simply.

His eyebrows shot up above the rims of his glasses. "Are you so sure of that?"

"I'm sure."

Jonathan studied me for a moment with curiosity. "Did you use your Psi ability on him? Your ability to connect empathically with another?"

I went very cold and still at his words. "Excuse me?"

"Don't be alarmed. It isn't common knowledge. In fact, I am one of the very few connected with *Countdown* that know of your hidden talents."

"What are you talking about? What Psi ability?" My heart was pounding loud and fast against my rib cage.

A frown creased his brow as he studied me for a moment. "Don't tell me you don't know what you can do. Didn't anyone ever tell you?"

I knew I had that…something. Something that made my head feel as if it might split open. Something that gave me an insight on whether somebody was good or bad. There were times I'd considered that it might be Psi-related, but I'd never been sure.

"Nobody told me anything," I finally said, fighting to keep my expression neutral.

He continued to study my face, perhaps to gauge if I was lying to him. Finally, he nodded. "Then it's high time you knew. All doctors keep special records on their patients— especially female children born after the Plague. A certain percentage have been found to be psychically gifted. According to your records, you are one of these girls."

"I am?" I'd never been told anything like this before. I had a doctor before, of course. My father had worked for the university, so he could afford it. We had gone once a year for a physical—blood work, body scans, everything. It had taken a whole day, and it had been really boring. My friends never had to go through the same thing. At the time, I'd envied them.

My last exam had been a week before my family was murdered.

But if anything like this had come out of those tests, I'd never been told a thing.

Jonathan nodded. "Perhaps you weren't informed since you're marked down as a low-level empath, which typically would not cause much interest from the scientific community." He walked toward the small window overlooking another gray building. "Other girls with high-level Psi powers are taken to the Colony as soon as their abilities are discovered, so they can grow up in a much more stable environment—given housing, education and access to peers who are going through the same experiences. Those with the low-level abilities are mostly ignored. But I spotted it in your files—in your DNA profile. I thought your abilities might help you along in the game in some small way. Perhaps I was wrong."

There was no smile on his face anymore as he turned from the window to look at me.

I struggled to process everything he'd said. I was a Psi, a low-level one. Somebody able to get a minor empathic read on another human being. That fit with what I'd discovered about myself already. It was as if a missing piece had just clicked into place for me.

But I'd failed this test by not being strong enough. If I'd been stronger, I would have had a better life. I'd be in the Colony right now, going to school, learning about my abilities.

Instead, I was here, lying in a hospital bed after being shot in the leg.

I didn't want to admit anything to Jonathan, but I needed more information. "If what you're saying is true, how did you think it would help me?"

"I wasn't sure, exactly. An empath—well, it isn't a tangible talent. If you were telekinetic it could be a different story. Even having a low-level telekinetic ability would be an asset in a game such as this. However, he doesn't fully believe in Psi abilities, so it doesn't matter in the long run."

Empath...someone able to sense another's emotions—and in my case, barely. Telekinetic...somebody able to move stuff with their mind. I could see how that would have been a major asset in this game. I had a fleeting fantasy of blowing up the digicams with the power of my mind. Just my luck that I'd landed a lame Psi ability.

I sat up higher in the bed. "Wait. Who doesn't believe in it?"

He hesitated before answering. "The producer of *Countdown,* Gareth. He's pleased with your showing so far, but doesn't feel that your minor Psi abilities have had anything to do with your success. Our Subscribers are also very happy with the inclusion of a female player. We've had a forty percent increase in viewing time since your game began, making *Countdown* the number one program on the Network. And the more they view our offering rather than switch to another feed, the happier Gareth is."

Gareth. At least I now had a name to focus my hatred toward. The producer. The reason I was here, fighting for my very life.

I tried to process everything Jonathan had told me. If my doctor had written in my profile that I had Psi abilities, did that mean my parents had known? They'd never discussed it with me. It had been a total surprise one day after my thirteenth birthday, when I'd touched somebody and felt...something. Luckily it didn't happen *every* time I touched somebody, because when this strange ability clicked in, it hurt really bad.

I wanted to ask Jonathan if it was supposed to hurt. But I held back my questions. Sharing *anything* about what I'd discovered felt as if I was exposing my vulnerabilities. Giving my enemies a chance to use them against me.

Still, why was Jonathan sharing all of this with me? How did this help the game? All he had to do was patch me up and let me get back to the game, but I would have sworn I saw concern in his gaze.

It was something. Maybe something I could work with. "Jonathan, you have to help me. Help *us*. I don't want to die."

"I know you don't." He nodded grimly. "Please, Kira, let me see your leg."

I shook my head.

"You don't trust me."

I didn't trust anybody. "Despite this little heart-to-heart, I can't think of a single reason why I should."

He rolled up his right sleeve and thrust his forearm at me. "Test your empathic abilities." He studied my face. "You *know* you have something, don't you? You've known for a while, even if it was never confirmed before today. Maybe it scared you. Maybe it hurt you. But, please, try, right now. Touch me and see if you can get a sense of who I really am."

I wanted to keep denying what he was saying, but words failed me. I waited for a long moment before I decided to do as he said. I tentatively reached out to touch the skin of his forearm just below his elbow, pressing my fingers against his flesh.

"Close your eyes," he said. "And focus. Flex your mind."

Flex my mind? I closed my eyes and tried to push away all other thoughts. Since my mind was currently rather full, this took a bit of effort.

When my mind had cleared enough that I was able to fully concentrate on my task, I reached out with that *something* inside of me, that strange thing I'd been aware of for three years that scared me. I reached out toward Jonathan…

Then it was there—like a dark pool before me. I waded into it ankle deep.

This was different than before. I was actually *trying* this time, not coming across this situation by accident. It was real, not just my imagination. I had proof now, even if it was only Jonathan's word. I had the chance to explore just a little deeper than I normally would.

And I wanted to test myself, to know what I could do. It suddenly seemed like the most important thing in the world.

I inhaled sharply as the sensations began to flow over me. It wasn't anything coherent or totally understandable. Just flashes of emotion. Snapshots of feelings.

Jonathan felt tired. He felt angry, determined. Sincere.

And guilty…about something. About *everything*.

A sensation of goodness swept over me. Sadness. Despair. Hopelessness. A man who'd been forced to do things he didn't agree with…

Then a spear of pain lanced through my brain, and I let go of him, pressing my palms against the sides of my head.

Agony!

Now *that* was a sensation I recognized.

After a moment, a cold cloth pressed against my forehead, and I opened my eyes slowly. The fluorescent lights above now seemed too bright, and I squinted. Jonathan held a wet towel against my forehead. He stared at me with wide eyes.

"You sensed something, didn't you?" he asked breathlessly. "I felt you in my mind."

The pain began to subside. "Did it hurt?"

"No." He frowned. "Though, it was a curious feeling. I knew you could do it. I *knew* it. Are you well?"

I pushed his hand away. "Well enough, I guess."

"What did you sense from me? Enough that you now trust me to help you? Were you able to see that I'm not trying to deceive you?"

"I wouldn't go that far, but I saw enough." If what I'd felt was real, I now knew he wouldn't take much pleasure in watching me or Rogan die on a Network death game.

Finally, I pulled at the sheets that covered my hurt leg. It was a small act of faith, but he seemed pleased by it. He undid the bandaging and inspected my injury.

"Very good. It's healed as well as I'd hoped."

I frowned and looked down. Where I expected to find an oozing bullet wound was only a soft, bright pink mark that had already nearly healed over. It didn't even hurt when he touched it gently.

Rogan had said I'd been out for eighteen hours. But even eighteen hours wasn't long enough to heal a bullet wound.

"How—?" I began.

"We have a great deal of technology at our fingertips here, Kira. The company I work for has always had a hand in research—be it computers and artificial intelligence or medical research. That is why I originally came on board ten years ago. Unfortunately, due to recent rules and regulations and the nondisclosure agreement I signed, I'm unable to share this research with anyone outside of the corporation."

I touched my leg, running a finger along it. The wound was flat. I was healed. From an injury that had felt as if it had torn my leg clean off.

"What kind of a company is this, anyhow? And who is this Gareth guy? He has people doing secret medical research? And *he's* the one in charge of this game?" I shuddered. "He sounds absolutely horrible."

"He wasn't always." Jonathan turned away from me to look toward the small frosted window on the opposite wall. When he returned his gaze to mine, it was flat, hard. The emotion I'd seen there a minute ago had left the building. "Now, I must fill you in on the next level of *Countdown*."

Tears of frustration stung my eyes. "But I can't keep playing. You need to help me. Please, Jonathan."

His jaw clenched. "I am sorry, but the only way you can escape the game is to win it. You used your empath skills to read me. You must know that there's nothing I can do to change what is."

I had read him. The overwhelming feeling I'd gotten from him before my head nearly exploded had been hopelessness.

We were silent for a moment.

"Jonathan," I began. "If I win…if Rogan and I both get through all six levels—"

"It doesn't have to be the two of you anymore."

My breath cut off. "What?"

"I know the rules were never properly explained to you.

Plus, they're different for each team who plays. For you, after level three, both you and Rogan don't need to survive to the end for one of you to be considered the winner."

I let this disturbing information settle over me. "What about the implants? We need to stay close."

"You still do. But if one of you is killed during a level, the other will be allowed to continue on."

I swallowed hard. He put such a horrible outcome so bluntly; it was as if someone had punched me in the stomach. "What happens if we *do* win?"

"The champion or champions get to choose his or her own prize."

It was still difficult for me to find my breath. "Would I be able to request transportation and entrance to the Colony?"

The smile reappeared on his face. "Certainly. First-class transportation to the Colony and a brand-new life."

"A brand-new life," I repeated. "I like the sound of that."

Jonathan smiled. "I think you'd do very well in the Colony, Kira."

I let all the wonderful possibilities, the dream of freedom and a brand-new life, drift through my mind. "But we can still both win, right? Both me and Rogan?"

"Yes, if you both survive, you will both win."

The tightness in my chest eased a little. "Maybe Rogan would like it in the Colony, too."

A crease formed between his brows. "You believe he's innocent."

I nodded and arranged the sheets back over my legs. "That's right."

"Did you use your empathic ability on him?"

I tensed. "I tried, even though I didn't know what it really was, what I could do. But I didn't have enough time to concentrate long enough on him. So I just asked him. He told me the truth. I believe him."

The grim expression on Jonathan's face was not setting my mind at ease. My heart began to race.

"I see." He rubbed his fingers over his short black goatee.

"You see what?"

I looked over at the door. Was Rogan still waiting outside? Had those men taken him away? He couldn't have gone too far since my implant wasn't giving off the ninety-feet-or-more warning signal.

Jonathan didn't say anything for so long that my anxiety peaked.

"Jonathan! You see *what?*" I said again, louder this time.

"It is not my place to say. In fact, I've stayed with you too long already. I was to check your leg and inform you that the next level is a reward level."

"I don't care about any reward unless it's a ticket to the Colony and out of this game." My voice had gone shrill and harsh. "What are you keeping from me? What do you know about Rogan?"

He shook his head. "I must leave."

I grabbed his arm and forced my gaze to soften. "I got a read on you, Jonathan. I know you're a good man inside, no matter what this Gareth guy is making you do. But if there's something I need to know about Rogan—" I hated to even question it, but... "He's...he's not really guilty of those horrible crimes, is he?"

I was afraid that I'd been a complete idiot to start trusting him—when I normally didn't trust *anyone*. An idiot to trust my *heart*. My heart had been closed up tight ever since my family had been murdered, but somehow with Rogan, it had started to open up just a little.

"I knew Rogan," Jonathan said. "Before any of this insanity began. His father and I were friends."

My eyes widened. "I had a feeling you already knew each other. I could tell when you helped him with his wound."

He nodded curtly and began pacing the length of the sterile, white room, wringing his hands. "I met Rogan two years ago when his father brought him to me to be put into a thirty-day youth treatment program I ran for Kerometh addiction."

I inhaled sharply. Kerometh had been the drug of choice ever since the Plague. Expensive, but easy to acquire, easy to take. I'd never experimented with it, but I'd heard that it put you into a state of disorientation. A deep, mindless bliss. But it lasted only a short time—a few hours tops. After that you immediately plunged into the painful withdrawal that could last weeks unless you got another hit. If you didn't, then violence and anger—they called it Kerometh-fury—took you over.

"Okay, so he had an addiction," I said. "So do a lot of people. Doesn't mean he deserved to go to St. Augustine's. Or Saradone."

Jonathan was silent for a moment. "There's a reason you were chosen to be Rogan's partner, Kira. Nothing is ever coincidental here."

"He didn't kill those girls. He couldn't have." I swallowed hard past the thick lump in my throat. "Don't you dare tell me he lied to me."

Jonathan shook his head. "No…he was telling you the truth. The murder of those nine poor girls was not his doing. He was charged and found guilty of the crime, but any proof was

inconclusive at best. But with his prior record for drug possession and other minor crimes, the courts didn't seem to care."

Relief flooded over me. "So he's innocent of murder?"

Jonathan was quiet for so long, I doubted for a moment that
he'd answer me. "I believe he's innocent of those murders.
But he is a murderer."

Something in his tone made me tense up again. "The robot
said that Rogan killed his roommate—that's how he got his
scar. But it was in self-defense."

"That's not the murder I'm referring to." Jonathan's expression was bleak. "I know you've started to care for him. That's
why it's vital that I tell you this now before it's too late."

I shook my head. I didn't want to hear what he was going
to say next.

"You have the right to know this." He hesitated, as if sum-
moning something inside of himself to speak the words to
follow. "One night during his treatment program two years
ago, Rogan slipped out of the facility. He was in withdrawal,
experiencing severe Kerometh-fury. He began breaking into
homes to steal enough money to buy more drugs. Yours was
one of the homes he broke into. Rogan is the one responsible
for murdering your family."

The silence that followed that statement was deafening.

"What?" My heart pounded, a thundering sound in my ears.

"He murdered your mother, father and sister. They were
not the first or last of his victims that night. Rogan doesn't
know you were connected to this act at all. He'd never seen
you before you met at the beginning of level one. His mind
is finally clear of his former addiction after spending the last
year and half in a secured and guarded juvenile detention hall.
But it doesn't change what he's done."

"What?"

I didn't want to believe it, but…it made sense. It made such horrible sense. No coincidences on *Countdown*. Of course, that's why they'd made us partners. Of course. They'd known all along who I was. Who *he* was.

Rogan, the boy with the beautiful ocean-colored eyes; the boy my gut told me was innocent; the boy I'd begun to believe in, heart and soul, even after such a short time.

He'd killed my family and taken everything from me. He'd stolen my life.

He should have killed me, too. I wish he had.

"I'm a very bad person," Rogan had told me only minutes ago. *"If you knew the truth about me, you wouldn't be looking at me like that. You'd hate me. And you'd sure as hell not want to be this close to me."*

I rocked myself back and forth for a long time, hugging my knees against my chest. Jonathan, the man my empathic ability had revealed to be truthful and honest and filled with guilt about the job he had to do, patted my back and gently wiped my tears away.

"I'm sorry, Kira. Perhaps I shouldn't have said anything, but I could see you growing closer to him. Too close. I cared for him once myself, I was like an uncle to him, but his addiction changed him so much—it created a monster. You don't deserve any of this, and I'm so sorry. All I can tell you is what I told you before…."

I waited for him to continue, but he didn't. "What?"

He cleared his throat before he spoke again, his expression stony. "Only one of you has to live to the end of *Countdown*. If Rogan dies in the next level, it won't be held against you.

You'll still get your ticket to the Colony. Do you understand what I'm telling you?"

I just stared at him. "I think so."

He nodded and took out a small black handheld device from his pocket. On its touch screen were a series of red and yellow buttons. "I'm very glad to hear it."

"What is that?"

His face was set in grim lines. "Now that I've determined you have healed enough, I'm afraid we must continue on to the next level. Are you ready, Kira?"

I shook my head. "No, I just need a little time. Just a little—"

"I'm sorry, but it's already begun." He pressed one of the buttons.

Everything went black.

LEVEL

4

I WOKE BUT STILL SAW ONLY BLACK. IT TOOK ME
a second to realize I was wearing a blindfold, and my hands
were bound behind my back.

Damn it. I hated the darkness. *Hated* it.

While I willed myself to stay as calm as possible, I concentrated on the announcer's voice in my head. The voice I'd
come to despise, ironically now the only thing keeping me
from freaking out.

"Yesterday in level three," he said, *"Kira received a bullet wound
to her upper femur. Without proper medical intervention, she would
have died from blood loss. She has now recovered enough to continue.*

*"She has performed to an exceptionally high level and the produc-
ers of* Countdown *are thrilled with your reaction to her and realize
you are hungry for more information about our first-ever female competitor. We thank you for your patience.*

*"Kira Jordan is sixteen years old and will be turning seventeen
in four months. It pleases her to know that you, as Subscribers, are
watching her every move as part of* Countdown, *as she and her*

*handsome but deadly partner, Rogan Ellis, fight for their lives in the
anticipation of winning the game.*

*"On the streets since she was fourteen, Kira survived as best she
could using her brain and her body to get what she needed. Desperate,
destitute and friendless, six months ago, she decided to use that body
to aid her survival. This is a path taken by many lost girls and it's
a story that inevitably ends in tragedy. Many prostitutes are beaten
or murdered every day. At the very least, they typically succumb to
Kerometh addiction.*

*"The client who was to be her first found Kira on her darkest day.
He was a man in search of a young girl—a lawyer who was the lead
partner at his firm. His wife had already left to enter the Colony, and
he was to join her in the days to follow. Little did Kira know that he
planned to torture and kill her—a hobby that he'd recently acquired.
She would have been his fifth victim.*

*"However, Kira had already decided that a life of prostitution was
not for her. A security camera in the man's house caught the action to
follow. As you can see on the video footage, when she asked to leave
he struck her and she fell to the floor.*

*"The lawyer's wife collected priceless antique china. A bowl had
broken next to Kira's prone form. As the man began to beat her, Kira
curled her fingers around the bowl, and she swung it toward his head,
an act that succeeded in knocking him unconscious.*

*"Before Kira fled the scene, she searched the man's body for his
wallet and took all of the money, which amounted to just under thirty
dollars.*

*"While his wife suspected her husband was unfaithful, neither
she—nor Kira—realized that he was actually a demented murderer.
Several bodies were later found in the backyard shed, and the man
was arrested and brought to justice.*

"Through this experience, Kira Jordan realized that stealing would

*help her to live to face the next day. To fight for survival in a dying
world. It has also led her here, to this very moment, to the next level
of* Countdown."

The blindfold was ripped from my face. I blinked. Two men
in white coats stood on either side of me. The skies were darkening with an approaching storm. I felt shaken at hearing one
of the lowest points in my life broadcast in a chilling singsong
voice. I'd had no idea until a minute ago that that bastard had
wanted to do anything but rape me—as if that hadn't been
bad enough. But he had planned to torture and kill me, too?

I hoped he was rotting in Saradone right now.

My wrists burned as the men released my bindings and one
of them shoved me. I staggered forward until I realized where
I was and stopped moving. At the top of a skyscraper. On the
very edge of the roof. If I'd taken another step I would have
dropped forty stories to the street far below.

"Kira!"

It was Rogan. Stretched between the tops of two skyscrapers was a small bridge, not more than eight inches wide. It
must have been fifty feet across between the two buildings.
In the exact middle was Rogan, lying horizontally, with his
arms stretched above his head. His wrists were bound to the
platform.

I looked down at myself. I was fully dressed again, in the
same clothes I'd worn before. My red shoes were still bright,
still new-looking, but the cargo pants were ruined, with the
bullet hole and dried blood evident on my right thigh. My
tank top had definitely seen better days.

"Welcome to level four," the hateful voice continued. *"Kira is
to rescue her partner by crossing a narrow and dangerous bridge high
above the city streets, and then the two must continue on to the other*

side to complete this level successfully. There will be no safety gear, no ropes, no tricks. All Kira has to work with is her sense of balance and self-preservation. Should they finish, they will be rewarded for their efforts. Our competitors have ten minutes to complete this level. Enjoy!"

My mouth went dry.

I didn't move. I stood in place and stared at Rogan. I'd always thought that my only fear was of the dark. Who knew about this nagging little fear of heights I'd managed to develop in the past two minutes?

Okay. So I had precisely ten minutes to rescue the boy who'd killed my family, all while trying not to fall dozens of stories to my death.

I scanned the area. The men who'd removed my blindfold and bindings were departing through the rooftop door. I ran over to it and tried the handle, but it had locked behind them.

I was all alone. Nobody to push me to do this. Nobody to force me.

Returning to the edge of the building, I eyed the narrow bridge.

"Nine minutes remain in this level of Countdown.*"*

I was going to die.

No, I admonished myself. *Let's at least try to think positively, okay?*

When I drew closer to the beginning of the platform, it was even narrower than I'd originally thought. I forced myself to breath normally.

When I was ten years old, I took gymnastics. I remember balancing on the beam, trying not to fall off. I'd been pretty good at it then, even been able to do a cartwheel or two. But the floor had been padded in case there were any tumbles.

That felt like a million years ago.

The platform seemed fairly stable. I tested it with my foot and it gave a little, but not much. Despite being healed by whatever medical magic Jonathan had done on me, my upper thigh ached. Still, it was way better than it would have been if he'd done nothing.

These *Countdown* people wanted their contestants to be in top shape before their precious Subscribers got to watch them die.

So sporting of them.

"Kira!" Rogan shouted again. He had his head up and looked at me. "Be careful!"

I ignored him. Thinking about him right now was only going to distract me. There was no time for me to be distracted. To say the least.

Don't look down.

The problem was, not looking down left me with very few options. The platform was so narrow that when I focused on it, I couldn't help but see the street so very, very far below me.

My right foot shook as I placed it on the platform, and I wavered for a second, holding my arms out to either side of me as I established my balance. I let out a long breath and tried to center myself.

Just like gymnastics. I needed to pretend that I was competing at the Olympics, if they were still being held. I wanted one of those gold medals I'd seen in the history books. I needed to focus on that gold medal. And nothing else.

"Eight minutes remain in this level of Countdown."

The voice seemed louder in my head than usual, which surprised me. I shook a little before managing to steady myself again. I took another tentative step.

"You're doing great, Kira!" Even from twenty feet away I

could tell Rogan's expression was strained. He pulled at his bindings and the platform shook.

"Don't do that!" I snapped. "Just stay still."

"Sorry!"

"Yeah," I muttered under my breath, and a line of sweat trickled down my forehead and onto my nose. "You're going to be sorry, you son of a bitch."

I couldn't think about anything negative. Nothing. All I could focus on was putting one foot in front of the other—

"Seven minutes remain in this level of Countdown."

—and doing it quickly.

Damn it. That voice was so distracting.

I took another step.

A silver digicam buzzed past my face, so close that I felt the breeze it created.

"How is Kira feeling right now?" the announcer asked. *"Is she ready to win* Countdown *and receive her ultimate prize? Does she want all of her dreams to come true in the Colony after surviving the last two years of hardship and loneliness?"*

I glared up into its lens. "Go to hell."

It flew away and out of my peripheral vision, but I could still see two other cameras whizzing around the air nearby.

Jonathan had told them what I wanted to win. Okay, so that made it official. I was playing for keeps. I wanted that prize more than I wanted anything else in the world.

Another step. *Balance.* Another step. *Balance.*

Rogan was much closer now, his head still propped up, and he watched me as I approached. His jaw was tense. The muscles in his arms tight. As I got closer, I was shocked to see a small grin appear on his lips.

"What are you smiling at?" I growled.

"Just the fact that you've come to my rescue. Does that make you my knight in shining armor?"

I didn't smile. "I haven't rescued you yet."

His grin faded. "Just watch your step. Don't fall. Here comes another camera."

It buzzed close enough that it almost touched me. "Are they trying to knock me off this thing?"

"They're not trying to give you a helping hand, that's for sure."

"Why'd you let them tie you up like this?"

He pulled at the bindings. The platform shook slightly. "As if it was my idea. They took me outside the room and knocked me out again. I woke up here. Trust me, it was a big shock."

I studied the ropes that tied him. "This is going to be tricky."

"I don't think the knots are too tight. It's just awkward."

I studied the face of the boy who'd killed my family. Blue-green eyes framed with dark lashes. Fading scar. He also wore the same clothes as before: bloody, dirty, ripped. I'd been drawn to him, despite what I'd been told. I'd let him charm me into believing in him. Or…at least, *begin* to believe in him.

His dark brows were drawn together as he frowned up at me. "Why are you looking at me that way?"

I blinked back tears. "Just shut up. I need to concentrate."

One lesson in gymnastics had been how to kneel down on the beam without losing my balance. It took me forever to learn that without falling off, but I had finally gotten it. However, that had been six years ago, and it was definitely not a skill that I used all the time.

I slowly crouched down far enough that I could fumble

with the bindings around his ankles just above his worn, black boots.

His body took up the entire width of the platform and then some. He couldn't move without shaking everything around, and I couldn't get past him.

He eyed his wrists. "Now what?"

A camera whizzed past my ear, and I swatted at it, hitting cold metal.

"Five minutes remain in this level of Countdown.*"*

I met his gaze and saw there was more than a trace of fear behind it. There was concern. For me.

My heart wrenched. Why was he concerned for me? I hated that I'd convinced myself he was a good person—and even now, after everything, I still had doubts about his guilt. Was it because I wouldn't allow myself to believe I could feel something for the boy who'd murdered my family?

"I'm thinking."

He blinked. "What they said earlier…about what happened with you and that lawyer scumbag—"

"It was true. All of it."

His jaw tensed. "If he wasn't already dead I'd find him and rip his heart out."

I willed myself to stay focused on the platform. "Nothing happened. I learned my lesson the hard way."

"I'd still kill him."

"Is it that easy for you? Killing?" My voice broke on the word.

His expression darkened. "I'll do it for a good cause. For the right reason. To protect somebody I care about."

"Are you saying that you care about me?"

"Sure." He looked away. "And now I care that you untie me so we can get this goddamned level over with."

"Don't forget it's supposed to lead to a reward."

"I don't care. I just want us to get through it in one piece. Now you're going to have to climb over me and untie me so we can keep going. There's not much time left."

I put a hand on his jean-clad thigh and slowly eased myself lower. He spread his legs so his feet dangled off the side of the platform to give me space to maneuver. Now on my knees, I slid myself closer to him until I couldn't go any farther. I placed my hands on his firm stomach, then one at a time on his chest, sliding up to his shoulders. I grabbed the platform above his head on either side of his arms. Our bodies were now firmly pressed against each other.

His breathing hitched. "Damn."

"What?"

"Is it wrong that I'm enjoying this a little bit?"

"Are you?"

"Kira…" His eyes locked with mine, our faces so close I could feel his breath, hot against my lips.

I leaned in closer and whispered in his ear. "Jonathan told me that you're the one who murdered my family."

His eyes went wide. "What?"

"You heard me. Two years ago when you were a Kerometh addict." A tear slipped down my cheek and fell into the empty air beneath us. "You escaped from rehab and broke into our home in the dead of night. You shot my father, mother and sister. And you would have killed me, too, if the cops hadn't arrived."

He shook his head. "No, Kira—"

"Shut up. Just shut up." My voice rose, pitchy and near hysterical. "That's why they picked me to be your partner. Because they knew what you did to me. They *knew*. Jonathan told me—"

"Jonathan's a damn liar," he spat out. "He's one of them. Don't you see? He's lying to you. I didn't kill your family. I swear to God I didn't."

"And I'd believe you? Why would I believe you?"

"You have to believe me."

"I don't have to do anything." I shook my head and slid past him, going hand over hand, pulling myself clear of his body. "I can leave you here. I don't have to save you, as long as I save myself. You can die at the end of this level and I'll live."

Something in his expression shattered. "You're the only one who's given me the benefit of the doubt in forever. Don't take that away from me."

I just held on to the platform and closed my eyes tightly.

He craned his neck to look at me, his expression haunted. "Kira, I've done bad things. I'll admit that. I killed my roommate in juvie. But I'd never kill anyone who didn't deserve it."

"Maybe you have a lousy idea of who deserves to die."

"I swear, Kira. I didn't kill your family."

"How would you even remember? Are you trying to say you weren't a Kerometh addict? That you weren't in Jonathan's treatment program?"

There was deep anguish in his expression as he strained to keep me in his gaze. "That part's true. I was addicted. I was a complete asshole back then, you have no idea, but I didn't kill your family. You have to believe me."

I brought the back of my hand up to wipe at my eyes and frowned so hard that it hurt. If he wanted to lie to me right now, desperate for me to help him get through this level, why wouldn't he just say he'd never taken Kerometh a day in his life?

But he had. He admitted it.

Lots of people screwed up their lives with drugs—but it didn't automatically turn them into murderers.

"There are three minutes remaining in this level of Countdown.*"*

But I'd read Jonathan. I *knew* he was telling me the truth. He was the one who'd told me about my low-level Psi ability in the first place.

But how did I know for sure that *this* was the truth? Because he read as being an honest man? Even honest men can lie when they had to.

When they were *forced* to.

What else had I felt? Guilt. Jonathan had felt a deep, bottomless sense of guilt.

Maybe because he was being forced to lie to me about Rogan.

If Rogan had killed my family and left me as an orphan who'd nearly had to sell her body just to avoid starving to death, then I hated him. But if he didn't do it—if he wasn't guilty of anything more than making some bad choices…

I couldn't know for sure. Not now and not with less than three minutes to go in this level. I didn't have enough time or the ability to concentrate, to touch Rogan, to try to read him, and even if I did, would that tell me anything? I'd gotten a decent read on Jonathan, but that had only left me with more questions. More confusion.

But I had to choose. Right now. One way or the other.

I couldn't trust words, not from anyone. I had to trust my gut.

I started working on Rogan's wrist bindings until they

dropped away. I watched them fall, the ropes getting farther and farther away as they got closer to the street. I felt dizzy suddenly and tried to get up to my feet, but my hand slipped on the wet platform. It had started to rain. I hadn't even noticed until now.

Rogan scrambled to turn around and gripped my wrists. He held me in place just before I fell off the platform. We waited, facing each other on our knees until the platform stopped shaking. I stared into his eyes as the rain fell around us, soaking through our clothes.

"I would have fallen," I said, willing myself not to look down again.

"I know." His gaze had turned hard, fierce and haunted. "You're the only one who believed in me, Kira. Please believe me now when I tell you I didn't do what Jonathan said I did."

"Two minutes remain in this level of Countdown.*"*

He didn't wait for me to say anything else. He slowly and carefully got to his feet. He held a hand out to me. I took it and stood up.

"Let's go," he said.

I nodded and swiveled carefully to face the other building. I took a step, and then another step, and then another.

"59...58...57..."

"Don't think about the countdown," Rogan breathed from behind me into my now damp hair. "Don't think about the rain. Don't think about anything but surviving."

I swallowed hard. "I'm afraid of heights."

"Me, too."

I almost laughed at that.

I took another step, and another. A camera whipped past me

at breakneck speed, and I stopped. I felt Rogan's hand press against my back to steady me.

"You're doing great, Kira, just keep going."

"7...6...5...4..."

With a last step I touched the roof. Another step and I was on it completely and jumped down off the ledge. Rogan landed next to me. I turned to face him as streams of rain hit the rooftop around us.

Our eyes met. And held.

He reached out as if to touch me, but his hand fell back to his side.

"Kira, I—"

"Congratulations to Kira and Rogan on completing level four of Countdown *successfully. This was also a reward level, so we hope that you will enjoy what we have in store for you next."*

I braced myself for the blinding pain that usually preceded being struck unconscious by the implants, but instead a helicopter approached. My wet hair whipped around on all sides. Rogan grabbed my arm to pull me closer to him as the helicopter landed next to us.

Three men in white coats jumped out. They held guns. I couldn't hear anything because the sound from the helicopter's propellers was too deafening. The men in white were yelling something. I turned away and tried to run, but one of the men clamped his arm around my neck so tight I couldn't breathe. I fought him, clawed at him, but he dragged me to the helicopter and pulled me inside. The other two grabbed hold of Rogan and did the same with him.

"Rogan!" I screamed, but couldn't even hear my own voice.

The helicopter lifted off from the roof and flew into the dark, stormy sky.

9

WHILE IN THE AIR, A MAN IN A WHITE COAT blindfolded me, while the other two held me in place. About ten minutes later, the helicopter landed and I was dragged out of it. The sound of Rogan yelling my name from the near distance was cut off as a heavy door slammed shut.

Someone ripped the blindfold off my eyes so I could see the two guns held on me by men dressed all in white.

"Strip," one of them commanded. His gaze slithered down my body.

Other than being totally white, the room had no other discernable features. "Forget it. You're going to have to shoot me, asshole."

He smirked. "Don't you want your reward?"

"I don't want any reward that starts with me getting naked in front of perverts holding guns."

I sounded a lot braver than I currently felt.

He cocked the gun. "Strip *now*."

The door opened again, and Jonathan entered the room. Despite the fact that I now considered him a total lying bastard, given my current predicament I was extremely happy to see him.

"Is everything going well in here?" he asked blandly, sending a hard look at the men. He barely glanced at me.

"Is everything going well?" I repeated. "Are you kidding me?"

He regarded me then with a neutral expression. "I'm sorry this has been difficult for you, Kira. Congratulations on finishing the reward level. I'm sure you'll be very pleased to enjoy some privacy after four difficult levels."

I narrowed my eyes. "You lied to me about Rogan. Didn't you?"

He didn't reply. Instead, he nodded at one of the men in white who threw something at me. I couldn't do anything except catch it. It was a robe, a bathrobe. White.

Big surprise on the color choice.

Jonathan nodded at the men. "We'll give you some privacy, Kira. Leave your clothes in here."

"Where's Rogan?"

Instead of answering me, he turned and followed the men out of the room. The door closed solidly behind him.

I stood there, shaking, looking at the terry cloth robe draping off my arm. Then I dropped it and ran to the door, pounding my fists against it.

"Where's Rogan?" I yelled. "What have you done with him?"

I turned around and looked at the small white room, my chest heaving. And I waited.

For a long time.

Nothing happened.

There was no sound. No movement. Nobody came in to

force me to take my clothes off. I was alone with nothing to distract me except my racing thoughts.

I felt the back of my hair, now matted and stringy from being caught in the rain. I touched the incision where the implant was. It wasn't giving off any warning signal.

He must be close.

I needed to talk to him. Why had I let myself trust Jonathan? It was obvious to me now that he was the liar.

Maybe if I'd had a chance to do a full empath read on Rogan I wouldn't have doubted him at all. But I found it so difficult to concentrate around him...and that wasn't only because of this insane situation we'd found ourselves in. No boy had ever confused me as much as he did. As he *does*.

Jonathan must have lied to me so the level would contain extra entertaining conflict for the Subscribers.

I *hated* being lied to.

And now that I thought about it, when I'd accused him of killing my family, Rogan hadn't looked guilty.

He'd looked disappointed. Completely, devastatingly disappointed that I would think that of him after saying I believed in his innocence.

I hugged myself tightly while trying to breathe normally.

"Hello?" I said out loud. "Announcer guy? What's going on now?"

There was no answer.

It was quite obvious, actually. They were waiting for me to change my clothes, and nothing would happen until I did.

Make them wait, I thought bitterly.

And so I waited—another ten minutes.

Then I couldn't stand the eerie silence a second longer.

As quickly as I could, using the robe to cover me, I slipped out of my wet, dirty clothes and let them drop to the shiny white floor. I kicked off my stolen red running shoes. I tied the sash of the white robe tight around my waist and stood there in bare feet.

"Now what?" I growled from between clenched teeth.

There was a whirring sound, and the door to my right opened up, moving from floor to ceiling. It was dark beyond. I approached it cautiously.

It appeared to be a luxury hotel room. It was large and grand, with rich fabrics and beautiful artwork. A large four-poster bed was to the right. To the left an archway led into a huge bathroom. A picture window looked out on a red, orange, pink and yellow sunset over a tranquil rippling lake. Trees waved gently in the breeze. Where were we? There was nothing like this in the city.

I moved closer and touched the window. The image flickered—it was instantly clear that it wasn't a window at all, but a display screen—ten times bigger than the one my family used to have. I now saw the slot on the right side where the disc containing the image files went.

So real. So perfect. It had completely fooled me.

Spread across a table next to the screen was a feast unlike anything I'd ever seen before. Fruit, breads, roast beef, lobster, shrimp, cheese. A large bottle of wine sat in a silver bucket surrounded by ice. I reached out, noticing that my hand was shaking, and plucked a green grape from the table and brought it to my mouth, crunching down through the skin. The sweetness burst in my mouth. I felt as if I hadn't eaten in days. And I hadn't. Not really. Not like this.

Level four led to a reward, Jonathan had told me.

This was my reward. Food and a bit of privacy. I hadn't even realized how hungry I was until I saw real food.

My stomach twisted with concern as my thoughts turned toward Rogan again. Was he in a room just like this one?

After another minute of worry, my hunger won out.

I started to shovel the food into my mouth. Cheese, crackers, more grapes. Ignoring the wineglasses, I grabbed the bottle and tipped it back, chugging the chilled wine. A couple months ago, I'd done a few shots of some really nasty vodka offered by some acquaintances who'd found a half bottle of it in an abandoned house, but I'd never had wine before. It was much sweeter than the vodka, and it went down as smooth and easy as water.

After the feast had filled me enough to concentrate on something else, I moved toward the bathroom and gasped. There was a large bubble bath waiting, filled to near over-flowing. A sweet, floral scent perfumed the steamy air—like roses dipped in honey.

I looked around, over my shoulder, all around, trying to see where the cameras were, but I couldn't see any.

Was Jonathan serious that part of my reward was some privacy? It seemed too good to be true. My suspicions only worked to make my now-full stomach start churning.

I paced for several more minutes, waiting for the other shoe to drop. Waiting for the digicams to burst out of the walls.

But nothing happened.

I wondered for the eightieth time where Rogan was. My implant wasn't giving off any strange beeping signals. Unless they'd disabled our implants, he was less than ninety feet away.

I slowly became aware of an unpleasant smell and realized with dismay that it was coming from me. I'd been running and sweating hard for two days now. Even after being drenched from the rainfall, I smelled completely disgusting.

Finally, I dropped the robe to the floor and eased into the tub, letting out an audible sigh. It had been so long since I'd had a real bath. I'd gotten by on quick showers whenever and wherever I'd gotten the chance. This was pure ecstasy. Still paranoid, I waited for a silver digicam to fly up and catch me naked, but there was only blissful silence.

There was a bottle of both shampoo and conditioner on the edge of the tub, and I quickly made use of each one, slipping beneath the surface of the water to rinse my hair clean.

When I was finished, I got out of the tub, toweled myself dry, and then put the robe back on. I went back out to the main room and tried to organize my thoughts.

I felt…good.

Which made no sense.

There was no time for relaxation or feeling good. I had to use this time to figure out how to get out of this game before it killed me.

The door whooshed open and Rogan appeared. He stepped inside the room just before the door slammed shut behind him.

He wore a matching robe. His dark hair was slicked back off his now grime-free face. His eyes stood out like blue-green jewels in the dim lighting.

Wow, I'd been right. He did clean up really well. Like, *really* well.

"Are you okay?" he asked.

"I'm…I'm fine. Thanks. And you?"

His gaze moved through the room, ending at the buffet table. "Did you have any of this food or drink?"

"Well, yeah. Some of it."

He hissed out a breath of frustration. "Didn't it occur to you that it was probably drugged?"

"Oh." I stared at him. "I didn't even consider that."

"Obviously." He drew closer, his worried gaze sweeping over me. "You *seem* okay."

My full stomach sank, but it didn't really bother me. Which only helped clue me in that the food likely had been drugged to help me relax. "Actually, now that you mention it, I am feeling weirdly better than okay right now."

"Damn it, Kira." He glared at me. "It could have been poisoned, not just drugged."

"I was starving to death. And I'm fine, just a little buzzed. See?" I turned around slowly, my arms out to my sides. "Not dead yet. Besides, why would they want to kill me when the cameras aren't even around to capture that special moment? They just wanted us to chill out."

"Don't have any more of it."

"Yes, sir." I saluted.

Yes, I was definitely drugged, thanks to the feast. I hadn't felt more detached from my actions in…well, I'd *never* felt this detached. This relaxed.

This was a bad thing?

He gave me a wary look, then sat down on the edge of the bed. "I'm glad you're okay."

"Ditto. So maybe a reward level is simply that. A reward. No poison. And apparently no digicams, either."

"Forgive me if I'm suspicious of anything that happens to us."

And I thought *I* was tense. Rogan was the very definition of the word.

I eyed his white robe. "They gave you a bath, too?"

He shrugged. "It was more like a thorough hosing down."

"You smell good." I couldn't keep myself from saying it. I mean, it *was* the truth. He smelled good. He looked good. Really deliciously good.

Oh, boy. I was so buzzed. Even with the shots of vodka, which had actually made me sick to my stomach, I'd never felt this drunk before in my life.

"Gee, thanks." He looked at me, his gaze moving slowly up my body to my face. "So do you." Then he frowned deeply at me. "They didn't hurt you?"

"No. I'm fine."

"I'm glad to hear it." His expression softened, but then he stood up from the bed suddenly as if he'd just realized where he'd been seated and how intensely he'd been looking at me. He glanced to the side, toward the plasma display.

My face felt warm. I crossed my arms over my chest. "About what happened on the platform—"

Rogan turned his gaze from the fake view to me. "I guess you have some questions for me, don't you?"

I nodded.

He started to pace the room, his expression darkening, and he raked a hand through his damp hair. "I didn't kill your family, Kira."

"I believe you." I tried to meet his eyes, but he looked away again.

"I don't want there to be any doubt."

I bit my lip. "Actually, believe it or not, there might be a way for me to know for sure."

"What is it?"

"It's just…I can do this thing. I've been able to for some time, but I didn't know what it was." I told him what Jona-

than had talked to me about, my low-level empathic ability that wasn't good enough to get me into the Colony and
a school for Psi girls but was enough to show up like a strobe
light in my file. The girl who felt other people's feelings, if
only a little—that was me.

Jonathan thought it might help me. So far it had only made
things more difficult.

I told Rogan all of this.

"If it hurts you, you shouldn't do it at all," he said.

"Sometimes it's worth it. Like now. I mean, if you're willing."

"I'm willing. But what about the drugged food? Won't that
make it harder for you?"

"Crazily enough, I think it might make it easier. I won't
try to fight it. I can just let it happen all relaxed and calm."

"That makes one of us," he mumbled under his breath. He
studied me for what felt like a very long time before he nodded. "Okay…let's try."

"You sure?" He was so guarded about everything, was it
really going to be this easy?"

"I'm sure." He took a seat on the edge of the bed again.
"What do you need to do?"

"Um, I need to…touch you. That's how it works. Don't
move."

I sat next to him. He watched me warily as I reached forward and placed my hand on his left shoulder, slipping just
under the edge of his bathrobe. His skin was warm and still
damp from his shower. I slid my hand down over his chest
and felt his heartbeat quicken under my touch.

He didn't say anything to stop me. He'd gone very still.

"Okay," I whispered. "I need to concentrate now."

And I did. I closed my eyes and focused my mind, building on what I'd done with Jonathan, what I'd done by accident in the past. It took a moment to clear my thoughts, to get to that place where this could work. But then it did.

The sensations, the emotions, flooded over me one after another.

He was alone, so alone. Tired. Angry, driven by a need for revenge. Despair poured from him, disappointment and so much betrayal. Again, just as I had with Jonathan, I felt that sense of guilt—very strongly. And such sadness it made me want to cry.

It didn't hurt yet—maybe I was right and the lightly drugged food was helping me. There was something else there, deeper in that pool of water, that beckoned to me.

I focused and tried to slide further into his mind to discover Rogan's secrets—to find out just what he believed he was so guilty of that he thought it would make me hate him.

If it wasn't killing my family, I didn't know what it could possibly be.

Before I could sense anything further, the pain knifed through my brain. I let go of him and slid off the edge of the bed to fall to the floor, holding my head and moaning.

Oh, God. The agony! Squeezing and squeezing until I was certain my brain would be crushed.

But then it finally began to ease. Sweet relief.

Maybe this was a side effect of being a low-level empath. Maybe it would never get better than this for me if I wanted to use this Psi ability. Or had I simply gone too deep this time?

I *had* gone deep. It felt as if I'd been only a second away from seeing everything—from actually reading Rogan's *thoughts*.

But that was crazy. I couldn't do something like that. No-body could. Could they?

Rogan had dropped to the floor beside me and gathered me into his arms. He stroked my still-damp dark hair back from my face. "Are you okay?"

"I will be in a minute."

"You scared me for a second there. But it worked. I felt you in my mind."

Without saying anything else—I'm not sure I could have if I tried—I wrapped my arms around him and hugged him tight against me. I hadn't been exaggerating before. He smelled good, so very good—like soap and something else, something both sweet and spicy. I let his scent fill my senses, and it helped to chase the pain away until I could think straight again.

Finally, I moved back, but he held my face in his hands, staring at me intently.

"You're a Psi," he said.

"I guess so."

"It's amazing."

"Low-level only."

That earned me a grin. "*Still* amazing. Seriously. Do you have any idea how rare this is? It's incredible."

I met his gaze directly. "I felt your feelings, your emotions. There were a lot of them."

"Yeah. That must have been an unpleasant journey for you." His smile fell away. "So, now what?"

While Rogan Ellis might be a screwed-up kid who had some serious angst to deal with, he wasn't evil. I'd never been more positive of anything in my entire life. But I needed more. If only I was better, stronger, I knew I could have read his mind. I'd been so close.

If I couldn't read his mind, there was only one way for me to learn the truth.

"Now," I said evenly, "I want you to tell me what you really think you're guilty of."

He tensed. "What?"

"You said before that you're guilty as hell of something I'd probably hate you for. I felt that guilt just now. It's eating you alive. And if it isn't the mass murder of innocent college girls, and if it isn't killing my family, then what else could it be?"

"Just forget it." He tried to move away from me, but I grabbed the collar of his robe.

"No, I can't forget it. Tell me," I said more firmly. The effects of the drugged food were quickly wearing off, but it still helped me feel braver than I might normally be. "We're not going anywhere until you do. And I don't want to use my empath ability on you again because my head just might blow up next time."

He gave me a careful look. "Honestly? You don't sound like a low-level Psi to me."

"My file said low. If it didn't, I'd probably be living in the Colony." It was a painful thought.

"Maybe."

"Don't try to change the subject." I stood up and moved toward the spread of food again, trying to focus my slightly cloudy thoughts. "You know a lot about stuff—stuff I wouldn't think some former teenage addict who was thrown into St. Augustine's should know. I didn't know about Psis. I didn't know for sure about the Colony, or about this horrible Network, or about *Countdown* itself. But you did. You know plenty. Why is that?"

His jaw tensed. "Kira…just forget it."

"No, I'm not forgetting it." I hesitated. "Just who are you, Rogan?"

His expression turned bleak. "Trust me, you don't want to know the answer to that question."

I knew this much—that he was in Jonathan's program for addicted teens. And Jonathan had and has a strong connection with *Countdown*. With the producer himself. But how did the two things connect?

"Do you know somebody named Gareth?" I asked.

As if I'd flicked a switch, his expression turned to stone. "How do you know that name?"

A chill went down my spine. "Jonathan told me that he's the producer of *Countdown*." I inhaled shakily. "Jonathan told me a lot of things, and even though I know he's a liar, it doesn't mean he lied about everything. Are you somehow connected to this game? To this Gareth guy? Why did they pick you? Why did they try to injure you at the very beginning so you wouldn't last long? And…why were you were framed for a horrible crime you didn't even commit?"

After another flinch as if each of my words pained him, his expression hardened. "You really want to know? Are you sure about that, Kira?"

I met his gaze unflinchingly, my hands curled into fists at my sides. "Yeah, I really am. Let's go one at a time. Tell me who this Gareth guy is."

Rogan studied me for what felt like an hour, but was probably no more than a minute, before he finally spoke.

"Gareth is my father."

10

I COULDN'T HAVE HEARD HIM RIGHT.

"Your father?" Rogan's father was the producer of *Count-down?* "How is that even possible? Why would your father put you in this game? Does he even know you're here?"

Rogan hissed out a long sigh and went to stand in front of the display screen with the beautiful but fake view of that perpetually setting sun. "He knows. It's…it's complicated."

I had just sobered up in record time. "Why would your father produce a horrible game like this? One that puts his own son's life at risk?"

He laughed, and it was a hollow, soulless sound. "See, now you've come to my true secret, Kira. The one I would have preferred you never found out. You really want to know how screwed up my life is? Maybe then you can go back to hating me."

"What are you talking about?"

He still refused to look directly at me. "This game we're currently being forced to play? It was my idea."

My eyes widened. "What?"

Now he turned to face me. "I'm still surprised you didn't recognize my name when the announcer used it. Not only because of what they sent me to St. Augustine's for—that was splashed all over the news when it happened, but you did say you don't watch the news. But my father's also one of the richest men in the world. Have you heard of Ellis Enterprises?"

I blinked, trying to process what he was telling me. "I think so. Sure. It's the huge company that makes all the computers, right?"

He nodded. "Among other things. My father came from old money, but he managed to double it, and this was post-Plague. He's a business genius." His expression grew pained. "He had two sons—one was set to rise in the family, to take over the business eventually. And then there was me. The loser. The junkie. The disappointment."

The billionaire Gareth Ellis. I *had* heard of him. I didn't watch the news feeds or pay attention to social media and city gossip, but some things were just common knowledge whether you cared or not about the lives of the über rich and influential. Gareth Ellis was a billionaire who owned half of this city.

And Rogan was his son.

"What happened between you and your father?"

He gave me a grim look. "Like I said, I was the rich kid who never suffered a day in his life—who could have anything he wanted, whenever he wanted it. Did I appreciate any of it? Not a chance. I was bored living here. I hated it. I could have had anything I wanted, could have gone anywhere I wanted. I could have helped people. But I spent my allowance on the most selfish things possible. Wasted it all. Then I *got* wasted. Regularly." He snorted humorlessly. "I was using coke and ecstasy regularly by the time I was thirteen. Drugs were exciting, made everything more interesting, but they were just for fun, just for a quick high. I could have walked away at any time. But then I found Kerometh...." His expression shadowed. "It took me away for days—took my mind away, anyway. I was in such a stupor that life didn't matter anymore. And I wanted to stay that way. Pathetic."

I pressed my lips together, letting him tell me all of this without interrupting. His expression was so pained, but I didn't want to stop him. He needed to get this out. And I needed to hear it.

"My father tried to get through to me, have me work part-time at his office. Give my life meaning, since I dropped out of school and refused to go back. He didn't force me. He was calm—it was eerie, really. I knew he hated my guts by then, that I wasn't living up to my brother's shiny reputation. He said I could work at Ellis Enterprises and see if I liked it. It was that or rehab. I chose work. He'd already gotten involved with the Network by then and was trying to create a game to compete with the others. Games were my thing—I loved them. Spent hours, days, months playing online—even when I was high. He gave me the task to come up with a game idea. That finally got me interested in the job, which made my father happy. I mapped it out for him. Six levels of dangerous, life-threatening challenges played by actual people instead of avatars. The Network wasn't interested in picking it up until my father sank a ton of money into developing an artificial intelligence program for them."

"Wait...artificial intelligence? Like the robot from level three?"

He nodded with a jerk of his head. "Yeah. Almost got taken

out by the same thing my father helped develop—that indi-
rectly *I* helped develop. Ironic, right?"

I took a deep breath in and let it out slowly. "Okay, keep
going."

He searched my face. "You sure you want to hear the rest?"

I ignored my racing heart. "No. But keep going, anyway."

He scrubbed a hand over his forehead and paced to the other
side of the luxurious room. "The game didn't do so well in the
beginning. There was too much competition from the other
shows the Network carried—it was televised like a regular
TV network three years ago. Then, trying to be a smart-ass,
I randomly suggested they take things underground. Make
all their shows, including *Countdown,* secret and exclusive so
only certain people could access it. That got the Network's
attention—and my father's attention, too. I swear, it was the
first time he ever seemed proud of me. Too bad I was too
high to appreciate it."

"So, it's underground, thanks to the Subscriber implants,"
I said. "Those weren't being used before."

"That's right. Cranium implants. Jonathan was my father's
best friend, and the head of the Ellis medical research department. It probably made my father feel better about his greed
to put a chunk of money into medical research…something
good for humanity, or whatever. Anyway, he had Jonathan
work with our tech guys to develop a chip. Within a few
months they were good to go."

I touched the back of my head to feel the incision mark on
my scalp. The knot in my stomach grew tighter with every
word he spoke.

His mouth twisted. "I was first in line, along with my father, to volunteer to test the implants. It was more father

and son bonding time. By then I craved it almost as much as Kerometh."

"Where was your brother?" I asked. "Did he have a part of any of this?"

"No. Liam was at the Colony going to university at this time. He came back now and then, but it didn't matter. Besides, we never got along that well." There was something wounded in his tone that made me shy away from asking more questions about his brother. At least, for now. "Jonathan fitted both of us with a prototype—that's the extra mark you found on my head—but they never worked properly. However, the next ones developed a couple months later worked perfectly, and Subscribers were put on a long waiting list to get one. My father's people paid off the prison to use their inmates in the game—the levels were getting more dangerous with each cycle played. I was the one to think of the levels—it was big fun. If they won they got a reduction in their sentences. But then, one day, one of them was killed by accident on camera during one of the levels. I was horrified. Thought I'd be blamed, since it was my idea in the first place."

"Let me guess," I said, my voice hoarse. "The Subscribers loved it."

He nodded grimly. "Yeah. Now a regular game wasn't enough for them. They wanted more blood, more death, more everything. And if it was only inmates—scumbags who were already in prison for life—what did it matter? But it did. It bothered me a lot. But I was just a sixteen-year-old kid—nobody paid any attention to what I thought."

Rogan stared at me then, as if expecting me to have a look of disgust on my face. I couldn't say this was an easy story to hear, but I knew he was being truthful with me. This was his secret shame—what he thought I'd hate him for. But I didn't. I was disgusted, but it wasn't with him. Like he'd said, he was just a kid. It might have been his idea, but it wasn't his fault that it had evolved into a sick and twisted show that killed people for the amusement of others.

Rogan paced to the other side of the room. "It made me a little crazy, I guess. Pushed me deeper into Kerometh— enough that I started to lose my grip on reality. My father put me into Jonathan's rehab program, but the withdrawal…" He shook his head. "It was like hell. And it only made everything worse, made me obsess about my mistakes, my choices. I knew I had to do something to fix the mess I'd made and keep anyone else from dying. Late one night, I escaped the group home, went to where we uploaded the feed to the Network, and I started pulling plugs and breaking the computers. My father tried to stop me, but I shoved him into a bank of computers. There was this power surge—a huge one that shut off all the electricity. By the time I got back to rehab, the police were there. It was my father—he called it in. He had me arrested. But it wasn't for breaking and entering and destruction of property. By the next day there were pictures of me, video captures—all fake—and the story was about the murders of those girls."

He rubbed a hand over his mouth, his eyes haunted. "My family turned their back on me. My father disowned me. And the court threw me into St. Augustine's just long enough for me to turn eighteen. If I hadn't agreed to play this game I'd be packing my bags for Saradone." He let out a short, humorless laugh. "I never thought my father wanted to see me again, and yet here I am. Maybe he wants to watch me die. Maybe that will give him some sort of closure—that his loser son is finally gone from the world."

He stopped talking, and I just stared at him, trying to take in everything he'd just said, and make some sense of it.

"So, you're trying to say that your father hated you that much?" My voice shook as I said it. "Enough to frame you for those murders? His own son? Why? Just to get you out of the way? To punish you for trying to destroy the game?"

"I never said it made sense. None of it does, but I've never talked to him since." He shook his head. "He never showed up for the trial. Never to visit me. Nothing."

"So, now everyone thinks you're a murderer."

"That's right."

I chewed my bottom lip. "When I read you empathically, I did feel guilt. You feel guilty about creating this game."

"If I'd never thought of it, it wouldn't exist."

"But the Network would still exist," I reasoned. "And you're telling me there are other games on it like this. *Countdown* is just one piece of it."

My words didn't do a thing to relieve the pain in his eyes. "Don't try to make me feel better about this, Kira. It's a waste of time. What I don't understand is why my father is fine with all of this. He was always an emotionless prick, but I didn't think he was actually evil." He shrugged. "Maybe he gets off on the violence like the Subscribers do. Maybe he likes seeing people who don't have a choice make the last mistake of their lives. But he never used to be like that. Maybe he's just greedy. Like I was. Like I still would be if none of this had happened."

My jaw clenched. "I don't think you're anything like that."

"How can you say that after what I just told you?"

I exhaled. "What you told me? That you were a self-involved stoner rich kid who was bored and helped create a dumb game that other self-involved people thought was cool? That might make you an asshole, but it doesn't make you a monster."

"That's entirely debatable."

"Whatever's happened to this game since you've been gone is your father's fault, not yours." I tried to think. "You need to talk to your father."

He laughed coldly. "He won't talk to me. I've tried to contact him before."

I tried to come up with another plan. There had to be something we could do to stop this. "Do you know anything about the game that could help us get out of it?"

"If I did, don't you think I would have done it already?" He looked at me with a challenge in his eyes to cover the pain there a moment ago. "Why are you even still talking to me? I thought you'd want to kill me for what I've just told you. If I didn't help create this game, your life wouldn't be on the line right now. You'd be safe."

I sent a glare his way. "You don't know much if you think life on the streets of this city is safe. That's where they plucked me from. Not some penthouse in the Colony."

His expression clouded and his brows drew together. "You're right. I shouldn't have said that. But—damn it, I don't know. All I know is, this is my fault. And getting to know you the last couple of days…it's only made everything worse."

A sudden, sharp pain in my chest made me wince. "Sorry I'm such a problem for you."

His gaze snapped to mine. "I didn't mean it like that. I meant—" He swore under his breath. "It's just that now I give a damn about somebody other than myself. It makes things complicated."

My heart twisted. "Rogan…"

He turned away. "Forget it. Just forget it. I shouldn't have said anything since it doesn't help. And if you say you don't hate me, then you're the liar now."

When he began moving toward the locked door, his shoulders stiff, I zipped in front of him to block his way.

His expression was tense. "What?"

"I don't hate you, Rogan," I said evenly. "And I am not a liar."

"Kira, you seriously need to—"

I grabbed hold of him, went up on my tiptoes and crushed my mouth against his. He didn't pull away. After a moment, his hands pressed against either side of my waist as he drew me closer.

"What are you doing?" he breathed against my lips.

"Kissing you."

"Why?" His brows drew together. I could feel the rapid beat of his heart against mine.

"Because I really, really want to."

His breath was quick and warm against me. "It's the food, the wine—the drugs they put in it—"

"Yeah, well, I didn't have that much. Besides, what I was feeling before has already worn off."

What I felt right now—it was real. No drugs required.

"But, Kira—"

I didn't let him say anything else, because I kissed him again. Hard.

His lips…they were perfect. Absolutely perfect.

Full disclosure: I hadn't kissed many boys in my life. I might have been five minutes away from selling my body at one point, but that had been an act of desperation, not any indication that I was experienced. But kissing—sure, it had happened a couple of times, before and after I lived on the streets, but it hadn't been anything special and definitely wasn't *with* anyone special.

Nothing like this.

Finally, I broke off the kiss, breathless. Our gazes met—his was fierce but uncertain. But only for a moment. Then he gathered me into his arms, sweeping me off my feet, and kissed me again.

Talk about levels. We'd reached a whole new one in thirty seconds flat.

Before I realized it, I felt the press of the bed at my back. His mouth never left mine.

His hands were at the sash at my waist, loosening it enough that he could part my robe, his palms gliding over my bare skin. I pulled at his robe, desperate now to feel his bare skin against mine.

"You're so beautiful," he whispered.

I looked up at him, tracing the line of his scar with the tip of my finger. "So are you."

I drew his face closer so he could kiss me again, knowing that this felt right. It didn't matter where we were, this felt so perfectly right with Rogan. His lips tracing the contour of my jaw, my ear, my throat…

I didn't want him to stop. My reward—this was my reward.

But then I saw it.

Out of the corner of my eye, in the ceiling.

A small pinprick of a light. Blinking.

I froze.

"What is it?" he asked, going very still.

I couldn't believe what I was seeing.

"Digicam," I managed, the word just a croak. "They're recording us."

He turned his face to look where my gaze had gone. His eyes narrowed, and he swore, softly at first, then more loudly.

He yanked the bed sheet up to cover me. "That son of a bitch. It's sick. He can't do this."

"He can do anything he wants," I said, my voice hollow now. I wasn't even embarrassed. I was furious, but it was a slow burn. On the surface, I barely seemed annoyed. Underneath, I was ready to kill somebody.

Reward level. Privacy.

Yeah, right. I'd been so stupid. It was all a lie. They wanted to drug us up with the food and drink so we'd feel relaxed enough to have sex on camera to entertain the Subscribers. They wanted to take what should have been a perfect moment and make it into something dirty and ugly.

And if I hadn't seen the camera, that's exactly what would have happened.

It was disgusting.

Rogan lowered his mouth to my ear. "We'll beat them, Kira. We'll make them pay for this. For all of this."

I clutched the sheets to my chest. "Damn right we will."

The door opened, and five men in white coats entered the room. Jonathan came in last.

"It seems the reward level is officially over," he told us.

"You said that I'd have privacy," I snarled at him. "It was part of the reward, remember? But they were recording this?"

His expression was unreadable. "You must know by now

that I'm a liar, Kira. There is no privacy in this game. Get dressed."

Rogan sent a venomous look toward the man. "You're going to pay for this, you son of a bitch."

"Perhaps. But it won't be today."

He nodded at one of the men, who threw a pile of clothes at us. But they weren't the clothes I'd had before: cargo pants, tank top and my stolen red sneakers. These clothes were new and black, with black boots that hit the floor by the bed with a clunk.

"You have three minutes," Jonathan said. Then he turned around and left the room.

Rogan swore again under his breath. "I didn't see any cameras. I honestly thought we were alone. So stupid of me."

"It's okay. It's done. Let's just deal with what happens next. Time's ticking."

"Isn't it always?"

I chewed my bottom lip and looked away as he swung his frame out of the bed and grabbed the new clothing. He pulled on a pair of black pants and slid a black shirt over his head. The clothes fit tightly against his body, almost like a costume. He sat on the edge of the bed and laced up the boots.

I eyed him. "You look like a superhero."

"If you say so." He met my eyes, his gaze heating as he looked at me wrapped in the bed sheet, then he leaned over to snatch the rest of the clothes off the floor. He handed them to me.

I turned the pieces over in my hand. "You've got to be kidding me."

"You'll look like a superhero, too."

As if things couldn't get worse. "Yeah, a slutty sixteen-year-old superhero. Just what the Subscribers seem to want. Do they know what total perverts they are?"

"I don't think they care."

My costume consisted of a pair of skimpy panties. A skimpier bra. A short pleated skirt that barely covered my butt. A tight, long-sleeved shirt, low cut in the front. Thigh-high stockings, and knee-high combat boots.

All black.

Since my other choice of outfit at the moment seemed to be bed sheets, I slowly put on the clothes while Rogan turned his back to give me privacy.

Still, the red light didn't stop blinking.

Rogan eyed me when I was done. "You look…wow. Really hot."

I glared at him. "This is no time for jokes."

Despite everything, he was fighting to keep a grin off his face. "You'd be beautiful no matter what those bastards made you wear."

He slid his arm around my waist and pulled me closer.

"I won't leave you," he whispered into my ear. "If you don't want me to, I won't leave you. Okay?"

My throat thickened. "Okay."

The door opened again and Jonathan appeared. "Rogan, we're going to have you wait for a bit. Kira, I'm going to need you to come with me. Somebody wants to meet you."

I didn't take one step away from Rogan. "Not really in the mood to meet anybody right now."

"That's too bad. Mr. Ellis, however, doesn't take audience with just anyone. Consider it a great privilege afforded to few others."

Rogan grabbed my hand. "I'm coming with her."

"No," Jonathan said, and he had his handheld device out, "you're not."

He pressed the touch screen, and Rogan roared in pain before he dropped to the floor.

I crouched down next to him to make sure he was still breathing before I glared up at Jonathan. "I can't believe I ever trusted you."

His face was expressionless. "If I told you I was truly sorry for all of this, would you believe me?"

"No."

"Then it's pointless for me to say anything at all. Come with me. Don't put up a fight."

I decided to put up a fight just for the hell of it. But after a few moments, the men in white coats easily managed to restrain me and drag me kicking and screaming from the room.

11

ROGAN'S ESTRANGED FATHER, GARETH ELLIS, sat in a large white room that had a small table in the middle. It reminded me of a sterilized prisoner interrogation room, like the ones I'd seen from watching my parents' collection of old movies. The men in white coats shoved me into the room and slammed the door behind me.

Gareth, in contrast to the room, was all in black—a suit that I didn't have to be an expert to know was designer and expensive. I restrained myself from rolling my eyes at the appropriateness of that color. After all, he was the bad guy in this piece, right? I bet he'd personally chosen the color for Rogan's and my new *Countdown* uniforms. I resisted the urge to pull the skirt down to cover the bared tops of my thighs. My bullet wound was only a small, flat pink mark now. Barely noticeable.

If I wasn't so damn angry, I'd be embarrassed—I looked like some old loser's wet dream.

Gareth Ellis was a handsome man—but how could he be anything else with Rogan as his son? His hair was a shade lighter than Rogan's, a lot shorter. He seemed very professional. Very suave and sophisticated.

His eyes were the same color as Rogan's—a jarring ocean blue-green.

There was no doubt that they were father and son.

Knowing what had happened to Rogan only fueled my hatred for this man before me.

"Kira," he beckoned. "Come sit with me."

"I'll stand, thanks."

"I wasn't asking you, I was telling you." His gaze hardened, but a small smile appeared on his lips. "If you please."

So this wasn't going to be fun. Call it a hunch.

Without taking my eyes off of him, I slowly approached the table and slid into the seat across from him. He studied me as if I were a project in a science lab, his gaze scanning every part of me visible above the white tabletop.

"Do you like your new outfit?"

"No."

"I'm sorry to hear that. I think you wear it well."

I just glared at him.

"You're our first female competitor," he said after a moment.

"I know."

"How are you enjoying the game so far?"

"Enjoying the game?" I repeated. "*Enjoying* it? You must be crazy if you think I'm enjoying your sick and twisted game."

He cocked his head. "You were enjoying it a half hour ago. And you would have enjoyed it even more, I'm sure, if given more time. Tell me, Kira, are you always so loose with boys you've known only two days?"

I clenched my fists at my sides. "Kiss my ass."

He smiled thinly. "A girl with a bit of spirit. It's refreshing, actually. Most of the girls I meet nowadays are so wrapped up with the desire to go to the Colony that they'll say anything if they think you could help them achieve that goal." ·

"I guess I'm not most girls."

He didn't reply to that, but continued to study me closely.

"So, what now?" I asked, completely creeped out by him. "Are you going to stare at me all day?"

"Just trying to see what my son sees in you. Do you think you're special? Do you think he's never spent time in the company of young women before? Many would have done anything to be with one of my sons in the past. After all, girls are inevitably motivated by money."

I just looked at him, seething on the inside.

"Are you falling in love with Rogan?" he asked. "Or is it just lust?"

"I don't know the whole story about what you did to screw Rogan over, but what I have heard doesn't make me want to have a long detailed discussion with you about my personal life. Sorry."

He raised an eyebrow. "I know that he told you what happened."

"Are you going to deny it?"

He shook his head. "No. Rogan got in the way of *Countdown* becoming everything it could be. I had to stop him from ruining my plans. It's that simple."

Simple. Sure. This guy was obviously off his rocker. "He was *sixteen*."

"That's more than old enough to get in my way, trust me on that." His gaze remained fixed on me, unwavering, unflinching.

He was incredibly intimidating, but I managed not to look away. "Are we done here?"

"No, we're not." He stood up and came around to lean against my side of the table. "I don't believe in psychic phenomena, Kira. I believe in science."

"I don't really give a crap what you believe."

He smacked me hard across my left cheek. I hadn't seen it coming; it took me completely by surprise. I pressed my hand against my stinging face and stared up at him, my shock quickly shifting to anger.

"Here's what I believe, Kira. You are a thief. Four weeks ago you picked my pocket on the street. You took my wallet, kept the money from it, and threw the rest away. I followed you and saw the squalor that you live in. But I liked the way you moved." His gaze moved down the front of me. "I liked the sheer desperation in your actions. I knew you had what it takes to be on my show. I asked my employees to research you. We got a sample of your fingerprints, your DNA. I know more about you than you probably know about yourself."

There was something about this man, something wrong. He was evil. I felt it down to my very bones. Whether that was my Psi ability kicking in or just plain old gut instinct, I didn't know.

A smile curled up the side of his mouth. "I analyze, Kira. I analyze and I study and I learn. And I use all of that to help *Countdown* grow stronger and stronger and better and better until one day it will spread itself across all of this city, this world, and the Colony itself." He leaned forward and banged his fist against the table. "Are you listening to me?"

My cheek throbbed as I leaned back in my chair and tried to look at ease. "Sorry, I think I just fell asleep a little bit, that story was so damn long. Were you saying something about your wallet?"

His mouth twitched, and it reminded me disconcertingly of Rogan when he smiled. Only with his father it wasn't pleasant and it wasn't a smile. There was something much darker behind it that made my skin crawl.

"You truly believe, as Jonathan believes, that you are a low-level Psi?"

My mouth went dry. "I don't know what I believe."

Only that you're a sadistic monster in an expensive business suit.

"If you had any significant abilities at all you would be in a study program in the Colony. Scientists would be prodding you daily trying to figure out what makes you tick."

"Oh, well." I tried to sound as bored as I could. My heart was beating so fast I was afraid he'd be able to hear it. He didn't believe that I had empathic abilities. I wasn't going to tell him anything to confirm it or deny it. I'd keep all the secrets I could in this game.

"So all you have in life is your ability to compete on *Countdown*. You should be thanking me."

I almost laughed. "Thanking you? You're kidding, right?"

"You dream of going to the Colony. With your means and background, winning *Countdown* is the only way you'd ever achieve that goal, and my son's only chance to stay out of prison."

I gripped the side of the table so hard my fingers went numb. "Why did you frame Rogan for something he didn't do? Something so horrible? There had to be another way, you heartless bastard."

"We're not talking about Rogan, are we? We're talking about you."

I didn't know why I even bothered asking. It was clear he wouldn't tell me anything useful. "Whatever."

"But now that you brought him up, I have a proposition for you. Something that, now that the two of you are romantically involved, will make for an interesting side challenge."

I glared at him.

He leaned closer to me, and I could smell his expensive aftershave. "There is very little chance of you surviving to the end of *Countdown*. In three years we have had more than eighty pairs compete. Only one of those pairs made it to the very end to receive their ultimate reward. You will die, Kira. And I promise you, it won't be pleasant."

It was all I could do to stay where I was seated and not leap across the table to try to strangle him. "Go to hell."

He grinned. "The Subscribers seem to like you a great deal. It may have something to do with that attitude of yours; or maybe it's that firm, young body that's now been exposed for all to see and enjoy." His gaze moved to my low-cut black top, which made me squirm in my seat. I resisted the impulse to cover myself up. "Maybe it's the growing connection between you and Rogan beyond the chips in your heads, I don't know for certain. But they like you. They want you to win."

"Then I'll win."

He shook his head. "No, you won't. You will die. In level five or level six. It won't matter. The odds are against you." He paused. "But I'm going to give you another option."

He waited until I made eye contact with him again. "And what's that?"

He moved closer still. "You will kill Rogan on camera. He's strong, so he might get the upper hand unless you're sneaky. But I know you can be sneaky when you have to be.

The Subscribers don't like him. They believe that, along with the crimes he was in prison for, he also murdered your family. They want you to seek revenge."

I shook my head. "But Rogan and I talked. He's innocent of all of those crimes. If the Subscribers were watching they would have heard that."

He looked at me smugly. "The Subscribers didn't hear that part. Technical difficulties, I'm sure. The Subscribers are now wondering why you would let the boy who killed your family nearly have sex with you on camera." He smiled. "But to each her own, I suppose."

I could barely control the fury that curled through me like fire. It burned like my face still did where he'd struck me. I'd already known he didn't play fair, but that didn't make this easier to digest.

"I'm not killing him," I said evenly, trying very hard to hold on to my patience before I did something that would get me killed on the spot.

"If you kill him, you will win the game, and you will start your new life in the Colony. A million people living together in a city where all their dreams can come true—not stuck here in a place filled with nothing but violence, uncertainty, and ghosts of the past. You could be one of the lucky ones, Kira."

I steadied myself, trying to breathe normally, in and out, in and out.

This man couldn't be this horrible, could he? He was Rogan's father. That had to count for something. But I'd never met anyone I hated more on contact, and I hated a whole lot of people. It was as if my gut was trying to tell me something. Something my eyes and ears couldn't sense.

He was sitting so close. Could I get a read on him? Could

I push past my anger and frustration and concentrate enough to sense what he was feeling right now?

I'd done it with Jonathan and Rogan. The only thing keeping me from doing it again was my own self-doubt.

I had to do this. I had to know if he was really this horrible or if he was hiding something.

Breathe. Relax. Focus yourself.

He studied me with a small frown. "You're refusing my offer?"

I exhaled slowly and tried to still my mind. "I am."

He nodded, his gaze cold as ice. "Then we're done here. At your inevitable elimination, don't say I didn't give you a chance."

As he was about to get up, my hand shot out. I grabbed his wrist and squeezed. "Wait."

Please work, I prayed.

I closed my eyes and concentrated harder than I'd ever concentrated in my life.

Nothing.

I frowned. There was nothing but darkness and silence in his mind.

Maybe I was doing it wrong.

"What are you playing at, little girl?" he growled.

I concentrated even more, peeling away the layers I found within him like a black, rotting onion. Layer after layer of darkness until finally I could see something down deep. Sense it. Feel it.

Regret.

That's all it was. Just a small shadow of emotion smothered under a blanket of icy darkness.

It was something I hadn't expected.

It was something that told me there was more to him, but it wouldn't be easy to uncover the truth. I had to ignore the pain—a pressure that had started to build in my head.

Something told me not to let go, to keep searching, to keep reaching with these strange abilities. I had to find some truth that could help me understand any of this.

Who was this man? Why did he feel regret when on the surface he was an evil, manipulative sadist who would sacrifice his own son's future with a smile on his face? That small piece of emotion felt as if it came from an entirely different person—someone who still had a soul.

I kept reaching...searching...I had to know the truth.

Then I felt it, sensed it, something small and barely discernible...

Pain, despair, horrible sadness. Something trapped and muffled, barely alive. Barely conscious.

"Let go of me before I call for my guards." Gareth spoke quietly, but his words were laced with poison.

I ignored him. Words were not emotions. They weren't real. His tone didn't match what I empathically felt.

With every ounce of my strength, I stilled myself and strained to concentrate. His buried emotions were very quiet, very distant...but very precise. Each one like a knife stabbing the soft recesses of my brain. I steeled myself against the mounting pain, trying to hold on for as long as I could.

Help me, Kira. Help my son....

It has me. I can't escape, but you still can. Find a way, any way.... An image appeared in my brain—an address. It was fleeting, flickering, and I had to grab hold and pin it down before it faded away. I didn't know what it meant, but I knew I had to remember it any way I could.

What was this? These weren't emotions, they were… thoughts. Actual thoughts. I was reading Gareth Ellis's mind.

And then the men in white coats were pulling me off of Gareth, my fingernails scoring his arm hard enough to draw blood. I was crying from the pain, shaking so badly that they couldn't keep me on my feet. I sank to the floor, sobbing and clutching my head.

My nose was bleeding, too; the warm thickness of it came away on my hand as I wiped at my face. My head felt as though it had split open right through the middle.

Gareth Ellis held his injured arm and looked down at me coldly "Perhaps Jonathan was right about you after all."

I stared up at him. This man—it wasn't the same one I'd heard in his mind. What was wrong with him? Possession, maybe? A split personality? I didn't know for sure, but it was something. Something that had turned Rogan's father evil.

Did he realize I knew?

Yes. I could see it in his icy gaze. He no longer looked amused with me, just annoyed that I'd discovered something he'd prefer no one knew.

He leaned over and grabbed my face in his hand and squeezed.

"Be very careful, little girl," he growled. "*Very* careful. Some secrets can kill faster than any level in this game."

He let go of me and wiped his hand on his black pants as if to remove any trace of me.

I was surprised he didn't order my death right then and there.

But he didn't. After all, the show must go on.

LEVEL

5

ANOTHER BLINDFOLD. MORE DARKNESS.

You'd think I'd be used to it by now, but, unfortunately, phobias don't work that way. You don't simply get used to what you fear. It gets worse and worse and harder to deal with every single time. Even if you tell yourself it's irrational to be afraid.

The darkness made me hear my sister's cries and my mother's screams again, replaying like a nightmarish song, over and over and over.

But suddenly something made the darkness even harder to deal with.

My implant began to beep, and pain raked through my brain.

"Rogan? Where are you?" I said aloud.

There was a man at my back who had my arms pinned behind me as he pushed me ahead of him. He was big and strong, and I'd given up fighting against him several minutes ago as they'd led me out of the building and into a car. I couldn't see anything, but I think we drove for about ten minutes before stopping again. I didn't know where I was, but I knew it had stopped raining. The wind was cold on my face.

I felt something else move past my face with a metallic whirring sound. A digicam.

And so it begins again.

A deep weariness filled me. Was Gareth right? Was I doomed to die in this game? Was my only chance to try to kill Rogan?

He'd offered me everything or nothing at all. A privileged life or certain death. That was the choice I was supposed to make.

I didn't know exactly what had happened to that man, but I did know that if I did what he asked, I'd be selling my soul to the devil.

I was still hoping beyond hope for a third option to present itself.

Soon would be good.

I heard something heavy and metallic clang against the ground close by, then I was shoved from behind. I staggered forward, going over on my right ankle when I tripped on something. Pain shot up my leg as I fell, hitting the ground hard.

The beeping from my implant was disorienting, and I took a moment to steady myself, hands out at my sides as I forced myself back to my feet.

Keeping my weight on my left side, I braced myself for the next horrible thing to happen. But nothing did.

It was silent then. Too silent.

"Rogan? Where are you?"

I felt for the back of the blindfold, hurriedly untied it and let it fall to the ground. It was dark outside. Night. The moon glimmered from behind the clouds and layer of pollution. Only one star could be seen and not very well at all. The north star.

I wished on it.

Please help me. Give me strength.

Perhaps not so much a wish as a prayer. My mother taught me how to pray. Since the Plague, not many people had much faith anymore, but my mother had believed.

She'd believed in something greater and more powerful than us. I wanted to, too.

I looked down at what I'd tripped over. A long, thin piece of metal with a hook on the end of it. A crowbar.

So much for praying. That wasn't helpful at all right now.

"Welcome to Level Five! Rogan and Kira are rested and raring to go on to the next level. The question is this…will Kira find Rogan before time runs out? Or will she go in the wrong direction and find nothing but death by straying outside of her ninety-foot boundary? The ties that young Rogan and Kira have developed in their strange relationship—the murderer and the thief—are now more tangible as the farther apart they go, the closer to death they are. Kira has a mere ten minutes to locate her partner. Part one of level five commences now. Enjoy!"

Part one? That wasn't fair. Now they were doing sub-levels?

Cheating. Totally cheating.

Yeah, as if Gareth or anyone associated with this game cared about fairness. All they cared about was giving the Subscribers what they wanted and getting as many of them as possible to tune in to watch us die.

The thought made me sick.

The sharp pain in my ankle brought me back to reality. I scanned the empty street. The darkness was oppressive, but at least I could see. The streetlights hadn't been properly maintained, and every third or fourth one along the street was dark, either broken or simply burned out.

"*Six minutes remain in this level of* Countdown," the announcer said merrily.

"Is this fun for you?" I asked aloud, speaking directly to that bodiless voice that tormented me with its inane cheerfulness. "Do you enjoy your job, you disgusting piece of garbage?"

There was no reply.

Big surprise.

"Rogan!" I yelled as loud as I could, and began to limp along the street. After a few feet the beeping in my head got louder, the pain so acute that I couldn't think straight, so I stopped and changed my direction.

It was like that old children's game my sister and I played long ago. The one where you hide something and the other is trying to find it. Warmer, warmer...colder...very cold. The warmer you were, the closer you were.

Okay. Well, in this version of the game, warmer meant no beeping and I was close to Rogan, colder meant that my implant beeped and hurt. Very cold meant that it was moments away from exploding.

Not as much fun as the good old days.

I tried not to think about how many ways Rogan could be hurt or injured or worse, how many reasons he might be unable to respond to me. If what I'd been told about the implants was true—the ninety-foot rule—then he couldn't be very far away.

But where was he?

That shouldn't have happened between us in the reward room. Even though it had felt so right, so perfect, being in his arms, it just complicated things. This situation was complicated enough as it was.

All contrived, too. Everything about this game was a setup—especially the reward level. I mean, I don't know how I hadn't seen it. Drugged food and wine, all spread out in a beautiful room with a big bed. And the huge, relaxing bubble bath just waiting for me to slide into. To put me in the mood. The whole thing had "we want you to do it with Rogan so the pervy Subscribers can watch" written all over it.

And, stupidly, I'd very nearly done exactly what they'd wanted me to.

I couldn't fool myself into thinking it had just been because of the drugged food and booze. I didn't know what I really felt for Rogan, but it was something. Something real. At least, I'd thought so.

Now I didn't know. I didn't know anything anymore.

My heart twisted. "Rogan! Where are you?"

"Five minutes remain in this level of Countdown.*"*

I slowed and stood in the middle of the street.

Think, Kira, I told myself sternly. *You've made it through four levels on this stupid game. Think.*

I ran as quickly as I could, my ankle shooting with pain as I went, and pounded on every door I could. All locked. I called Rogan's name out again and again.

Nothing.

I turned around and around, but there was no clue. No cars. No trees. No high wires. No platforms. All the doors were locked. I couldn't see any sign of him.

And yet my implant had stopped beeping.

That meant he wasn't far.

My ankle throbbed. Did that guy mean to shove me so I'd

twist it? The bastard. I glanced down at it, thinking I might be able to see the swelling through my new black lace-up combat boots, when I saw something a few feet away on the ground.

A sewer grate. But it wasn't like the others that were old, grimy, and rusted.

This one glinted under the edge of moonlight.

"Two minutes remain in this level of Countdown.*"*

I hobbled over to it and crouched down, pressing my fingers against the edges of it. It was awkward and heavy. There was no way I'd be able to lift it up.

"Rogan!" I tried to peer through the tiny openings. "Are you in there?"

This sewer grate hadn't been here for years. It was the only thing that didn't look at least twenty-five years old on this street. Well, other than me.

But it was hopeless. How was I supposed to remove the cover to check?

Then I gasped.

The game had rules after all. Structure. It wasn't a free-for-all chaos session. The answer could often be found in the level itself. In the beginning, we'd been given the keys to our locks; we'd simply needed to figure out how to use them properly. The Dumpster had held the bell that had triggered the door to Jonathan's office. The man we were supposed to kill in level three hadn't been an innocent, he'd been a robot, and if we'd been paying closer attention, we would have figured that out earlier than we did.

The game gave us the tools and clues to help us get through the level. We just needed to figure out when and where to use them.

I hobbled back to where I'd started and grabbed the crowbar. Then I hurried over to the sewer grate.

"*45...44...43...42...*"

It took me a few seconds to pry up the cover. After it was partially removed, I could get my fingers under it and move it to the side. It made a heavy, scraping sound against the cold, hard pavement.

I peered into the darkness and it gave me chills.

"Rogan?" I asked, but was still met with silence.

A wave of fear and doubt crashed over me. I couldn't crawl down into the darkness. I couldn't do it—I couldn't even move. What if I was wrong? What if I was wasting time I didn't have right now?

No, that was wrong. I *could* do it. I had to do it. I had no choice.

A cry rising in my throat, I thrust my hand down and felt around for something to hold on to. It was warm and moist in there.

My hand brushed the underside of the opening, and it felt slimy. I shuddered.

"*25...24...23...*"

There was no time. I'd failed. We were going to die.

I plunged my hand deeper into that hateful darkness and touched the metal bars of the ladder.

"Rogan—I'm sorry...I'm sorry I'm too slow—"

I screamed when something grabbed hold of my wrist. It held on so tight I thought it would pull me down into the bottomless darkness. I tried to pull away but couldn't.

"*10...9...8...7...*"

Rogan's face appeared from the darkness. He held my wrist

tightly as he climbed up the ladder and flung himself onto the pavement, his chest heaving.

"Congratulations to Rogan and Kira for completing the first half of level five successfully."

I collapsed to the ground next to him and started beating on his chest with my fists.

"You asshole!" I yelled. "Why didn't you say anything? Why didn't you tell me it was you down there? Damn it, Rogan!"

He stilled my hands and held them until I finally relaxed.

"I'm sorry." He searched my face. "When you were meeting with my father they had me in another room. They told me that if I said a word to help you locate me they'd kill you on the spot. I couldn't reveal where I was until I got out of there."

My heart slowly returned to a normal speed. "Oh."

His grip on my hands tightened as his brows drew together. "Are you all right? Did my father hurt you?"

I shook my head, then touched his cheek. "Did they do this to you?"

His face bore a red mark that ringed his left eye…before too long it would darken to a bruise. His bottom lip was cut and slightly swollen.

He grimaced. "Let's just say that when they make a point they try to make it a memorable one."

I reached up to touch his face but stopped myself. "Well, let's look on the bright side, shall we? You weren't down there long enough to smell like a sewer."

He gave me the edge of a grin as reward for my awkward attempt at humor. "Good to hear. I'd rather not experience another involuntary hosing down if I can help it."

He got to his feet and then helped me up.

He frowned as he watched me limp a few steps. "What happened?"

I shrugged. "Went over on my ankle. I'll be fine."

"They did that, didn't they?"

"Maybe I'm just clumsy." I scanned the street. It was still vacant, still very dark. The shadows and light from the street lamps slid across the road like ghosts. "Rogan, I need to talk to you about your father—"

Then I heard a hard, metallic sound—like the crowbar hitting the pavement earlier. I looked down the street. In the distance I could see two figures standing a block away. I couldn't see much, apart from that they were large and male. The metal sound was indeed another crowbar that one of them had tapped against the ground. They stared at us but didn't say a word.

I got a strange feeling that I shouldn't wave my hand and try to be friendly.

"Who are they?" I whispered.

"Not sure." Rogan didn't take his attention from the silent figures.

"*Welcome back to* Countdown!" The announcer's voice made me jump. "*Rogan and Kira continue to make a terrific team as they work their way through every level with ease.*

"*You've met Kira already, now let's give you some insight into the mind of convicted murderer Rogan Ellis.*

"*Born into a life of privilege and leisure, Rogan grew up attending only the best private schools in the country. His father, Gareth Ellis, CEO of Ellis Enterprises, built his company to be a forerunner of all things technical, including the creation of the Ellipsis tablet that, just before the Great Plague, had taken over sales of both Microsoft and*

Apple. His two sons, Liam and Rogan, were the pride and joy of a loveless marriage to socialite Lissa Bartholomew Ellis.

I wondered if the Subscribers were getting a video feed to go along with the audio—pictures and clips of the family, like a documentary feature playing in their heads.

"But before too long it was evident that Liam was the favored son and was being groomed to take over the family business. Rogan, even in his early teen years, showed signs of being a sociopath who took pleasure in hurting others. His increasingly violent tendencies forced Gareth Ellis to hand him over to San Carolina's, an exclusive mental hospital for the very rich, for schizophrenia and drug abuse. Rogan's loving family feared he would never recover enough to properly function in society."

Rogan hissed between clenched teeth at the lies.

I squeezed his arm.

"The day he was released, his mother and Liam picked him up from the hospital to bring him back to the Ellis mansion. Despite being sedated, Rogan was reportedly acting erratically, and tried to take control of the car, which spun out of control and careened off the side of a cliff. His mother and brother were killed instantly. Both of Rogan's legs and six ribs were broken, and he also sustained a punctured lung."

My throat constricted and I looked at him.

"That's how they died," he said softly. "But I only tried to take control of the car because it was out of control on a slippery road. I wanted to help, not hurt anyone. They picked me up from my school that day—it was the last time I was there." He blinked hard. "My father later said that he'd wanted to send a driver, but my mother insisted she and Liam come to get me together." His Adam's apple jumped as he swallowed hard. "Took me a couple months in hospital to recover from that accident. That's when I first got into Kerometh. It helped me forget."

"After their deaths, Rogan became more despondent, and despite continuous help offered from his father, he began to sink deeper into drugs and violence. Gareth Ellis is quoted as saying, 'Had I known what my son would be capable of, I would have had him locked up in San Carolina's and thrown away the key before he could harm anyone else.'

"He refers, of course, to the night of terror when Rogan broke into the city university dormitory and systematically went door to door in his path of heinous violence. A nineteen-year-old woman who escaped that night said she returned the next day to 'walls coated in blood,' the word bitch *scrawled over the dorm room wall of every girl Rogan murdered that night, in his drug-clouded, misogynistic rampage. This was the same night two years ago, when, if you'll recall, there was a citywide blackout. Rogan used that darkness to his advantage to also murder the family of Kira Jordan.*

"He returned home that night, drenched in the blood of his victims. His father recalls Rogan laughing at what he'd just done. Sickened, Gareth knew there was no helping his son. He called the police and turned Rogan in. Since then, Gareth has contributed over fifty million dollars to a fund in the murdered girls' names for the prevention of violent crimes against women, both here and in the Colony.

"Rogan was sent to St. Augustine's Juvenile Detention Center where he was to remain until his eighteenth birthday. Three months ago, Rogan attacked his two roommates, leaving one dead and the other seriously injured. He was sent to solitary confinement where he remained until being released to take part in Countdown."

Rogan's arm was steel beneath my grip, his expression rigid and furious. I wished I could block out the sound of the announcer's voice, somehow shield Rogan from having to hear these horrible things being said about him, but the feed was directly through my implant and into my head, so I could do nothing but listen, as he did.

The other figures continued to stand in place in the distance, tapping the crowbar against the ground.

"Rogan and Kira have been unaware that another team has also been given the chance to be contestants on Countdown, *in a game that has run tandem to their own, and have also successfully completed four levels in this competition."*

My breath caught. I had thought we were the only ones.

"Kurtis Grimm was an inmate at Saradone, convicted of first-degree murder, specially chosen to compete in this game due to his background. His partner, Mac Zebowitz, is someone that Rogan might recognize. Mac was one of Rogan's roommates at St. Augustine's—the one severely injured by Rogan's rampage, which left their other roommate dead. Mac has personally sworn vengeance against Rogan. Today, with help from Kurtis, he will get that chance.

"Level five is an official death match. Only one pair shall go on to level six, the final level. Competitors, your countdown begins at thirty minutes. Kill or be killed. And to our Subscribers…enjoy!"

At last the announcer's voice left my head, leaving only the thudding of my heart and the dull noise of the crowbar hitting the ground to break the silence.

"Mac," I managed. "That's the boy who gave you that scar?"

He nodded. "Along with his pal, he attacked me in the middle of the night with a knife they smuggled in. Thought they might be able to extort some money from me or my father. When they realized he didn't give a damn about me, they just tried to kill me. I fought for my life and almost lost. I was damned lucky. I never thought I'd see him again."

"And they teamed him up with somebody from Saradone. A real murderer." I stared at the dark silhouettes. "Why are they just standing there?"

"They're waiting."

"Obviously. But for what? What do we do now?"

"I'm thinking."

"Think fast."

"Hey, Rogan!" one of them called out. "Long time, no see. You're mine now. And you know what? Thirty minutes is a long time. We can play with you and your girlfriend lots before the end of this level."

I didn't want to know the details of what he planned to do to fill that time. I was willing to bet that it wasn't reminiscing about the good old days over a beer and a plate of nachos.

"How's that plan coming along?" I asked.

"Slower than I'd like."

"We're going to be okay, Rogan. We're going to make it." I moved closer to him so I could feel the warmth of his body. "What are they waiting for?"

The crowbar tapped a steady tattoo on the street ahead. Every five seconds without fail.

Rogan didn't take his watchful gaze away from them. "I won't let them hurt you. I'll do whatever it takes, but we don't have any weapons."

"There is that handy crowbar from before."

He snorted. "Against a convicted murderer twice our size and a psychopathic teenage dickwad?"

"Gee, don't sound so confident."

I didn't hear the tap anymore. I watched the shadowy figures warily.

Suddenly, with a yell, they started running toward us as fast as they could.

We had no weapon good enough to defend ourselves for very long. And no plan forming to get us through the next thirty minutes alive.

Fight or flee.

I chose door number two.

"Come on." I grabbed a hold of Rogan's arm. "We have to run. We have to run now!"

13

HAPPILY, HE DIDN'T ARGUE WITH ME.

We ran past the shifted sewer grate cover, and I snatched the crowbar off the ground. Rogan started toward a door to one of the surrounding buildings.

"They're all locked," I told him. My ankle cried in pain with every step I took. My hand was sweating, but Rogan clutched it tightly in his as if he didn't want to let go of me.

"*All* of them?"

"I don't know. I—I thought I checked them all when I was looking for you!"

Because of my twisted ankle, I wasn't running as quickly as I could, and the other team was gaining on us. Fast. Their heavy boots slapped against the pavement as they ran.

Rogan glanced over his shoulder. "I'll hold them off. You hide."

"Bad plan."

"Why's that?"

"The ninety-foot rule? You go too far away and our heads will explode, remember?"

He swore under his breath, his expression tense. "You're right."

"And besides, I'd rather not stand by and watch them beat the shit out of you."

He raised an eyebrow at me. "I could hold my own for a while."

"Yeah, a valiant battle before they cut your throat. No way. We're in this together, no matter what."

He glared at me. "Give me the crowbar."

I decided not to argue and handed it to him just as my already injured foot hit a piece of gravel. I stumbled, and Rogan caught my arm before I hit the ground. We didn't stop moving, but we slowed considerably as we turned the next corner. Another dark street with no cars. All concrete and cold stone and brick.

There was the shadow of something in the middle of the road ahead, though. Something much larger than a piece of gravel. I met Rogan's gaze before I picked it up, feeling the cold, black metal in my hand.

It was a gun.

The show provided what we needed to finish a level. Just like the crowbar earlier. I stifled a feeling of gratitude toward whomever had left it there for us to find, which helped to manage some of the fear. At least now I wasn't helpless.

I stood clutching the gun with both hands, Rogan at my back holding the crowbar, as Mac and Kurtis caught up to us. I saw their shadowy faces, the hiss of breath hitting the cold night air. Just like us, they were also wearing the ridiculous new black *Countdown* uniform—or just like Rogan, anyway. I was the only one of the four of us that looked like a slutty superhero.

"That didn't take long at all," the older one, Kurtis, said. He had a shaved head and thick eyebrows that met between his eyes. "Damn, she's even prettier up close than she is on camera. Almost prettier than you are, Rogan."

He held a short-bladed knife while the younger one, Mac, had the crowbar. Mac was tall and wiry with sharp features and greasy blond hair tied back in a ponytail. I was surprised that he didn't look any older than me, but there was a hard edge to his gaze, and a coldness to his grin that chilled me. They walked in a slow circle around us, still keeping some distance between us—for now. Rogan and I stayed back to back as we turned, keeping an eye on the two murderers.

"I don't think my old friend has anything to say to us," Mac said with a smirk. "Is that right, Rogan? You got nothing to say?"

"Nothing comes immediately to mind," Rogan growled.

"Did you miss me?"

"Obviously, I must have missed you if you're still breathing. But I promise I won't miss again."

My arms already ached from trying to hold the heavy gun steady. "Look, guys. We're all in this together. We don't have to fight each other. Maybe we can get out of this if we work together."

Kurtis laughed hard at that. So hard that he had to put his hands on his knees to support himself. "That's hilarious. Where did they find this chick? I thought *Sesame Street* went off the air decades ago."

My jaw clenched. Okay, so much for trying to make friends with the enemy.

The convicted murderer eyed me slowly, from the toes of my combat boots up my thigh-high black stockings to the embarrassing amount of bare thigh on view, and the too-short black skirt barely covering my ass. He licked his lips and focused his attention on the skirt.

"Give me five minutes with you, baby," he murmured. "Just five minutes."

"Lay one finger on her and you'll be spending the rest of the level searching the city for it," Rogan snarled.

I refused to show that Kurtis's taunts were getting to me. I kept my chin up, my gaze guarded but steady. I'd shoot off more than his finger if he tried to touch me.

"I don't mean to interrupt," I said. "But I do have a gun. See?" I waved it. "Why don't I shoot the both of you and we end this level right now?"

Mac's beady eyes scanned the length of me. "Kira, right? Yeah, during a rest period, the show let us tune in to you and Rogan getting to know each other a bit better. Feel free to get naked again anytime."

I felt bile rise in the back of my throat at the thought that he'd been watching, but I tried to focus myself.

Unfortunately, while his taunts weren't doing much more to me than making me physically ill, they seemed to be working on Rogan.

"I'm going to kill you," he snarled. "Both of you."

Kurtis snorted. "You can try."

"Rogan, try to stay calm," I said.

"Yeah, Rogan," Mac said. "Listen to your girlfriend. She'll protect you from us."

"Don't think I won't." I raised the gun a little and pulled the trigger. The bullet hit the wall just over his right shoulder. His eyes widened and he took a shaky step backward.

"Didn't think I'd do it?" I snapped at him. "I'll do it. I'll shoot both of you in the head. I'm thinking it's no big loss for humanity."

"There are twenty-five minutes remaining for this level of Countdown."

"She's got some spirit to her." Kurtis's eyes glittered in the darkness surrounding us. "That why you like her, Rogan? Does she remind you of the pretty little girls you killed?"

"That was a lie," I said. "He's innocent."

"Is that the lie that got you into bed earlier? Did he convince you he was wrongfully convicted?" Kurtis snorted. "Yeah, we're all innocent here, aren't we? That's why we're playing this game."

I trained the gun on him. "Go to hell."

He cocked his head. "I heard the part when Jonathan told you Rogan killed your family."

I went cold inside. Of course there were cameras in the room with us then. There was no privacy in this game. Everything was fair game as entertainment for the Subscribers.

"I don't care what you heard."

"It's funny, though. That convo made me remember something."

"Oh, yeah? And what's that?"

There was a grin on his ugly face. "Just before I went to prison a couple years ago I'd been hired to kill a little girl tagged with Psi abilities."

My stomach turned, but I fought to keep my face blank. "Fascinating."

"Psis are a dark stain on humanity—a mutation caused by the Plague. A lot of people think that. Some of them have the money to hire guys like me to help cleanse the world of filth like you." His expression darkened. "Your daddy put up a good fight trying to protect you. I wasn't going to kill him or your mother and sister, but I shot them all just for giving me a hard time. Had to bolt when I heard the police. What a coincidence, huh? Both of us here playing this game. It's almost like they planned it that way." He took a step closer and peered at me. "Got to say, I am curious. *Can* you read my mind, pretty girl? Can you see into my soul?"

I squeezed the trigger, and he jerked backward. Blood flowed from his shoulder wound, although it was barely noticeable against the black fabric that covered it. Lousy aim, though. I'd been targeting his heart.

He yelled out and clamped a hand to his shoulder, his face contorted in anger and pain.

Pure red fury filled my vision and pushed all other thought out of my head. "You're the one? You killed my family? And they knew this?"

"Those bastards know everything," Rogan said from his back-to-back position with me.

"I'm going to kill you!" I yelled, and I aimed and squeezed off another shot at the murderer.

The chamber clicked empty. I pulled the trigger again and again, but there was nothing.

Two enemies. Two bullets.

The show had given us just enough to kill them and nothing more.

I screamed and threw the gun at Kurtis who'd slumped down to his knees on the ground, staring at the blood that gushed out from between his fingers. Rogan's crowbar made contact with Mac's—I could hear the crash of metal against metal, and then a grunt of pain as Rogan managed to clobber Mac. Then he dragged me behind him as we began to run again as fast as we could, trying to put distance between us and our pursuers.

I shook with fury. Kurtis had admitted what he'd done so freely, as if he was proud of it.

"Here." Rogan stopped running in front of a door, and I skidded to a halt next to him. The street lamp was angled so that its light was cast like a spotlight showing us the way. There was a chain across the door, and he whacked it a few times with the crowbar until it broke. When he tried the handle, it swung open. "Come on."

My cheeks were wet with tears of frustration and rage. I wasn't sad; there was no time for that. I'd finished being sad a long time ago, and now there was only anger left behind.

He took me by my shoulders. "Kira, I need you to focus right now. Can you do that?"

"He killed my family."

"I know. And I'm so sorry. But I won't let him kill you, too."

"How are we going to stop him? Stop both of them?"

"There are fifteen minutes left in this level of Countdown."

Rogan's jaw tensed. "Looks like we have fifteen minutes to figure that out."

We went into the building, and he shut the door behind us. There wasn't much light inside, only a faint glow from a bare lightbulb dangling from the ceiling, but we could see that we were in a small foyer that led to a staircase. Rogan moved toward the door and slid the lock across about two seconds before there was a loud, resounding bang on it from the other side.

"Come out, you little bitch!" Kurtis's bellow held a tense, pained edge to it. He was hurting bad from that bullet.

Good.

There was a creak as the door gave a little with the last pounding.

This space was too confined. And too dark. I couldn't function here.

I eyed the stairs. "We need to go up to the roof."

Rogan met my gaze for a tense moment, then he nodded. "Let's do it."

He started taking the stairs two at a time until he remembered that I was hobbling around on an injured ankle, and he thundered back down to my side. He put an arm around my waist and helped support me as we went up flight after flight of stairs. I was in pretty good shape, but by the time we got to the top of thirty flights, I was panting.

Rogan pushed open the door at the top, and we burst out onto the roof. I sucked in fresh air until I got my breath back, then moved to the edge and looked over.

"There's a fire escape over here. I think we can climb down."

"Seven minutes remain in this level of Countdown," the announcer said, loud and clear in my head.

"What are we going to do then?" he asked. "We can keep running, but it won't help either of our teams in seven more minutes. We'll both be dead."

My heart raced. "But I shot Kurtis already. And you hit Mac really hard. You don't suppose that counts, do you?"

The roof access door swung open, and Mac emerged onto the roof. Kurtis glared at me from behind him, still holding his hand against his shoulder.

"No," Rogan said as he met my tense gaze, "looks like we'll have to do this the hard way."

MAC BLED FROM A WOUND ON HIS TEMPLE, BUT he still held tightly to the crowbar.

"Five minutes remain in this level of Countdown," came the voice of the announcer.

"How time flies when you're having fun," Kurtis said, although the sound of his voice, raspy and out of breath, didn't really fit the words. He clutched his left shoulder, dark red and shiny with blood from the bullet wound against his black game outfit.

When he took a few steps closer, Rogan stepped in front of me.

"Back off."

Mac laughed at that and drew closer. "You're dead, rich boy. So dead."

Rogan's eyes narrowed. "You first."

"Nah. *You* first."

Mac swung his heavy crowbar at Rogan's head. At the last moment Rogan blocked the death blow with his own weapon. Metal crashed on metal.

Mac's fist made contact with Rogan's jaw, and he went sprawling to the other side of the roof, his crowbar knocked out of his hand. He got to his feet quickly, stormed back toward Mac and grabbed hold of his black shirt.

Fear for his safety distracted me long enough for Kurtis to move closer to me. Too close.

"No weapons now, huh? Too bad."

I didn't realize I was backing away from him until my legs hit the short barrier at the edge of the roof.

"Three minutes remain in this level of Countdown.*"*

His shoulder wound momentarily forgotten, he cracked his knuckles. "So, here's how this is going to go, pretty girl. I'm going to put my hands around your neck, and I'm going to squeeze until I hear something pop. And then I'll keep squeezing until your tongue rolls out of your mouth, until your eyes bug out from your face, and you go limp. Then I'm going to throw you off this roof and watch as your pretty red guts smear the pavement down there."

I felt the cold brick wall that pressed against my hands. The edge of it came up to the backs of my thighs. "Were you serious when you said that you killed my parents? Or were you told to tell me that to get a reaction for the cameras?"

He smirked. "Don't you believe me?"

"I don't know what to believe anymore."

He grabbed my wrist. I shrieked and tried to pull away, but he was too strong. "How 'bout I do you one favor before I kill you? If you're really a Psi, why don't you give me a read? Take a look at my soul and *you* tell me if I did it or not."

I searched his face for something to tell me that he wasn't a horrible, evil man who'd ruined my life. He could be lying.

For all I knew, they could be forcing him to say this. Like I said, I didn't know what to believe anymore.

Still locked in hand-to-hand combat, Rogan looked over at me and shouted my name when he saw I'd been cornered. He tried to move toward me, but Mac stopped him, pushing him back, and swung his crowbar like a baseball bat. Rogan roared in pain and fury.

"Two minutes remain in this level of Countdown.*"*

My wrist was trapped in Kurtis's grip. He was smiling at me, an amused smile, as if he were daring me to try to break away from him. My despair and confusion *amused* him.

"Maybe you're not a Psi, after all. Maybe you're just another nobody. Can't do it, can you?"

I met his gaze full on. "Oh, yes, I can."

I closed my eyes, focused my mind and ripped into his.

Funny, the more I did this, the easier it seemed to get.

Emotions drew me in: dirty, filthy feelings, anger, betrayal, rage. Certainty, pleasure, lust.

Deeper, deeper, just like with Rogan's father, I moved into his mind, peeling away layers. Searching for more than what could be found on the surface.

I needed to know the truth.

I began to sort through pictures in his mind like flipping through an album, memories, sensations, experiences—something I'd never done before, but it came naturally to me, like breathing. So many flashes, dark and bright, until I found what I wanted. A flickering image of a familiar man in a dark hallway—my father—a fight, a gunshot. His body slumping to the ground, blood forming a pool beside him. My mother's terrified face, my sister coming to her bedroom door before he gunned them down.

Now I'll kill her. I'll collect the other half of my money when it's done.

I was getting more than emotions and images, now. Thoughts. Actual thoughts.

The pain tore through my brain and I let go of him. It was even worse than before. Even worse than with Gareth. I was momentarily blind with the pain of entering this bastard's mind. He was everything he appeared to be—scum of the earth.

And I now knew for sure that he was the one who stole my life two years ago.

When my vision cleared and I was able to focus again, I saw him staring at me with awe.

"It's true. You can do it. I felt it. You saw into my soul."

I cast a fearful look over at Rogan and Mac. Rogan was bleeding, but he was still fighting hard. I returned my attention to the bastard facing me.

"Yeah. I saw into your soul."

He pulled his knife out of his front pocket. "All the more reason for me to slice you open and watch you bleed."

"Kira!" Rogan yelled.

When Kurtis flicked a glance in his direction, I slammed my fist into his injured shoulder as hard as I could. He screamed in pain and dropped his knife, but before I could twist away from him he grabbed my shoulders so hard I thought he was going to crush my bones. I fought back against him, as hard as I'd ever fought before. Nails, teeth, fists; everything was in motion as I slashed and hit anything I could touch. I tried to trip him, winding myself around his legs, and succeeded in making him fall.

He still had a hold of me as he crashed against the side of

the roof, and we rolled across it, and then suddenly there was nothing under my feet. I screamed and scrambled to grab on to the edge of the building as we fell off the side.

My already short fingernails broke. My hands were sweating, slippery, but I clung to the building, trying to get a foothold below me.

The countdown began to thunder in my brain.

"*45…44…43…42…*"

"Kira!" Rogan yelled again.

Hand over hand, scraping roughly over brick, I tried to pull myself back up to the roof. Just before I got a firm hold on the siding, I felt a hand on my ankle and then a heavy weight. I looked down. Kurtis was dangling off the side of the building, a few feet lower than I was, and he had a hold of my left boot. He stared up at me, his expression frantic.

My hand slipped a little as I struggled to hold on.

"Help me!" Kurtis pleaded. "Please don't let me fall!"

"*21…20…19…*"

I forced the words from a throat that felt more like screaming. "I read you, Kurtis, with my disgusting Psi mutation. And do you want to know what I saw deep inside of you? Deep inside your soul?"

"What?"

"Nothing worth saving."

His hand slipped off my boot, and he was hanging on to the side of the building for a few seconds by only a couple of fingers. And then, with a terrified scream, he fell thirty stories to the street below.

Just before he hit, I heard a loud bang from the roof. It scared me so much I almost lost my remaining grip.

"Rogan?" I managed. "Rogan, are you still there? Are you okay?"

It felt like an eternity, but it was only a few seconds until I felt hands gripping my arms, pulling me back up to the roof. Rogan, bloodied and beaten but still alive, crushed me against his chest.

"Congratulations, Rogan and Kira, for completing level five successfully."

"What happened?" I asked after a moment, pulling back enough to look at his injured face. I touched it gently, wincing.

"Ninety-foot implant rule," he said. "When Kurtis fell, he broke it."

I braved a quick look to the other side of the roof. A body lay there, very still, a dark stain where its head should have been.

I rested my head against Rogan's shoulder. "The song 'Pop Goes the Weasel' is playing in my head right now for some strange reason."

"I think that's very appropriate." He managed to give me a small grin.

I sighed, feeling bone-weary. "Kurtis begged for his life at the end. I couldn't help him, but even if I could have, I don't think I would have. I'm glad he's dead. Is that wrong?"

"Not in my books. The bastard had it coming."

"Rogan and Kira have only one more level to complete before they are considered the second set of winners ever in the history of Countdown. *Will they be successful? Or will the last level finally pull them apart forever? Stay tuned, Subscribers. This game isn't over yet!"*

That freak seriously sounded as if he was introducing a baseball team. Or doing an infomercial. Not hosting a game where death was the consolation prize.

I frowned. "Rogan, I really need to talk to you about your father."

His eyes lost their warmth. "What is it?"

"I was able to read him—and it was so strange. I don't know what's really going on. But he's not really—"

Just then, Rogan clutched his head and roared in pain just before his eyes rolled back into their sockets, and he fell to his knees before slumping over on his side unconscious.

Wide-eyed, I waited for them to trigger my own implant to knock me out, but nothing happened. I looked around at the three silver cameras that circled the area.

"What now?" I yelled at them. "What do you want from me now?"

The announcer's voice boomed through the darkness. *"Kira Jordan was given a choice earlier. If she eliminates her partner on camera she will automatically win the game and receive everything she's ever desired—a new life, riches beyond her dreams, a bright future. What do you say, Kira?"*

"What do I say? How about this?" I gave the cameras a good shot of my middle finger.

One of the cameras hovered closer. A small spotlight shone down on the roof, highlighting the knife that Kurtis dropped there earlier before he, well…*dropped.*

"Pick it up, Kira," the cheerful voice urged.

I resisted, but then felt a jolt of electricity zap through my implant. I stooped down and snatched up the knife.

Rogan lay on the ground, his face bloodied but peaceful in sleep. His arm was sprawled across his chest, almost as if he was lying in a comfortable bed.

If I killed him, I could have everything I ever wanted.

"The Subscribers want you to kill him, Kira. According to a recent poll, they want you to win."

A long breath hissed out between my clenched teeth. If I killed Rogan in cold blood right now, I might get everything I ever dreamed of. But it wouldn't really be winning.

I'd never do what they wanted me to do. I didn't care what the penalty for that would be. They didn't own me. And they didn't control me—nobody did.

I turned my face up toward the digicam. "Tell the Subscribers to go screw themselves."

I threw the knife over the side of the building.

There was deadly silence for a full ten seconds.

Then pain ripped through my brain, and everything went black.

LEVEL

"KIRA, WAKE UP."

I woke slowly. I was lying somewhere soft. Rogan was next to me. His hand was on my forehead, stroking the hair off it. I blinked slowly until he came into focus.

"Morning," he said.

"What…" My voice was thick with sleep. "What's going on? Where are we?"

"Not entirely sure about that."

"How long have we been here?"

"Not sure about that either, but it's light outside." He nodded toward a window to the left.

I focused further and saw that we were in a small bedroom. It looked like a motel, a cheap one. But everything seemed clean enough at first glance. A small amount of light shone through the window through gray clouds overhead.

A quick check under the sheets told me that I was still fully dressed, even wearing my boots, and so was Rogan.

"We must have been asleep for hours." I tried to sit up. My

body ached from head to foot, so I settled back down on the comfortable bed. "I still feel like crap."

"Me, too."

I touched his face, studying it for the first time up close since yesterday. He was covered in bruises and small cuts. "Ouch."

"Yeah," he said flinching. "I'm a wreck. As if this damn scar wasn't bad enough."

He touched the scar that bisected his eyebrow and ran down to the center of his left cheek.

I grabbed his hand. "You must have been really vain when you were a rich pretty kid. I hate to even tell you this, in case it swells your ego any further, but scars are hot."

He raised an eyebrow. "Is that right?"

I nodded solemnly. "In fact, I don't think you have enough scars. This game has obviously not been difficult enough for you."

"Yeah, it's been great. I can hardly contain how much fun it's been so far." His smile faded, and he looked around the room. "Listen, yesterday in the reward room…"

My stomach clenched. "What about it?"

He gave me a sidelong look. "I'm not sure what happened."

"Really? Because it was pretty clear to me. Don't worry about it. It's not like anything serious happened. Luckily, right?" I said it jokingly, but inside I felt a twinge of something. I wasn't sure I wanted to hear his reply to that.

He didn't say anything for a moment. "Nothing happened?"

"Well, I mean, stuff *happened,* but nothing…like, regrettable. Or…I don't know. Whatever. It doesn't matter now." I hated this. I hated feeling awkward about something that had felt so right at the time, but now, knowing they'd been recording us, seemed wrong.

When he didn't answer, I finally chanced a look at him, surprised to find that he was smiling at me.

"You're kind of funny, aren't you?" he said.

My cheeks heated. "Yeah, hilarious. My goal in life is to amuse you."

"You're definitely amusing…for starters. It's kind of a new thing for me."

"What's a new thing for you?"

"You are." He captured my gaze for a moment that made my breath catch. Then his expression darkened, and he looked away. "For two years I've lived a life where it felt like nobody cared if I lived or died. Even my own father. Damn it. Why would he turn his back on me like that? I would have been there for him. If the situation had been reversed, even if I thought he was guilty—" He shook his head. "I can't see myself totally abandoning him like he did me."

He needed to know there was something wrong about his father—something that was beyond the real Gareth Ellis making him do these horrible things. And that the real Gareth was still in there somewhere trying desperately to survive… just like we were.

The thought made my blood run cold.

"Where do you think the cameras are?" I whispered.

"Don't know. They could be anywhere. They're probably recording us right now." He pressed back into the bed and stared up at the ceiling. "Those digicams…they have artificial intelligence programming chips in them. That's why they move like they have minds of their own. Because they do."

My mouth felt dry. "Like that robot did?"

"Not exactly like that. Just enough that they can fly about on their own, keeping us as their targets. They have receivers on them. Our implants are connected to the digicams. And the digicams are connected to the game's network at Ellis Enterprises."

I pulled him closer so I could whisper into his ear. "Why can't we just run? As long as we stick together our implants won't mess us up."

His jaw tensed. "They'd know."

"So, there's no way of getting away?" I was saying it so softly. If there were cameras hidden in the room I didn't want them to hear me.

"Not with those damn cameras around."

"Rogan," I whispered quieter. "I need to tell you something. It's important."

"What?"

My heart began to race. "You said that you didn't understand why your father would abandon you like that. Well, I—I think I know why. Part of it, anyway."

"Why?" There was strain in his quiet words. "Tell me."

Then a loud alarm sounded, and the room we were in split down the very center. Right through the middle of the bed. The room parted as if on wheels, and Rogan stared at me with shock as we moved farther and farther away from each other.

The roof rolled back, and instead of stucco, it showed the cloudy skies overhead.

I realized with a sinking feeling—a feeling I'd gotten used to having on a regular basis in this game—that the motel room we'd been in was actually a set. All fake, like something out of Hollywood. All created to be the background for our "emotional pillow talk scene." There must have been microphones all over the place. Hidden cameras. They'd probably been hoping for another explicit make-out scene, but instead when I'd been about to reveal what I knew about Gareth, they'd put an end to it.

Frozen with shock, I watched as my side of the bed moved away from Rogan until we were stretching our ninety-foot rule to the limit.

"Kira!" Rogan jumped up from the half bed. Another step took him off the makeshift set and onto the pavement of yet another abandoned street. He looked around at the surroundings quickly before focusing again on me.

"Welcome back to Countdown! *Kira and Rogan are all rested up for the final level—level six!"*

Three silver ball cameras zoomed into view, bobbing and moving along the street. They got to Rogan first and circled him like a nest of wasps as he glared at them.

"In a recent poll amongst our beloved Subscribers, Rogan Ellis received only a thirteen percent approval rating. This is as low as any contestant in the history of the game. It is obvious to anyone watching that, despite his attractive appearance, a cold heart lurks inside this boy's chest."

The cameras left Rogan's side and swarmed toward me instead. They spun around my head, and I could see myself reflected in their black, shiny lenses.

"Kira Jordan has been a very popular player on Countdown. *It goes to show that, despite her fragile exterior, a female competitor is not necessarily going to be outplayed by her male counterparts. Kira has earned a seventy-two percent approval rating, a rating that improved with every successive level.*

"Kira, do you have anything you want to say to the Subscribers who have enthusiastically supported you in the game so far?"

One camera came down to eye level. It reflected me from my waist to the top of my head.

"Absolutely." I forced a smile to my lips. "I just wanted to let you know that every one of you Subscribers disgusts me. Why do you sad, pathetic scumbags keep watching this? They're forcing us to play. We have no choice. You want to see people killed? You're sick! All of you are sick!" I literally spat at the camera.

There was a long pause.

"We are very sorry, but we lost our audio feed for a moment. We strive to bring you the best of entertainment, but we are slaves to our cameras, I'm afraid. Kira wanted you all to know that she appreciates your support and that she's thrilled to have been able to bring you hours of entertainment. She would love to thank you all personally if she could, but there simply isn't enough time. Not if we want to get on with the show!"

I tried to calm down. It just made me sick and furious to know that the Subscribers, however many of them there were, were sitting back comfortably watching in their mind's eye as Rogan and I fought for our lives.

"Everything has led to this final level. Kira and Rogan have forged a partnership, found common ground, learned to work together and nearly given in to their desires. We have been thrilled to share all of this with you.

"They helped each other when the other was down, for without one's partner, one is nothing in Countdown.

"That is, until level six."

The digicams separated. One stayed in front of me, another zipped through the air toward Rogan, and the third hovered between us.

"Weapons have been placed under each side of the bed. Will the contestants please retrieve these weapons now?"

I looked over at Rogan. He stood next to his side of the

bed, his fists clenched at his sides, while I hadn't moved an inch from where I lay. The sheets tangled around my legs.

A digicam zoomed closer to me.

"Please, retrieve your weapon, Kira."

I glared into the black iris of its lens. "Please, kiss my ass."

Three small green lights just above the camera's lens swelled slightly in intensity. I flinched as I felt a zap of pain to my implant. A warning.

I forced myself up off the bed and crouched down to look underneath. It was a gun. I wrapped my fingers around the handle of it and pulled it out.

I stood there next to the half a motel room, right next to the gray of the pavement, holding the gun, and tried to fight past the rising panic in my brain to figure this out.

Rogan had his gun in hand as well. He held it loosely at his side.

"Rogan and Kira have fought side by side in victory thus far, but now they must fight against each other. For only by defeating the other can one of them win the game.

"Rogan fights now to clear his name of his crimes. Should he win, he will be able to start life with a clean slate, a clean record and the forgiveness of his father.

"Kira fights for a fresh start, as well—in the Colony. There she will find her new life awaiting her, including a luxury apartment and enough money to last her to her dying day. The only thing now standing in her way—in either of their ways—is each other.

"Whoever is standing at the end of level six…whoever still breathes…shall be crowned the winner.

"Should neither of them succeed in killing the other in the time allotted, the level will be forfeited and both competitors shall be eliminated.

"There is a five minute time limit for this level…which starts right now. Enjoy!"

When the announcer stopped talking, I stood there, completely stunned. I looked at the gun in my hand.

They wanted me to kill Rogan.

And they wanted Rogan to kill me.

Kill or be killed.

And if nobody pulled the trigger, *both* of us were dead in five minutes anyhow.

Then they'd start a new cycle with new contestants, and soon nobody would even remember us.

A line of fury ripped through me, and I fought hard to hold in a scream. The rage burned just beneath the surface. I'm sure that as I raised my gaze to look in the lens of the camera any Subscriber would have been able to see exactly what I was thinking. How much I hated them, those rich, faceless, bloodthirsty bastards who got off on violence and pain to fill their mundane lives, out there somewhere watching every move I made.

I was so lost in my thoughts for a moment, so distracted, that I didn't hear Rogan approach. At the last second I heard his boots slap against the pavement as he drew near.

"Don't come any closer." I automatically raised the gun and pointed it at him, and he stopped running. He held up his hands.

"Easy, Kira, easy."

"Easy?" I managed. "There's nothing easy about this. You heard what he said. Just stay back."

"There are four minutes remaining in this level of Countdown.*"*

He eyed my gun uneasily. "You're going to shoot me?"

My hands were steady, but the rest of me trembled. "That's

what they want. They want us to kill each other. Jonathan and your father already made me this offer. I could have killed you in an earlier level and won the game."

His jaw set. "Jonathan made me the same deal."

"What? When?"

"Voice in my head during level four."

A shudder went through me. "But you didn't do it."

"No. I didn't."

I searched his face. Did I really trust him? Now that it had come to this—him or me—did I honestly think there was a way we could both survive this?

One bullet, one press of my index finger, and I could have everything I ever wanted.

I'd once told a friend that I'd kill to get to the Colony. At the time, I'd meant it. She'd laughed and told me she would, too.

Rogan raised his gun toward me.

"What are you doing?" I asked shakily.

"Don't really like having a gun aimed at me when I'm not doing the same. Even when it's you. Makes me feel a little too vulnerable."

"Wouldn't want that."

"No, vulnerable can be bad." His brows drew together. "Vulnerable can be good, too. Depending on the situation."

I didn't think he was talking about guns anymore.

A million different scenarios sped through my brain. There *had* to be a way out of this. I looked at the digicams that were greedily taking everything in. Everything in this game seemed to revolve around those digicams and the chips in our heads. They were connected.

"Three minutes remain in this level of Countdown.*"*

I exhaled. "These digicams see everything, don't they?"

"That's right. Eyes in the sky. They know where we are, can find us no matter what."

"So, there's no escape from them. Is there?"

His gaze was steady with mine. "No escape."

"That really sucks."

"Yeah."

"Because if we could get away from those cameras…"

"Too bad we can't."

"Right."

I glanced at the digicams, now circling us, recording our last conversation to be replayed over and over again for the entertainment of the Subscribers.

"What now, Kira?" he asked.

"Do you think that you can kill me, Rogan?" My throat was tight. I noticed that his attention had left me to look at the cameras.

He didn't answer for a moment. "I should ask you the same thing."

"If it meant your life or my life—and, guess what, it *does*—can you pull that trigger when it counts? Do you have a good enough aim?"

His attention shifted back to me. "I used to do target practice with my brother all the time. Don't worry about my aim."

My arm was beginning to burn from holding the heavy gun up. "Will it be worth it to shoot me? To clear your record?"

"What do you think?"

"Personally, I'd shoot somebody to stay out of Saradone. Do you have any idea what they'd do to a cute eighteen-year-old boy like you there?"

"Cute, huh? I was hoping you found me devastatingly handsome." His lips quirked for a second before his gaze went cold. "But, yeah, I have a few vivid ideas of what they'd do to me in prison. And you? Would you shoot someone for a shiny new life in the Colony?"

"In a heartbeat." I spoke without hesitation.

His lips thinned. He inspected his gun for a moment. "Got enough ammo in this gun to make sure we don't miss. They haven't taken any chances this time."

"Two minutes remain in this level of Countdown."

"So, shoot already," I told him. My heart beat so loudly, I could barely think.

"Not yet. Haven't given them a good enough show yet. I'm surprised they set it at only five minutes. They could have stretched this out way longer."

"I'm not going to miss."

His lip curled to the side. "You shot Kurtis in the shoulder when I know you were trying for a kill shot. I'm going to go out on a limb and say that you have lousy aim."

"Okay, now you're just being mean. I can hit something if I have enough ammo. Don't worry about that."

Silence fell between us. I alternated checking where the digicams were and keeping an eye on Rogan's trigger finger.

"Not long now," he said.

"59...58...57..."

A shudder of fear and dread went through me. Less than a minute until I found out just how good a shot I was. And Rogan, too.

It had to be perfect. If I didn't aim perfectly, then I was going to die.

"The time has come," the announcer said, and his normally singsong voice was a bit breathless now. *"The facade of partner-*

ship and amity has faded away, leaving only two raw competitors be-hind. Who will be victorious in the remaining seconds?

"30...29...28..."

"So sick of that guy," Rogan growled.

"Yeah. And if I never hear another countdown, it'll be too damn soon."

"See, we still agree on a couple of things."

"Yeah, I guess we do."

"So, I'll do you one last favor." He raised an eyebrow. "You can try to take the first shot."

My hands were sweating. "I'll do more than try."

"7...6...5..."

I swallowed hard. "Ready?"

His eyes narrowed and his grip tightened on his gun. "Do it, Kira. Now!"

I swung my arm around and pulled the trigger. The camera that was in the process of getting a close-up of my face, of any potential emotion that might be found there, went flying backward.

Then I heard gunfire, shot after shot after shot from Rogan's gun—each making me jolt. I focused on the one digicam on the ground, sputtering and sparking. I shot it until my gun was empty before I frantically looked back at Rogan. Two silver digicams had crashed to the ground near him.

He looked at me, his chest heaving, a sheer gleam of perspiration on his forehead.

I met his gaze. I half expected the chips in our heads to spontaneously combust as punishment, but nothing happened. "Now what?"

He offered me the barest edge of a grin. "Now we run like hell."

16

"I THINK I KNOW A PLACE WE CAN GO!" I YELLED as we thundered along another side street, sprinting as fast as we could. I ignored the pain from my sprained ankle and clutched my gun.

"Where?"

I had the brief glimmer of the location in my head—the address that had flashed through my mind when I'd read his father. It wasn't much to go on, but it was all we had.

"We're almost there," I said. "I hope you were right about those digicams being the link between us and the Network."

"Since we're still conscious, I'm guessing we were right. Nobody's triggered us into painful unconsciousness yet. I'd have to bet that blowing the cameras glitched up their system and their ability to track us for a short time—based on our current and continuing consciousness. But it won't be long before they can find us."

"Up ahead. Turn left on that street."

The village was about a mile away from where we'd been

for level six. We slowed to a jog as we turned the corner. My ankle sang out with pain.

It was jarringly different from where we'd just been—a deserted part of the city that made me think nobody else in the universe existed except for Rogan, me and the disembodied voice of the announcer. Here in the well-populated village, I was reminded that the city, while definitely dying, was not yet dead.

This large neighborhood flowed with people moving along the sidewalks. The road was trafficked by small, energy-efficient cars and mopeds. This was how the entire city had been once upon a time. Alive. Busy. Full of people with jobs and families.

Hiding our guns, we weeded through the crowd while getting some sideways stares at our costumes. Black, shiny and tight didn't really go with the muted colors of business casual we were bumping up against. An old woman eyed my black thigh-highs and short skirt, sneered at me with disapproval and muttered an insult.

I thought about running up to her and grabbing her hands, begging her to help us, to hide us, but I stopped myself. I took a deep breath and let it out slowly as I clutched Rogan's arm tightly and continued to hobble along, favoring my right ankle, which was even worse for wear after our escape. I knew that we couldn't drag anyone into our problems. No one would offer us sanctuary. No one would even believe us. Everyone was too busy worrying about their own lives, their own problems, their *own* safety.

"Up ahead," I said to Rogan. "Number three-fifty-eight."

He led the way without questioning me again. We'd tucked our guns into our waistbands. The black of the weapon blended against the black of our *Countdown*-supplied outfits. The cold metal against my skin gave me a meager sense of calm, although it didn't help my heart to stop racing. It was so loud that I was sure the people passing us would be able to hear it.

My gun was out of ammo since I'd used it all up on the digicams, but I didn't throw it away. Just having it calmed me. Most people would cower away from the sight of a gun; there was no need to even pull the trigger.

Just before we reached the address, a man stepped in front of us. I felt Rogan tense up as he blocked our way and gave us a huge smile.

"You two look like fun kids."

"Get out of our way," Rogan growled.

"I have something you might be interested in."

"What is it?" I asked, my voice strained.

He produced a tri-fold flyer printed on light blue paper. "Have you been wanting to get away? Want to figure out how to finagle a seat on the Colony shuttle while you're on a working class budget? Well, I have just the thing for you right here."

"Not interested," Rogan said. "Get yourself and your scam away from us."

"Scam? Not even slightly. In my course, I will give you the top ten ways to get to the Colony and away from it all. There are always other options, other solutions. Just picture it— perfect temperatures all year, no pollution, silver skyscrapers, more jobs than you can shake a stick at, streets lined in gold! A perfect place for a perfect life, the Colony is. And you can get there with my help."

"It's a course?" I asked, disappointed.

"Yes. It's called Ten Weeks to Paradise. Five hundred dollars and you, too, can realize your dreams." He thrust the flyer at me.

"Not interested." Rogan's voice went cold at the edges. "Get out of our way. Don't make me say it again."

The man cleared his throat and withdrew another flyer from his inner jacket pocket. "Not interested, I can understand that. Perhaps a vacation a little closer to home? I can provide you with a steady supply of Kerometh to make every day a holiday—"

Rogan shoved him out of our way, and we started walking again.

"Dream dealers." He said it under his breath, sounding pissed off. "Almost forgot they're everywhere."

I looked wistfully back at the man. How many people had he conned into taking his course that offered no promises? He preyed on the dreams of the people stuck here. People like me.

Not that I ever would have had five hundred dollars to spend on a stupid course of any kind. Education was for the rich, not for girls like me, girls living on the streets.

I pushed those thoughts out of my head as we closed the distance between us and our destination. The street number was set in brass above the large door.

I tried the door and was surprised when it swung open at my touch. We slipped inside, and the door closed behind us. The noise from the street vanished. We were now in an unadorned hallway lit only by a small window. I let out a shaky breath as we began to move along the passageway.

"What is this place?" Rogan asked.

"I'll explain in a minute. Come on."

Every time I came close to mentioning his father I'd been interrupted. I didn't think that was a coincidence. The digicams had to be long gone, otherwise we wouldn't have made it this far, but I wasn't prepared to risk it. Not yet.

The passage went along straight for about twenty feet and then turned sharply to the right. The front of the house that faced the avenue had just been a facade.

Ahead of us there was a light above a red door. It had a buzzer next to it. On the door was the street number again.

This was the right place.

Rogan studied the door skeptically. "Kira, are you going to tell me what's going on?"

"If I knew for sure, I'd tell you everything."

"So, now what?"

"You know when people who haven't been screwed over a million times try to think positively?"

"Yeah?"

"Let's pretend to be those people."

I pressed the button. The sound of a buzzer was deafening.

I half expected the door to swing into darkness and some monster to appear, grabbing us and dragging us inside. But nothing happened. Absolutely nothing.

We waited in silence for what had to be five full minutes.

Rogan raked a hand through his dark hair. "So, how long should we wait here? I'm trying to be patient, Kira, really I am. But you have to talk to me. Now."

He was right. It was time.

I told him everything I knew—which, to be honest, wasn't all that much. Everything I'd learned from using my Psi ability on his father. That this monster who'd kept the game going, who'd likely framed his own son to get him out of the way, who'd kept a game running that caused pain and destroyed lives…

Something wasn't right. It wasn't him. I'd heard the real Gareth Ellis—literally *heard* him—deep inside the shell of his body. He wasn't in control.

He was the one who'd given me this address. To help me, to help Rogan.

He wanted us to escape.

Rogan listened to me in silence, his expression like stone. When I was done, I waited for his reaction. It took a moment.

"Why didn't you tell me this before?" he asked quietly.

"I tried to, on the roof after Mac and Kurtis…and again just a little while ago before the room split. They were listening. They didn't want me to tell you so they wouldn't let me."

His forehead creased into a deep frown. "You make it sound like my father's possessed."

"I know it sounds crazy, but that's what it felt like. He's not in control of his actions right now."

I watched emotions play on Rogan's face. Disbelief changed to anger, to the slow, grudging acceptance that this might be a possibility. Then his gaze snapped to mine.

"You said you read his thoughts? Literally read them?"

I nodded, still stunned myself by the possibility. "Same thing happened with Kurtis on the rooftop. It wasn't just emotions, it was more than that." Rogan was still giving me an odd look. "Why? Is that bad?"

"Not bad, just…" He didn't speak for a moment. "Just… not low-level."

"What?"

"Jonathan told you that you were a low-level, right?"

"Yeah."

"Maybe Jonathan lied. Maybe you're not a low-level empath."

My heart skipped a beat. "Why would he lie about something like that?"

"Why does he lie about anything he does? I don't know." Rogan looked at the door again. "We need to get out of here. There are other places we can hide."

He was right. I'd hoped this might be something—some help offered in an unexpected way, but it could just as easily be a trap. And it would become a trap no matter what if we stayed here while the Network pinpointed the location of our implants.

We turned back to the passageway just as the door leading to the street slammed shut and heavy footsteps approached.

Rogan pulled his gun out of his waistband and gave me a tense look. Without hesitation, I did the same.

Just then I heard a popping sound and something in the back of my head began to tick.

"Unable to detect implant signal." It wasn't the announcer this time. It was a computer-generated voice. Inhuman, unemotional. *"Please return to proper signal range. Not complying will result in implant self-destruction in fifteen minutes. Countdown begins now."*

Oh, shit. I looked at Rogan with wide eyes.

He raised an eyebrow. "Just keeps getting better and better, doesn't it?"

"What now?"

"I guess we'll soon find out."

I gripped my gun with both hands as I pointed it at the semidarkness of the hallway. I hoped Rogan still had ammo. A moment later, somebody appeared in front of us. He also held a gun, raised toward us.

It was Jonathan. He was dressed in dark pants and a long-sleeved shirt, but he wasn't wearing his white lab coat. His forehead was shiny with sweat.

"Drop your weapons!" he commanded.

"You first," Rogan snarled.

"Rogan, you need to do as I say and drop your weapon."

"Not exactly taking orders from you right now, asshole. I will pull this trigger and waste you without a second thought."

Jonathan's gun shifted in my direction. "Shoot me and I'll shoot her. I know her gun's empty. I was counting. And you only have one bullet left."

Rogan flicked a tense glance at me, then back to him. "One bullet's enough to kill you."

I hadn't expected him to come here. It was more proof that this had been a wrong move on my part. Damn it. My hatred for this liar surged to the surface, but I knew getting upset wouldn't help. I tried to stay as calm as possible given the situation.

"How did you know we were here?" I demanded.

"Are you going to listen to reason, Kira? Or are you going to be stubborn like Rogan?"

"Since you just threatened to shoot me, I'm thinking stubborn sounds pretty good to me."

I studied him for a moment, holding my useless gun so tightly that it began to cut into my skin. I remembered when I'd used my empathic ability on him—with his coaching.

Why would he have lied about my abilities being low-level?

One thing I remembered very clearly, the moment that had fooled me before, was that he gave the distinct impression of being honest and truthful. But there was an ocean of guilt mixed in—enough guilt to drown in.

"What do you think you're guilty of, Jonathan? Answer me that right now."

Surprise flickered across his expression, but he didn't lower his gun. "I'm guilty of a lot of things, Kira. I don't even know where to begin."

"But you feel bad about what you've done."

His expression darkened. "Of course I do. That's why I'm here. That's why you need to hear me out."

"Am I a high-level Psi?"

He blinked, surprised. "Yes."

I gasped. "Why did you tell me I was low-level?"

"I didn't want *him* to know. And I hoped that your ability might help you in the competition. And it has. You're here. But there's no time, you have to trust me. Drop your gun. Please, Kira."

Trust him? After he'd lied to me over and over?

He'd told me I was low-level so Rogan's father wouldn't know. So he wouldn't see me as a threat. So I could read him if I got the chance. So I could know the truth.

Was it possible that Jonathan really was trying to help us?

Only one way to find out.

I stared at him for a moment longer, and then I dropped my gun and held my hands out before me.

"Kira, what the hell are you doing?" Rogan growled.

"Trusting my instincts."

"Your instincts are going to get you killed."

"My gun was empty, anyway."

Jonathan's gun was still trained on me.

"I did what you wanted," I said evenly, despite my shaking on the inside. "Now talk."

"Your implants have started their self-destruct sequence,

haven't they?" When neither of us confirmed it, despite the constant ticking in my head, he continued. "I was notified the moment you escaped the game and moved out of network range." A smile twitched on his lips. "Well played, by the way. Well played."

"No thanks to you," Rogan said, each word coated in poison.

A muscle in his cheek twitched. "I've done what I can. I healed you, Rogan. I healed Kira's leg after the shooting. But now you've escaped. They know you must still be in the city."

Rogan glared at him. "And let me guess. You've notified them that we're here. Isn't that convenient?"

Jonathan shook his head. "No. They don't know. I'm the only one who knows where you are. They assume that when they do find you, they'll be retrieving two dead bodies after the implants self-destruct."

"Then I guess it'll be three bodies they find. You were wrong about how many bullets I have left—there's more than one in here. Now lower your weapon away from Kira or I swear to God I'm going to fill you with so many holes that you'll be able to see out of your own ass."

"Rogan—" My throat was so tight, it made it difficult to form words. "I honestly don't think Jonathan wants to hurt us."

He gave me a sidelong glance. "Why? Because of your empathic instincts?"

"Call it gut instinct."

"Sorry, not good enough for me."

Jonathan let out an exasperated sigh. "There's simply no time for this." He bent over and placed his gun on the ground. Rogan stormed toward him and grabbed his arm, swinging him around to shove him up hard against the wall next to the door. He jammed his gun against Jonathan's head.

"Now tell me why you're here."

"I'm here—" Jonathan's words were partially muffled by the fact his face was squashed against the wall "—because you pressed the buzzer. It's connected to a device I wear at all times. It informs me if someone has found the safe house your father had me set up." He nodded as much as he could. "I could see you through the hidden camera, so I came straight away."

I glanced up and saw the subtle glint of a small black lens in the corner of the ceiling.

More cameras. God, how I hated cameras.

Rogan grabbed Jonathan's shirt and swung him back around roughly. "Explain more."

"Your father is not himself."

"I know."

"You know?" Jonathan's eyes widened. "You know about the A.I. virus that corrupted his implant?"

Rogan shot a look at me. My eyes were wide, my chest tight.

He was possessed—I'd felt it. I didn't know if it was a demon, an evil spirit, or a psychotic break that had split his personality in two.

But I hadn't expected this.

"What do you mean?" I managed. "A virus? Like a computer virus?"

Jonathan nodded. "It happened the night of the blackout—the power surge. He couldn't fight it. We never could have expected anything like this. We created a monster through Ellis Enterprises's billion-dollar artificial intelligence research and development department. And that A.I. monster now controls your father."

Rogan swore. "You expect me to believe this nonsense?"

"Nine minutes until implant self-destruction," the tinny voice announced.

Jonathan's chest heaved. "There were times in the beginning when the real Gareth was able to give instructions without the virus knowing. He attempted to stop what was happening. In the end he lost the battle for control of his body, but he was able to do some small things, such as set up this safe house. You are the first to make it here."

Rogan looked at me, and I could see the strain in his face at hearing all of this.

"We need these implants out," he said.

Jonathan sighed. "Yes, you need them out or you're both going to die. Now take your damn hands off of me, boy, so I can get to work."

17

JONATHAN UNLOCKED THE DOOR AND touched the light pad inside before hurrying into the small house. "Follow me."

He disappeared into another room through a narrow archway.

"Eight minutes remain until implant self-destruction."

With that announcement I began to feel a disturbing burning sensation at the back of my head. I was again reminded of what was left of Mac's body on the roof after his implant exploded and turned everything above his shoulders into pulp. Shuddering at the memory, I followed Jonathan into the next room—a narrow kitchen with a stove, refrigerator and small wooden table.

"Sit there." He nodded at a chair to the side of the table.

Without argument, I did what he said, easing myself onto the hard wooden chair.

Jonathan produced a gauzy piece of fabric from his pocket, which he unrolled on the table in front of me. There were several silver medical instruments in it, all very sharp, all very dangerous-looking. He flicked a switch on one, and a bright orange light began to glow.

"If you hurt her—" Rogan warned.

"If you keep distracting me with that gun, I may do just that by accident." Jonathan had a syringe in his hand and he filled it with a small amount of clear liquid from a tiny glass vial. "There's no time to put you completely under, Kira, so a local anesthetic will have to do."

I eyed him uneasily.

"Wait—" I held up my hand as he approached. "Rogan, didn't you say that the implant will detonate if removed wrong?"

Before Rogan could say anything, Jonathan replied instead. "That's absolutely true. However, I am one of the very few who know how to remove such devices properly. But you must stop talking and hold completely still."

So, even though Jonathan had lied to me several times, I was now forced to put my life in his hands. It didn't seem all that smart.

Unfortunately, we'd officially run out of choices.

"Put the gun down!" Jonathan snapped at Rogan. "Or I won't do this at all."

I glanced at Rogan, who met my gaze. Finally, the muscles in his arms flexing, he lowered the gun and placed it on the counter next to the stove. His expression stayed full of menace. I sensed that if Jonathan made one wrong move, Rogan would reach over and break his neck.

Oddly enough, the violent image was reassuring.

All thoughts, reassuring or otherwise, disappeared from my mind as I felt the jab of the needle to the back of my head. A few seconds later, my eyesight went a bit blurry and a numbness began to spread across the back of my scalp, out to my ears, and down to my cheeks and jawline.

Rogan sat down next to me. I reached for his hand, and he didn't pull away.

"It'll be fine," he told me, his expression tense.

"If you say so."

It'll be fine, I repeated internally, trying to focus on anything other than the ticking in my head.

Jonathan reached forward and chose a scalpel. I clutched Rogan's hand, squeezed my eyes shut, and tried to be brave. Despite the freezing, I could still feel the knife score my skin, right where the original incision was. An ooze of warm blood slid down the back of my neck before Jonathan wiped it away with a cloth.

The instruments rattled together as Jonathan took something else from the selection. First, he dabbed something on the wound.

"I'm neutralizing the connection," he said. "It should prevent the implant from exploding when I remove it."

"It *should* prevent it from exploding?" Rogan repeated. "You better be sure."

I squeezed Rogan's hand tighter as I felt a strange pulling sensation.

Then there was a pain so intense and pronounced that my eyes snapped open, and I couldn't help it—I screamed.

"Damn it." Jonathan sounded strained. "Rogan, hold her still!"

Rogan took a tight hold of my shoulders, and I gripped the edge of the table. I felt a series of painful snaps—one after another after another until I thought it would never end.

Then, for a horrifying moment, I saw nothing at all. I'd

gone completely blind—and the total darkness felt as if it was smothering me. But just as my paralyzing fear of the dark was closing in around me, my vision cleared. Jonathan tossed the bloody implant into a metal canister. It landed with a metallic *thunk*.

He grabbed another instrument, the one he'd flicked on earlier. It was red-orange on the end, and I knew it was because it was extremely hot. He pressed it to the incision. The sickening, charcoal-like scent of burning flesh wafted under my nose as he cauterized the wound.

The ticking countdown was gone. It gave me a small measure of relief, but we were only halfway there. And there wasn't much time left.

I looked down at Rogan's hand. I'd clutched it so hard that I'm made little half-moons that filled with blood from where my fingernails had dug in.

"Sorry." My words were still slurred from the freezing.

"Forget it." He gave me a grin. "You're brave."

I managed to return the expression. "Thanks."

"How long do we have?" Jonathan asked.

Rogan tore his gaze from mine. "Two minutes. Might not be enough time, I know."

Anxiety spiked inside me. "Hurry."

Rogan and I switched places, and I held his hand, being careful not to hurt him again as Jonathan began working on him. Rogan kept his eyes open through the operation, breathing steadily through his mouth, his expression tight.

"How long now?" I asked.

"One minute," Rogan replied.

"Jonathan, hurry!"

"Believe me," Jonathan said, "I'm going as fast as I can."

I didn't want to look, but couldn't help myself as Jonathan quickly numbed the area and then cut a line into his scalp about two inches long. He held back the flaps of skin to reveal the implant, which was an inch square. Little blue and red wires as thin as hairs disappeared into the skull itself.

"Twenty-five seconds." Rogan's grip tightened on my hand.

Without replying, Jonathan dabbed the implant with the colorless neutralizing solution and then inserted a flat instrument underneath the implant. When he pulled up on it, Rogan's grip on my hand grew painful.

This must have been the part where I'd screamed.

Now the implant was attached to the tissue only by metallic hairs. The implant, along with the attaching wires, suddenly reminded me of a spider. I shuddered at the thought. I hated spiders.

"Ten seconds…"

Jonathan used a tweezerlike instrument to pluck those thin wires out of the tissue connecting it to Rogan's skull. When they were detached, the implant itself finally gave way.

Rogan's teeth were clenched together. "That was damn close."

His pained gaze slid to mine. I nodded encouragingly. "You're brave, too."

He snorted weakly at that. "Thanks."

"What about Rogan's other implant?" I asked Jonathan. "The prototype from years ago?"

Jonathan closed the wound and used the cauterizer on it. "That would be a deep cranium operation. I don't have the time or the facilities to accommodate an operation of that magnitude. It's not a priority right now."

He flipped Rogan's implant into the canister along with

mine and took it over to the counter. He dumped the contents into a blender and hit the on button.

With a churning, metallic grinding sound, the implants were destroyed.

I finally let out the breath I'd been holding.

"Are you okay?" I asked Rogan. I couldn't help but notice his face had paled considerably during the operation. I'm sure mine was the same.

He raised an eyebrow. "I'm still breathing. And you?"

"Never felt better."

"Glad to hear it." He glanced at Jonathan, and his gaze turned wary. "Thank you for helping us."

"You're very welcome." Jonathan came over to the table and sat down heavily in a chair facing us. "Now we must see what we can do about getting the two of you to safety."

Rogan's eyes narrowed. "That's all you have to say to me? After the bomb you just dropped on me about my father? I am grateful for you removing our implants, but that doesn't mean you've made up for everything you've done. Before you go anywhere, I need more information."

Jonathan's lips thinned. "An unexpected and powerful computer virus attacked the Ellis mainframe and attached itself to the artificial intelligence program that we'd been creating. Your father's implant was among the systems compromised during the power surge. In just milliseconds, the A.I. program...adapted. It evolved. It's incredible."

"Incredible?" Rogan bit out. "How can you say something like that?"

"I'm a scientist. A researcher. If one looks at this strictly from that viewpoint, it was a breakthrough in cybernetic technology—a body of flesh and blood fused together with artificial intelligence. This virus has been using Gareth's power and influence to grow stronger with every passing day."

"How is this even possible?" I asked. Even back when I did go to school, science and computers had never been my best subjects. It was all I could do to keep up with this discussion.

But I understood enough. Rogan's father was possessed, just like I thought. But instead of a demon, he was possessed by an artificial intelligence computer virus that had become sentient. After everything I'd experienced as part of this game, and what I'd found out about Rogan's father, I'd been searching for an explanation of how all of this could have happened. This was far-fetched…but it also made a weird kind of sense.

"This is a very important part," Jonathan said. "This A.I. virus—it feeds off the brainwaves of the Subscribers through their implants. Every week that has passed, he's become more and more powerful. And with the Ellis fortune to back him in a city with an eighty percent poverty rate, all he has to do is throw money around and he has a legion of employees willing to do whatever he wants. Most of them believe they're simply working for a power-hungry billionaire with very little moral fiber."

Feeds off brainwaves. The thought made me shudder. "How has *Countdown* remained a secret all this time?"

"Fear," Jonathan replied. "Those who come to work closely with Gareth sign a nondisclosure agreement which, if broken, has extremely harsh penalties."

"Who would sign an agreement like that?" I asked.

"You'd be surprised what money can buy."

"This is insane," Rogan breathed. "All of it."

"Yes, it is. But that doesn't make it any less true. Currently there are over fifteen thousand Subscribers fitted with an implant, who each pay upwards of a million dollars a year to gain access to the Network feed." He snorted softly at that. "Ironic. The feed that feeds Gareth. And there is no end to his appetite."

I did the math in my head. This shadowy Network was netting a minimum of fifteen billion dollars a year—and *Countdown* was only one of its horrible games.

"Does the Network have any idea about this feed? About what the virus is doing?" I asked.

"Not that I'm aware of. Not that they'd likely care if they knew, as long as they continue to turn a profit."

"Why haven't you tried to stop him?" Rogan clenched the side of the table. His knuckles were white.

Jonathan pressed his lips together. "What makes you think I haven't? I've been secretly working behind Gareth's back on a plan to stop this before it gets worse. Before Gareth manages to take things wider—toward a day when everyone on the planet is fitted with an implant. I know that's where this is all headed. The Network—"

"The Network's not my concern. Only my father," Rogan said bluntly. His jaw tightened. "I can help you."

Jonathan shook his head. "The best thing for you to do is to get as far away from here as possible."

"Wrong. He's my father—"

"Exactly. You're too close to the situation. You will only interfere with what I have planned. Besides, it's my duty to do what I can. After all this time, I've waited too long..." Anguish filled Jonathan's expression, and he squeezed his eyes shut.

"And you feel guilty about it," I said. "I read you when I was in the hospital room. I felt that guilt."

"So much time has passed, and I haven't known what to

do. I've watched my dear friend slip away and a monster take his place, and all the while my fear for my own safety kept me from taking the necessary action to stop it. Including what happened to you, Rogan. Words will never express how sorry I am for everything you've been through."

Rogan's face was tight. He didn't say anything in reply.

Jonathan met my gaze. "If your father saw the same test results I did—and I'm sure he would have—then he knew about your Psi abilities. But he kept it secret, even from you. I understand why he was afraid. There are those in this society who wish harm to anyone different from them."

I swallowed hard. "Like Kurtis. He'd wanted to kill me for what I was. What I *am*. He said it was a mutation of the Plague."

"In a way, it is. But I don't think it's a bad thing. I believe it's an incredible gift."

I shook my head. "I don't know if I'm really high-level. I mean, I read you as being honest, but you've lied to me over and over."

His expression shadowed and he looked away. "I'm sorry for all of that."

"But—but it doesn't mean you're *not* honest. You have helped us. And you were the one who told me about my ability. And you want to stop this virus. A few lies and bad choices don't change who you are deep inside."

"I don't know anymore. I hope you're right. I really do." Jonathan stood up from the table. "I've arranged for two tickets on the next shuttle to the Colony for the both of you."

My breath caught. I didn't expect this at all. "Are you serious?"

He nodded gravely. "This city is not safe for you—not now,

not ever again. You must go to the relative safety of the Colony. There is less corruption there, at least for the foreseeable future, and a large enough population to lose yourselves in."

There was silence at the table.

"When does the shuttle leave?" Rogan asked. "How do we get to it?"

"You'll find a set of train tracks behind this house. At precisely three o'clock, I've arranged for it to stop to pick you up. It'll look like a normal passenger train, but it will bear this symbol—a mayflower—to let you know it's the right one." He reached into his jacket pocket and pulled out two tickets with our names on them, along with a white flower with five petals in the top corner. "It will then take you to another train that will continue your journey to the Colony."

We each took one. I stared at it, certain my eyes were deceiving me. I'd been wanting this for so long that now it seemed surreal to actually be holding it. This was all it took? This little piece of shiny paper was enough to change my life forever?

"I've contacted the Iris Institute already, Kira. It's a private school for girls who have high-level Psi abilities like yours. I know it's been difficult for you, especially with no training. I promise that the more you use your ability, the less pain you'll experience. It's like exercising a muscle, you see. You will grow stronger and they will help you. I've written the address on the back of your ticket."

I turned it over and stared at the small, precise writing. "This is— It's...too good to be true." My gaze shot up. "What's the catch?"

This earned me the edge of a smile on his otherwise deathly serious face. "I understand your doubt. But it's all true."

A school that could help someone like me. Where I could meet other girls who had Psi abilities. Where I could make friends and take classes and have a place to belong—after all this time of not belonging anywhere.

I drew in a shaky breath, my throat tightening. "Thank you."

He nodded. When he turned his attention to Rogan I noticed that Jonathan's eyes were now shiny with emotion. "As for you, Rogan. I cannot express to you how sorry I am for all the pain you've been through."

Rogan's throat jumped as he swallowed. "It's over now."

Jonathan nodded. "As I said, your father has had a few sentient moments. He was able to arrange for a bank account to be set up for you. By the time you reach the Colony your criminal record will be cleared, so your name will cause no red lights upon your arrival. The account number is written on your shuttle ticket. Your father wanted you to have enough money to last the rest of your life. He wanted you to enroll at the school Liam went to. He believes you have incredible potential—more than you ever gave yourself credit for. Some admissions tests will be required, but again, I've made a call and explained the situation, leaving out some of the more unpleasant details, of course."

"You would have had to leave out a lot."

Jonathan raised an eyebrow. "Let's face it—money speaks volumes when delivered in the right amounts. The school is aware you might stop by, and they said that they're looking forward to it."

Rogan stared at the ticket as if in disbelief. "My father wanted this for me."

"Yes. He loves you, Rogan. He always has, whether or

not you realized it." Jonathan pressed his lips together. "You should know, he begged me to kill him while he was still in control of his body, but I couldn't do it. Now he doesn't trust me—this technological monster that possesses him believes I'm working against him, but he has no proof yet. He has associates who shadow me wherever I go."

Alarm rose inside me. "Then how were you able to get away today without being seen?"

He crossed his arms. "After your escape, Gareth was furious. The headquarters were in chaos. I had a feeling that you might be headed here, and when you pressed the buzzer, I managed to slip away unseen. I'm afraid I won't be able to stay for much longer, though. In fact, I should leave immediately. They'll be looking for me."

"I'm coming with you," Rogan said firmly.

"No, you're not. My plan does not involve you. I must do this myself."

"What's your plan?"

His expression was tense as he fished into the front pocket of his pants and pulled out a small card. "Take this. I will find a way to contact you in a week to tell you if I was successful. However, if you don't hear from me, it means I have failed. Wait a month until everything has calmed down and then use this information to get in touch with a man named Joe. I believe he might be able to help fix this if I can't."

Rogan didn't look convinced, but he took the card, anyway. "But why can't I help you now?"

"Because the moment they see you they will kill you. They'll kill both you and Kira for escaping from the game. There's still a risk once you arrive at the Colony, but it's substantially reduced from the risk of staying here, I can assure you."

I shuddered at this blunt statement. Then I glanced at the card. It had an H-like logo on it and an address here in the city. The logo looked familiar to me, but I couldn't place it.

"What is this place?" I asked.

Jonathan's lips thinned. "Just a small glimmer of hope after years of darkness. After all this time, I still hold on to the hope that things can change—even when they seem at their bleakest."

I eyed him. "Well, *that* is annoyingly vague. Can't you tell us more than that?"

"Sorry. I've already told you too much as it is."

Rogan took a step closer to Jonathan. I wasn't sure what he was going to do until he thrust out his hand toward the other man. Jonathan shook his hand firmly.

"Thank you for what you have told us—and what you've done to help us," Rogan said, his voice tight. "And good luck with your top-secret plan, whatever it is. Please do what you can to save my father."

"Be safe, Rogan."

When Jonathan glanced at me, I offered him a genuine smile. "See, I *knew* you were a good guy after all."

"No, you didn't." He smiled, too, but his eyes remained sad.

"No, you're right. I didn't. But I do now. Thank you for the tickets and for the—the school thing." Words failed me. How could you thank someone who'd forever changed your life for the better?

He gave me a gracious nod. "The shuttle will arrive at three o'clock on the dot. Stay inside the house until only a few minutes before. Understand? There are clean clothes upstairs if you'd like to change. I'm sure you're ready to get out of those ridiculous costumes."

"It's like you're psychic, too," I said, which drew a short laugh out of him.

"Goodbye, both of you. And good luck."

He turned away and left the kitchen. A moment later I heard the door slam behind him.

Rogan looked at me.

I stared back at him, my mind reeling, my heart racing—I honestly didn't think it had slowed to normal since I woke up in that silver room chained to the wall.

"My head is still killing me," Rogan said, deadpan. "I have no idea why."

"Might be because a big piece of metal just got ripped out of it."

He snorted and I couldn't help but grin.

"Yeah, that could be part of it." He glanced in the direction Jonathan had just taken to leave the safe house. "I shouldn't have let him leave yet. I should be helping him."

"You heard him. He has a plan."

"I wish he'd told me what it was." His expression was grim. "But after everything we've been through, I just want to get as far away from here as possible."

"I'm so sorry about your father." Looked as if we were both orphans. Even though his father was still technically alive, Rogan had really lost him two years ago.

He nodded. "Yeah, so am I."

I reached around to the back of my head and felt the hard ridge of cauterized skin. "I can't believe the implant's gone."

"I know."

"And here I thought I was going to have to get used to having you within ninety feet or less for the rest of my life."

He gave me the edge of a smile. "Good job they're out, right? You can finally be free of me. You'll be happy in that private school, Kira. I know it."

"I hope they like me."

"What's not to like?"

I rolled my eyes and tried not to grin. "I'm going upstairs and check out that change of clothes Jonathan mentioned."

"You do that."

I turned away from him, leaving the kitchen. Around the next corner was a flight of stairs to the second floor.

Once we got to our destination we'd go our separate ways. Was I thinking we'd stick together indefinitely? There really wasn't any reason why we would. I would go to the Iris Institute—which sounded both terrifying and amazing. And Rogan would go to university, like his brother had. The Colony was huge—a thriving city of a million people. We'd both get lost in the crowd.

If my father had seen the results of my tests, that I was a high-level Psi, maybe he'd been planning to take me to this institute so I could develop my abilities and learn how to control them. What would my life have been like now if that had happened? If instead of living on the streets of this dangerous, desolate city for the past two years, I would have lived those years in the Colony.

However, then I wouldn't have met Rogan.

We'd been thrust together, neither of us had had any choice in the matter, and we'd dealt with it the best we could. Now it was over, and the moment we reached our destination I might never see him again.

This was the way it was supposed to be.

Even though I knew that, it still hurt like hell.

THE CLOTHES WERE UPSTAIRS IN A CLOSET.

They weren't perfect—I didn't think whoever had stocked the closet, probably Jonathan, ever expected a girl to be here. I grabbed the smallest pair of jeans I could find, cinching them with a belt, and a T-shirt I had to tie at my waist. There were no shoes close to my size, so the black lace-up boots I already had would have to do.

Then I busied myself with taking a shower and washing my hair before I slowly got dressed. I stared at my reflection in the foggy mirror after clearing it with my forearm.

Still me. I looked the same as ever. Tired, though. And a bit bruised. I had a small cut on my cheek that I hadn't noticed before.

I tidied up and left the bathroom. Rogan was waiting in the hallway.

"Finished?" he asked.

"Yeah, it's all yours."

"Thanks." His hand brushed against mine as we passed, and he closed the door with a click. I stood there for a moment, studying the door separating us, listening to the sound of the shower turning on, as well as to the sound of my suddenly racing heart.

I spent the next two hours exploring. The house was small, but fully furnished. It reminded me of the house I'd grown up in, even though it didn't look much the same. Maybe it was just the fact that it was a real house, not some crappy place I could crash for the night to get off the streets.

There was a small view screen set into the wall, and I activated it, flipping through the channels. I stopped on a news feed, half expecting to see mine and Rogan's faces splashed across the pixels as dangerous, escaped criminals.

There was nothing, of course. We weren't criminals. And the only thing we'd escaped from was something that very few people had any idea existed.

In another room I found a bookcase with some old hardcover novels. I pulled one out, brushing my palm against the torn, dusty cover. After a second, I recognized it as a book about a boy wizard and couldn't help but smile sadly. My mother had read this book to me and my sister—even though my sister had always thought she was too old for such things. Still, it hadn't made her leave the room when Mom had pulled this book, and others, out.

I read a few chapters, lost in nostalgia, before slipping it back onto the shelf.

Soon I'd be sort of like that boy wizard. Only, you know, I wasn't a boy. Nor was I a wizard. But I'd be going to a school where they'd help me learn how to use my special kind of magic. And to think, only a few days ago I'd been stealing red shoes and depending on French fries for my meals.

I glanced at the clock for the hundredth time. It was two

o'clock. Still an hour to go until the shuttle arrived. The house was cold, and I hadn't found a temperature control yet. I decided to grab a sweater before we left. At the top of the stairs, in the room I'd been in before, I tapped the light pad on the wall so I could take a better look in the closet.

The floorboards behind me creaked—Rogan had moved into the doorway and was standing there, looking at me.

"You've been keeping a low profile," I said, not taking my attention from the closet of fascinating men's clothes. "Two hours apart. I think that's a record for us."

From the corner of my eye, I could tell he smiled at that.

"Yeah, well, I guess we should get used to it."

I forced a grin to cover up the flash of pain I felt at that. "Do you know what subjects you'll take in university?"

"No idea." His words were dry and fairly clipped. He wasn't making eye contact with me anymore. "I'll deal with that when I get there."

"Good idea." I pulled a blue sweater from its hanger and slipped it on. It would do fine.

"Kira…"

"What?" I turned back, surprised that he'd drawn closer. I waited for him to say something else.

He didn't.

"What is it?" I prompted, pushing the closet door shut with a click.

His throat worked as he swallowed. He studied a small picture of a lake on the wall over my shoulder. "So, you're definitely going to that girl's school."

"Well, yeah. Of course. I can't think of anywhere else I should go."

"Just don't let anybody tell you that being a Psi is wrong—like that bastard did. It's not. Jonathan's right, it's a gift."

"All the more reason to go so I can be around other kids like me. Otherwise, I would think I'm a total freak."

"You're not a freak."

"Thanks for the vote of confidence." I pressed back against the wall. It hadn't been this awkward talking to Rogan before, had it? Now that I knew we were parting ways, everything seemed harder. "What are your plans if you don't know what you want to study?"

"Other than waiting for news about my father, not much." He shook his head. "Actually, I have no damn idea what I'm going to do next."

I nodded and tried to push away some of this overwhelming sadness—it was crazy to be so sad over saying goodbye to a boy I'd only met a handful of days ago. "Well, I wish you luck."

"Yeah, you, too."

"Like, seriously, Rogan. I don't know what I would have done if you hadn't been with me through all of this."

"I feel the same way."

Silence fell, and I began to feel very awkward again, and at a total loss for words. He moved back toward the door, but paused there, blocking it as I was about to move past him.

I eyed him. "Do I need to pay a toll?"

His lips curved. He studied a spot on the ground by my feet. "No toll."

But he didn't move.

"Well?" I prompted.

He snorted softly, and finally raised his gaze to capture mine. "It's going to be a little strange."

I bit my bottom lip. "What's going to be strange?"

"Not having you around anymore."

My heart began to pound faster. "I thought you'd be glad to finally get away from me."

"Glad isn't exactly what I'm feeling right now."

I hesitated. "What are you feeling?"

He shrugged and finally stepped out of my way. "Forget it. I know the past few days have been bad for you, Kira. Don't worry, the worst is over now."

I moved past him, but he caught my wrist.

"There's just one thing I really need to know..."

My breath caught. "What?"

He captured my face between his hands, and then his mouth was on mine in a deep kiss that made me gasp against his lips from the sheer force of it. He pressed me up against the wall, and the picture of the lake went crashing to the floor.

The reward room experience had ended in such embarrassment that it had tainted the moments we'd spent together, made me doubt what I'd begun to feel. But this kiss—so unexpected, so right. It made me realize that the only bad thing about that moment with Rogan had been the interruption.

"What did you want to know?" I asked as we parted for a second, my heart going a million miles a minute.

He grinned. "If you'd kiss me back."

I was going to laugh, but his next kiss stole my breath.

His warm hands slid under my sweater to circle my waist, pressing me tight against him. There was no future, no past, only this moment. All I knew for absolutely sure was that I never wanted to let him go.

But then the sound of a slamming door made me freeze.

"What the—?" Rogan didn't waste any time. He grabbed his gun and ran down the stairs. I was right behind him.

We turned the corner at the bottom of the stairs to see that Jonathan had returned. He stood by the sink in the kitchen with his back to us.

I let out a long breath. "Jonathan, thank God it's only you."

Rogan grabbed his shoulder and turned him around to face us.

I gasped. Jonathan looked terrible. His face was as white as snow and damp with sweat. The skin around his left eye was dark purple, the white of it filled with red. He clutched at his upper chest with his right hand and supported himself against the counter with his other.

"What happened to you?" Rogan demanded.

Jonathan shook his head. "There's no time to explain. I learned that the shuttle would be here early and had to tell you. You must leave now…you have only minutes to catch it. Gareth and the others—they know…they're…they're coming for you…"

"What? They know about this place? Did you tell them?"

"They know that I…that I helped you. They've been suspicious ever since I gave you the antidote. They think I helped you escape."

He slid down to sit awkwardly on the floor.

"What did they do to you?" My heart was banging painfully against my ribs. "What can we do to help?"

"Be safe."

Then his expression stilled and his eyes glazed over. His hand dropped away from his chest to reveal a large, bloody wound. It was just like the wound Rogan had had when the game had begun—the wound from the knife dipped in calcine poison.

Rogan dropped down beside him and pressed two fingers to Jonathan's throat. He looked up at me grimly. "He's dead."

I stared at him in shock. "He can't be dead!"

"They killed him, Kira. And they're on their way to do the same to us." He leaned forward and closed Jonathan's eyes, and then got to his feet. "We need to leave right now."

I didn't want to believe it, but it was true. Jonathan was dead. The only one who cared enough to try to help us...and they killed him *because* he helped us.

Rogan's hand closed around my upper arm, and he roughly guided me along with him out of the kitchen as a banging sound came from the front door. Someone, or a lot of someones, was trying to get in. They were from *Countdown*. They were trying to get me and Rogan and take us back or kill us or torture—

"Kira, come on," Rogan urged. I shook my head trying to clear it enough to keep putting one foot in front of the other. We slipped out the back door just as I heard the splintering of the front door behind us. The back of the safe house looked out on a yard encircled by a small fence. A few hundred feet beyond the fence lay a set of train tracks.

A train was pulling up right now.

"That's got to be the shuttle." Rogan's voice was strained. "We're going to miss it."

"Are you sure? Maybe there are lots of shuttles that go past here."

"Maybe. But this one has the symbol on it."

He was right—it did. However, at first glance and if I hadn't had the mayflower symbol pointed out, it didn't look any different than any other train I'd ever seen.

When we got there, the pain in my ankle obscured by the

racing of my heart, a white-haired man reached out to me from the side of the shuttle. "Do you have a ticket?"

"Yes!" I showed him the ticket Jonathan had given me. He eyed the ticket, then eyed me. If he saw anything strange or suspicious, either he didn't show it or he didn't care. Maybe he saw a lot of panicky people about to board. In fact, I'm sure he did. This wasn't just a train, it was the promise of a better life.

Scratch that. It was the promise of a *life*. Period. There were no such promises in the city.

"Welcome aboard," he said with a nod.

I climbed up on the shuttle and turned around to look at Rogan.

"Ticket?" the man asked Rogan.

Rogan looked back at the house.

"Rogan!" I tried to get his attention and reached my hand out to him. "Come on, there isn't any time. They're coming."

"I know."

There was something glinting in his eyes when he met my gaze. Resolve. Determination.

It worried me deeply.

The man frowned down at him. "The shuttle's leaving, young man. On or off?"

Rogan shook his head. "I'm sorry, Kira. I can't go with you."

I stared at him. "What?"

"Now that Jonathan's gone, I have to stay." There was anguish in his eyes.

Panic clawed at my chest. "No. No, Rogan! You have to get on this shuttle right now."

"I can't just turn my back on him knowing what I now know—about...about my father."

This couldn't be happening. Not now when we were so close to escaping! "We can think about what to do later when we're somewhere safe. Those men—"

"Those men are being controlled by something evil that needs to be stopped." His expression was strained, but fierce. "I want to come with you, but I can't leave. I have to stop him."

The shuttle let out a sharp whistle.

We had tickets. The shuttle was here. It was about to leave, to take us somewhere we'd be safe. My dream come true of starting a fresh new life, finally after all this time—it was everything I'd ever wanted.

"I need to go now," Rogan told me, his voice strained. "I have to do this, Kira. You see that, don't you?"

"Yeah," I managed. "I see it."

I jumped off the shuttle to land at his side.

"What in the hell do you think you're doing?" Rogan growled. "You were on the shuttle. You were leaving."

"I know. And now I'm off the shuttle and I'm staying."

"I can't wait any longer, miss," the man said.

I turned to look at him grimly and tucked my ticket back into my pocket. "I understand."

"Very well." He nodded and blew a whistle. The shuttle began pulling away from where we stood.

"There's no guarantee you'll be able to find another shuttle," Rogan said.

"Well, that's just the chance I'm going to have to take, isn't it?" I clenched my jaw. "Now, are you going to stare at me all day, or are we going to get out of here before those white-coat-wearing freaks figure out where the back door is?"

He chanced a glance back at the safe house and then sent a pained look at the departing shuttle as if he couldn't believe

I'd just sacrificed a first-class trip to the Colony to stay here with him.

Yeah, me neither, actually. But here we were. "Do you need a literal countdown all the time to get your ass in gear, or what, rich boy? Let's go!"

"You drive me crazy, Kira. You know that?"

I felt his anger at my decision like a heat wave emanating from him. He crossed his arms in front of him, and I saw that he'd tucked his gun into the waistband of his new jeans. He started walking along the outer line of the fence. We didn't say another word until we found an opening and were able to dart through a neighboring yard, and then along a side street that took us back out into the village. A cool wind had picked up, and it blew my hair around my shoulders as we emerged on a well-populated street.

"So what's the plan?" I finally asked.

"The plan is to get you somewhere safe, and then I'm going to the location on the business card Jonathan gave me to see if I can find this Joe person. I just wish Jonathan told me more before he—" His voice broke. "Damn it."

"You want me to go somewhere *safe*?" I repeated flatly.

"That's right."

"Forget it. I got off that shuttle for one reason and one reason only, and that's to help you stop the virus and save your father."

He laughed. It was a cold laugh that sent a chill through me.

I narrowed my eyes. "What's so funny?"

"*Save* him?" he repeated bleakly before his eyes went hard with resolve. "Actually, my plan is to *kill* him."

19

I COULDN'T HAVE HEARD HIM RIGHT. "WHAT
did you just say?"

His jaw tightened. "You heard me. Jonathan said it himself. My father begged for Jonathan to kill him when he had
the chance. It's the only way to put him out of his misery and
to get rid of the virus once and for all. It's evil, Kira. It has to
be stopped before more people get hurt. It's the only way."

I'd sacrificed my chance at the shuttle to help Rogan with
a rescue mission, not to be an accessory to murder. "There
has to be another answer."

He gave me a sidelong look as we hurried along the crowded
sidewalk. "Oh? And please tell me what it is, being as you're
so technically savvy."

"Sarcasm not terribly appreciated right now. I don't know
anything about computers or viruses or anything, but I can't
believe the only option is to kill him."

He hissed out a breath. "Don't make this more difficult
than it has to be."

"You're not a murderer, Rogan."

"I killed that kid in St. Augustine's."

"Only because you had to. But this is your own father."

He glared at me again as if he couldn't figure out why I was giving him such a hard time. "This is difficult, don't think it isn't. Why didn't you stay on that shuttle? Then at least I'd know you were safe. Damn it, Kira. Why did you have to jump off?"

Because I think I'm falling in love with you.

But of course I didn't say that out loud. The thought, which came out of nowhere, shocked even me, since I hadn't realized the truth of it until this very moment. My throat tightened. "Because...because you need my help. I'm in this just as much as you are, you know. And even if I had made it to the Colony doesn't mean that your father's men would have stopped looking for me. Can you promise me that they won't? That they won't try to hunt me down wherever I am?"

His jaw tightened. "I can't promise anything right now."

I crossed my arms and kept walking. "Didn't think so."

My now implant-free brain was working overtime. Computers. Viruses. Artificial intelligence. Stuff that could have been pulled straight out of my parents' collection of old sci-fi movies. I'd seen things while playing *Countdown* that I'd never seen before in my life—things I never dreamed possible. Holoscreens, cranium implants, a freaking talking evil robot that had shot me in the damn leg.

It was all way, way out of my league, and I knew it. Sure, I could pick a pocket or con somebody into buying me lunch on a good day, but apart from my Psi ability, which I was only starting to get a hang of, that was about where my talents ended.

I looked around the street. This area suddenly seemed familiar to me. "Where are we headed, again?" Rogan handed me the business card. I studied the logo that looked like an H. "I've seen this somewhere before, but I forget where."

"Wherever it is, I need to talk to this Joe guy," he said. "But Jonathan didn't tell me how he might be able to help or what this place is."

My eyes widened as it finally clicked for me. "Wait a minute. I do know what this is. And I know somebody who goes there all the time."

"Who?"

"Oliver. The guy from the mall, remember? I've been friends with him for months. This place...I know it because he wears the logo on a T-shirt. It's an underground gaming den. If he's not at the mall, he's there. He hangs out there for hours, sometimes days."

Rogan stared at the business card, his brows drawing together. "This is a gaming den? You're sure? How did Jonathan think some guy who can be found at a place like that's supposed to help us?"

I shook my head. "No idea."

"Maybe he gave me the wrong card to throw me off so I wouldn't get in his way. For all I know, maybe he didn't have a plan to stop my father in the first place."

"He died to help us and to give you that card. Let's make sure he didn't die in vain, okay?" I touched his arm to stop him from walking. "We can check it out. Maybe Oliver will know who Joe is."

He looked grim. "Yeah, maybe."

"Considering that your other option at the moment is storming one of the biggest office buildings left in the city and trying to take out the CEO by force, I'd say this is something that we look into."

"If I tried walking through the front doors of Ellis Enterprises right now, I have no doubt they'd shoot me on sight."

I nodded firmly. "Then let's go to this place and hope Oliver's there. If anything seems off, then we'll get out of there and look for him at the mall instead."

He didn't say anything for so long, I was sure he was going to argue with me some more. But he didn't.

"Fine. I still think it was a bad move for you to jump off that shuttle, Kira. But…" His gaze locked with mine. "Thank you."

"You're welcome," I said as he drew closer to me. He leaned toward me, his attention shifting to my lips. I suddenly forgot how to breathe.

Then suddenly, somebody banged into us and totally ruined the moment.

"Watch where you're walking," an old man snapped as he gave us the evil eye. "Get off the sidewalk and get a room. Damn useless kids."

The perfect moment for another kiss had been destroyed, but it was probably for the best, given the gravity of our situation. "We need to get going. The place isn't far from here."

Rogan tore his gaze away from me to study the sidewalk stretching out before us. "Then lead the way."

Years ago, kids used to get together and play networked video-games in secret underground dens, staying for hours and hours working their way through the levels—fighting against each other or working in teams to accomplish their digitized goals.

Not that much had changed, really. Ever since the Great

Plague, new technology offered to the general public was both rare and exorbitantly expensive, so the same sort of games being played twenty-five years ago were still popular today.

Oliver was one of these kids, bringing his ratty old laptop computer to his secret gaming headquarters to get plugged in. He had always bragged to me about how amazing he was and how nobody could beat him. He was "a god among gods" when it came to kicking ass and taking names in the digital jungle. At least, according to Oliver himself.

To me, playing games that earned you nothing but wasted time was, well, a waste of time. Therefore, I'd never paid too much attention to computers.

That was before a walking, talking computer put a bullet in my leg.

Now I was ready to take a stand and say that I wasn't a big fan of them.

"Here." I nodded when we got to the location on the business card around an hour after leaving the safe house—and saying goodbye to the Shuttle of My Dreams. The front door had no marking other than the H-symbol. I remembered now. According to Oliver—when I'd asked him about the logo on his T-shirt—it was the *Hagalaz,* a rune symbol that stood for "controlled chaos."

Welcome to the Secret Society of Gamer Geeks.

Rogan nodded, pushed the door open and we went inside.

I still had hope, but it was waning with every passing minute. How was somebody from this place supposed to help us? All I knew for sure was that I didn't want Rogan to get killed by trying to assassinate his father, so any other option was better than that.

But I also knew the man had to be stopped. Some way and somehow. There was no other choice.

And the familiar geek playing the war-zone videogame in the corner of the dark basement at the bottom of a sketchy flight of stairs might be just the person to help us stop him.

The only light in the basement came from the flickering screens of ten computers. All of the guys—and they were all guys, no girls—sat staring at their computer screens as if hypnotized.

Any socializing between them was being done on screen—and it looked as if there were a lot more people playing than the handful in this room. I knew those gamers could be anywhere on the planet if they had the cash or connections to get on a good network. Each screen showed a different piece of the digitized action. Each player was fitted with a visor that hooked into his computer. Oliver told me once that he owed a small fortune to the owner of this place for the extra equipment, but it made everything seem more real—as if he was really playing a game of life and death.

Having experienced the real deal, I had to say that playing for your life wasn't nearly as much fun as he might think.

There was a stale smell of sweat in the basement, along with something sweet and a little sickening, and a very faint odor of urine.

Lovely.

I didn't always stay in the nicest, cleanliest five-star resorts, but this was not up to even my low standards. In fact, I'd rather not see what might be crawling around in here if they ever turned on the overhead lights.

"Nice place," Rogan whispered to me as he surveyed the room. "You come here often?"

"Oh, yeah," I replied drily. "Every day. Can't get enough."

"There's your friend." He nodded in the direction of Oliver, who was hunched over with his back to the stairwell.

"Wait here," I said to him. "Or somebody might recognize the infamous Rogan Ellis."

"Wouldn't want that."

The floor was carpeted and seemed a little squishy under my boots. *Gross.* I glanced back at Rogan while I moved through the dark room—luckily not quite dark enough to trigger anything but a niggling sensation of my phobia. As long as I could see what was going on around me, I was fine. Mostly fine.

Oliver was completely focused on his computer screen. His hands, encased in cybergloves, gestured, pointed and waved as he worked his way through the game. Onscreen, his game avatar walked down a darkened hallway with dirty walls. The tip of a weapon was visible at the bottom of the screen—a big gun, maybe even a flamethrower.

Despite my disinterest in the gaming world, I recognized the game. It had something to do with the bad guys trying to take over the world and the good guys trying to stop them.

The first thing you had to do was decide which side you were on.

"Oliver." I reached forward and closed my hand over his shoulder.

He shot up from the seat and let out a hoarse scream. Onscreen, the door in front of the computer-Oliver burst open, and I could see the outline of a figure who immediately opened fire. Digital blood trickled down from the top of the game screen.

Words then appeared:

YOU'RE DEAD, LOSER! NUCLEARXXX KILLED YOUR SORRY ASS! EVIL REIGNS!

Oliver swore and whipped off his gloves. Then he took off his goggles and furiously spun around to face whoever had just made him lose his fake life.

His eyes widened when he saw it was me.

"Kira!" he squeaked. "What are you doing here?"

I grimaced and nodded at the screen. Typed-in taunts were coming in from other players. He wasn't being mourned for his great on-screen sacrifice in his battle for good, that was for sure.

"Sorry about that," I said.

He looked regretfully at the screen, where the latest message read: LMAO UR A LOSER!!!!!!

"Yeah, well, whatever." Then his gaze shot back to me. "Kira, what are you doing here?"

I bit my bottom lip. "I need your help."

His brows drew together. "Didn't you ask me for help in the mall before you went all psycho and took off? I thought you were mad at me or something."

Definitely *or something*. "No, I'm not mad. The psycho thing might be debatable, though." I'd wanted to keep from drawing him into this mess, but now that the game part was over for me and Rogan, Oliver could be just the help we needed. "I've been really distracted lately. I'm sorry if I seemed like a bitch to you."

"You told me to leave you alone."

I forced a smile. "I was having a really bad day."

Fear slid behind his gaze. "You were with that guy—"

He hadn't seen Rogan yet, standing to the side of the room cloaked in shadows. "Oliver, listen to me. I need your help."

"She needs help. Nice." Another kid next to Oliver peeled off his visor. "You need some time alone? Oliver, I didn't know you had a girlfriend. She's hot, too." His gaze raked me from head to foot.

"She's not my girlfriend," Oliver said very coldly. "She'd rather be with guys who have police records. Sorry I'm not up to par yet, Kira. Where's your new friend?"

"Right here." Rogan appeared at my side. "Is there a problem?"

I sighed. I didn't think his presence would be very helpful when it came to getting Oliver to talk. Call it a hunch. But too late now. "I thought I asked you to wait over there."

He raised an eyebrow at me. "I guess I don't take orders very well. Sound familiar?"

I shot him a look. He was still pissed that I hadn't gotten on that shuttle.

Rogan looked at Oliver. "Now, I believe that Kira was asking you for some help. Are you really saying no to her?"

Oliver's eyes widened. "I…I…don't know. Um…"

"Just chill," I said to Rogan, getting worried now. "We don't need everybody in here freaking out right now."

The other kid took a step closer. "You're Rogan Ellis."

He didn't seem to be freaking out. Which was a good start.

Rogan studied him for a moment. "That's right."

"You can call me Snake."

Rogan eyed him. "Snake?"

"It's my screen name and I prefer it to my real one. Dude, I can't believe this. Rogan Ellis standing three feet away from me."

My mouth went dry. I didn't want a confrontation right here. Not now, there wasn't time.

"Let me guess," Rogan said drily. "You collect the signatures of convicted murderers like me."

"Nope." Snake shook his head. "You totally didn't do it."

Rogan's eyebrows shot up. "I didn't?"

"No." The kid frowned. "Why, are you saying that you did?"

"No...it's just—" Rogan closed his mouth for a moment, and his gaze flicked to mine. "It's just that everybody always assumes I'm some kind of monster."

The kid flicked his hand dismissively. "You were set up. It's obvious to anybody with half a brain. I have a website devoted to proving the conspiracy that got you locked up."

I eyed Oliver. "Did you hear about this?"

Oliver nodded. "Yeah, but Snake's theory is that it has to do with aliens. I never took it too seriously."

Snake glared at him. "Shut up, loser."

Oliver didn't even look at the kid; he stayed focused on me. "I tried to show you one of those sites a few months ago as a joke but you blew me off. Said you weren't interested in some dumbass rich kid. Guess you're interested now, huh?"

Rogan glanced at me for my response. "Dumbass rich kid?"

I cleared my throat. "Well, um...right. Now that you mention it, I think I do remember."

Hindsight sure had a strange sense of humor.

"Listen, Oliver," I said, trying very hard to get us back on track. "We're looking for somebody you might know. Somebody named Joe. Do you know him?"

Another gamer had taken off his visor and gloves and stood to the side watching our interaction silently. The remaining seven players continued on as if nothing existed outside of their videogame.

"I'm Joe," he said. His expression was anything but friendly. "And you're Rogan Ellis."

Rogan eyed him. "Then you're the one I'm looking for. I was told you could be found here."

"I'm always here. I own the place." He scanned Rogan slowly. "I'm glad to meet you."

The owner of the place Jonathan had a business card for was glad to meet Rogan. That had to mean something. Hopefully something good.

"Glad to meet you, too," Rogan replied.

"A lot's changed since the last time we saw each other."

Rogan now studied the guy suspiciously. "We've met before?"

"Not officially. I saw you in passing three years ago when I came in to interview for a job at Ellis Enterprises." Joe leaned back against the table. "We shared an elevator."

"Sorry." Rogan shook his head. "I don't remember."

"I'm sure you don't. But I do."

"Oh, yeah?"

"I was completely floored to be sharing the same air as you. For a kid barely fifteen, you were so…I don't know. Impressive, I guess. Thought I'd take a moment and try to break the ice, so I commented on your father's secretary's ass. She had a very fine ass." His lips thinned. "When we got off the elevator you told your father not to hire me. I heard you."

Rogan forehead creased as if he was trying to think back. "I don't remember that at all."

Joe shrugged. "Hey, whatever. It's been a long time. You've been through hell since then, I know that. You're out of juvie already? Were you proven innocent of those crazy charges?"

"Yeah. Something like that."

I looked at Oliver. He was watching the conversation intently. The other kid, Snake, had gone back to playing his game.

Oliver gave me a pinched look. "I can't believe you'd want to be with this guy."

There was dark venom attached to those words—and more than a little palpable jealousy.

If you asked me, the hairy eyeball he was giving Rogan probably had less to do with the fact that Rogan was a wrongly convicted murderer and former spoiled-rich-kid drug addict, and more that he was a good-looking guy in my company.

"Oliver—" I began.

He held up a finger. "I have to take a leak."

He turned his back on me and left the room.

"Okay," I said slowly. "Never mind."

"So, what are you doing here?" Joe asked.

Rogan reached into his pocket and pulled out the business card. "A man named Jonathan gave this to me. He told me to find you, that you might be able to help me. He worked for Ellis Enterprises, too."

Worked. Past tense. I shivered.

Joe shook his head. "Sorry, I have no idea why he'd give you that card. I don't have anything to do with Ellis Enterprises. I mean, I don't work there, do I?" He gave Rogan a humorless grin. "No hard feelings, of course."

Rogan studied him for a moment. "Have you ever heard of something called *Countdown?*"

"Rogan..." My heart pounded. It felt almost like a magic word; say it too loudly and the bad guys would bust in and grab us or something.

I waited, but nobody busted in. I was embarrassed to realize how relieved that made me feel.

"Countdown," Joe repeated slowly. "Now, you *could* be referring to a listing of the top pop songs of the week, or you could be referring to a death game on a secret televised network. Given your expression, the second seems more likely. Survive or die, right? Yeah, I've heard of it. Thought it was just a rumor."

"Just a rumor?" Rogan said. "Then why do you have a folder on your desktop labeled *Countdown?* Just a crazy coincidence?"

Even in the half darkness I could see Joe blanch.

He swore under his breath as Rogan grabbed his shirt and threw him against the table. All the computers shook.

The other gamers removed their goggles to see what the disturbance was.

Rogan glared at them. "All of you, get out of here right now."

He said it with enough menace to clear the room immediately. They fled up the stairs and out of the building.

Joe didn't fight back against Rogan, but he looked a bit more afraid now.

"Talk," Rogan growled.

"Okay, okay. After I didn't get that job, I was pissed. And I wasn't pissed at myself. I blamed you one hundred percent. That was a wicked opportunity my father set up. He said it was a sure thing and then some smart-ass rich kid had to blow it for me. I hated your guts, and I admit I celebrated when your life took a nosedive."

Rogan didn't let go of him. "So you hated me. Join the club, it's a big one. What then?"

"I went home and sank into a mega depression. I worked hard on a little present for Ellis Enterprises to get back at you—and everyone else. I was bitter, of course. And, hey, I had a lot of time on my hands being unemployed. At the time I lived with my father—him and Mr. Ellis went to college together. That's how he knew your father well enough to get me the interview. Same circles and all that. I'd heard a rumor about *Countdown,* and that's where I wanted to be. I wanted to be a part of something for real that I normally just played online. It would have been so sweet."

"What was the present you're talking about?" I asked.

He eyed me. "Well, first I had to hack the Ellis mainframe before I could do anything. Took me a while to do that until I finally got in."

There was silence in the room.

"And when you got in, what did you do?" Rogan asked quietly.

"I uploaded a virus. A nice juicy one I'd made specially for you. One that would know its way around and sink into everything and start eating all of Ellis Enterprise's precious data. I uploaded it and waited to hear news of the system going down. Of your future fortune going up in flames. But other than the blackout that night, there was nothing. However, the next day you got your ass arrested for those murders. I figured my virus was a failure, but karma had worked its special magic, anyway."

My eyes had widened with every word he'd said. The virus. The virus that had seeped into the artificial intelligence program and uploaded itself into Gareth Ellis's implant during the power surge.

The thing that had ruined Rogan's life.

All because of a job opportunity lost for a throwaway sexist remark.

A flap of a butterfly's wing turning into the proverbial hurricane.

Rogan laughed then, and it sounded just this side of insane.

"What is it?" I managed. "What's so funny?"

Rogan finally let go of Joe. "My father's secretary—she was really nice to me whenever I came to the office. Now I don't even remember her name."

Joe shook his head. "She had a great ass."

I couldn't believe this. Jonathan must have known. He'd known that Joe was the one responsible for the original virus. That's why he'd told us to come here.

But why? Why would he care who created the virus? What difference would it make now? And, if it could make a difference, why hadn't Jonathan come to Joe himself?

Maybe this was his last resort if he couldn't find another solution. And maybe Jonathan was being watched too carefully. I mean, one wrong step today had gotten him killed.

I moved closer to stand at Rogan's side. Joe was pale and breathing hard, but he didn't look guilty for what he'd done; he looked annoyed that he'd been caught after all this time.

He didn't know what had happened. He honestly thought his virus hadn't worked.

"Is there an antivirus?" Rogan asked.

Of course! An antivirus. That had to have been what Jonathan was after.

Joe raised his eyebrows. "An antivirus? After all this time? Why would you even care anymore?"

He had asked; so Rogan told him. Rogan told him all of

it—about the virus, the blackout, the corruption of his father's implant.

It wasn't long before sweat slid down Joe's forehead. "You're serious, aren't you?"

"Trust me," Rogan said. "I wouldn't joke about this."

"Ever since my virus failed…" Joe paced back and forth in the small, dark space. "Or since I *thought* it failed, I've been obsessed with all things Ellis, especially anything to do with *Countdown*. I even reapplied for a job there a few months ago. Your father interviewed me personally, which surprised me since he's, you know, Gareth Ellis, the freaking all-powerful billionaire. Anyway, he offered me the job. Then he told me about the implants. Still sounded cool, so I got fitted with one while I made my decision on the job offer. I got to actually watch a few levels of *Countdown*. Man, I was so stoked." He rubbed his hand vigorously over his forehead. "But then I saw somebody get eliminated. They killed him right on camera. Mr. Ellis laughed it off like it was nothing. Told me that this was the future and I should get used to it. He showed me the contract. He pretty much wanted me to sign in blood. Then somebody approached me. He told me that he'd help me get out before it was too late. He removed my implant and told me to run. I did. That was Jonathan."

"What happened then?" I asked.

"I've been in hiding ever since. I know *Countdown* is a big secret. I knew I'd learned too much for my own good. My father died in a car crash a week later." Pain shadowed his expression. "I know Gareth Ellis arranged for his death, but I don't have any proof. That's what this folder is. It's research. I know about the game, the levels, how they select competitors. I know about the implant linking." He shook his head. "You don't know what the show's like now. It's hell."

"We do know," Rogan said. "We've been playing it for three days against our will."

Joe's mouth fell open, and then he swore under his breath. "If that's true, then how did you get here?"

A flash of everything we'd endured went through my mind, and I shivered. "We escaped."

Joe's eyes widened. "You *escaped?*"

"Yeah. So, if you have an antivirus," Rogan said and there was a sharp edge of strain in his voice, "then we need it. It could be the only way to stop the virus."

A door clicked shut as Oliver returned to the room. "What are you guys talking about now?"

I approached him cautiously. "Oliver, I know you're pissed at me. I can understand that. But if you trust me at all, I need you to leave here. Go somewhere safe."

His brows drew together. "What?"

"Just take off. Come back here tomorrow or something."

"If you say so." He tried to smile, but his cheeks twitched too much to allow it. And just like Joe, Oliver was now sweating buckets, even though it wasn't hot in here. "Sure. Okay. I'll go. Um…I'll leave right now."

Why did he sound so nervous? Was it just being around Rogan? Or…was it something else?

I got a really bad feeling it was something else.

"What's wrong with you?" I asked him.

"Nothing. I'm fine. Never better."

I didn't know if it was my Psi ability kicking in without skin-to-skin contact or if it was simply my gut telling me that something was desperately wrong here.

"I'll see you soon, okay?" he said, turning toward the staircase.

"Yeah, sure. Oliver?"

When he turned back to me, his gaze guarded and fearful, I gave him a tight hug. He stiffened, as if not expecting the physical contact, before he relaxed against me.

Then I slid my fingers into Oliver's hair at the back of his head hoping very hard I wouldn't find what I was looking for.

But there it was.

Oliver had a freshly installed implant.

He took a step back from me. "I'm sorry, Kira."

My throat felt thick. "Why are you sorry?"

The boy was literally trembling now. "I had no idea you had anything to do with the game. They hired me on last week—thought my computer skills made me an asset to the team. I wanted to tell you my great news, but you've been avoiding me lately. They fitted me with an implant so I could watch." His expression tensed. "And they stationed me in the mall to see if you'd try to get me to help you. But you didn't. You ran away. With *him*."

Rogan now stood beside me, his gaze filled with fury. "Where did you just go, Oliver? Did you make a call? Did you let them know we're here?"

He wouldn't make eye contact with either of us. Then he nodded once. "They'll be here any minute."

My chest tightened—a familiar sensation of fight or flight I recognized very well by now.

I was voting for "flight."

Another countdown commences.

"I'm sorry," Oliver whispered.

I opened my mouth to say something to him—to scream

at him for selling us out—but Rogan took a step toward him first. That was all it took. Oliver staggered back from him and tripped on a wire. He fell and hit his head against the side of the computer table, managing to knock himself unconscious.

I grabbed Rogan's tense arm. "What are we supposed to do now?"

"We hope Oliver's wrong about our time line."

Joe's eyes had grown very large. "They're coming *here?* Somebody go up the stairs and lock the damn door."

I didn't need any more prompting. I thundered up the stairs as fast as I could, still favoring my sore ankle, and turned the dead bolt.

When I got back downstairs, Rogan was staring straight at Joe. "We need the antivirus and we need it now."

I was certain Joe was ready to run. I was equally certain that Rogan wouldn't let him, but we didn't have time for a physical confrontation. Not here. Not now.

To my surprise, Joe nodded sharply. He turned and sat down heavily in front of his computer and put his fingers on the keyboard. "I know it's around here somewhere. It's been a while, man. I hope I didn't trash it."

"But will an antivirus actually work?" I asked. "I don't know much about computers, but wouldn't the virus have progressed too far for that by now? Besides, it's not in a computer anymore, it's in a person."

Joe shrugged with one shoulder as he whipped through folder after folder, which appeared and disappeared in flashes of light and color. "That's entirely possible. But the virus isn't really in a person, it's in an implant inside a person. And that implant is directly connected to Ellis Enterprise's artificial intelligence server. If you can get to that server, shove in the antivirus disc, and launch it, then I think you'll be able to do some serious damage."

"Wait a minute," I said. "We have to put the disc in the server itself? We can't do this remotely—like from here, if you can hack into their network?"

"Unfortunately, no. They've totally upgraded their security. If you can't physically get to the server itself, this has no chance of working."

Rogan gripped the back of Joe's chair as the scrolling files appeared on screen. "I wish I knew where the A.I. server is now. It used to be on the second floor."

"It's in the sub-basement now," Joe said. "I walked past it during my orientation tour and I'm betting the guy leading the tour told me way more than Mr. Ellis would have wanted him to on an intro tour of the facilities."

"Do you know any more details? Like what room it's in?" I asked.

"Damn, why can't I find it?" The files scrolled down the screen faster than I could read them. "Where did I put it?"

"Joe, which room is it? Do you remember?" I said it louder this time. By my estimation, we had less than a minute left to get out of here.

"Yeah, I remember. It's marked as Mr. Ellis's office, even though I know his real office is on the top floor. The room has a computerized lock that only certain employees can access. The only people who were able to get in have a red clearance tag, if that helps. I remember that because those tags made me think of blood. *My* blood. And I didn't want to spill any of it either then or now."

Just then I heard a bang, and I nearly jumped out of my

skin. At the top of the stairs somebody was pounding on the outer door.

They were here.

"It's a strong door." Joe's voice trembled. "Trust me, paranoia will take you places. Especially dark, well-locked places. We have another minute before they can get in."

Rogan's expression was bleak as he met my gaze. Jonathan had been certain that if they ever found us, we were dead. "I'll hold them back for as long as I can," he said. "And you try to escape. Maybe I can talk some sense into them."

Was he crazy? "I don't think they'll be too interested in talking. They'll just kill you."

"Don't be so sure. I have a hunch that my father—or the thing possessing him—will want to see me personally one last time. He'll want to find out how we beat the system. I'll be questioned before they kill me."

My throat constricted at the thought. "Rogan—"

"I found it!" Joe shouted, sounding very relieved. "I just need to get it on a disc for you."

He opened a drawer next to him and fumbled through its contents. He closed his fingers around a small, blue plastic disc about the size of a quarter, pushed it into the slot on the side of the computer, and clicked a few keys. After another moment he pulled it out and handed it to Rogan.

"If you can get into that room—and I don't have any idea how you're going to do that—shove this into the A.I. server. If it's going to work, it'll work."

Rogan studied the disc with a frown. "How will I know if it worked?"

Joe hesitated. "That's a good question. I figure if it works... you'll still be alive."

"Great," Rogan said drily. He eyed me, and looked at Joe again. "Is there another way out of here?"

Joe swallowed hard. "Unfortunately, no. But now that I think of it, that would have been a really good idea. Escape routes, and all that."

Crap.

The pounding on the front door increased. We were cornered with only one way out.

Rogan looked at the small disc. Then he eyed me. "Can you do me a favor?"

"Sure. Anything."

"Hide this for me until later?"

He handed me the disc and I looked at it. "Where should I hide it?"

"Put it in your bra," Joe suggested, and then blanched at a look from Rogan. "I mean, I can think of a couple other places, but, uh, a bra's probably your best bet."

I didn't hesitate. I tucked it into my bra, glad I'd decided to keep wearing the one that had gone with my *Countdown* costume.

"I'll want that back." Rogan's gaze met mine. "Soon."

"Ask me nicely and it's all yours."

The edge of a smile appeared on his lips. "I just thought of something hilarious."

"Oh, do share. I could use a laugh right about now."

"Before—I had no idea how I was going to break into Ellis Enterprises without getting caught. Security's tight."

"And now?"

"I think we're about to have an in."

"Great. Just try not to die first."

"I'm going to try real hard."

Rogan took my hand in his and squeezed it.

Then several sets of feet pounded down the staircase as Gareth Ellis's men came for us.

ENDGAME

20

ELLIS ENTERPRISES WAS A FIFTY-STORY BUILD-
ing made of silver and glass that sat in an otherwise empty
section of the city like a cold, sparkling gem under the overcast skies.

Rogan was seated next to me in the back of the SUV. Both
of our hands were bound behind our backs. He was currently
unconscious. He'd put up a pretty good fight against the five
men in white lab coats who'd come for us. They'd easily dis-
armed him of his gun and then knocked him out. Frankly, I
was surprised they hadn't killed us on the spot.

I was sure it was only a matter of time.

Joe hadn't gotten off so lucky. He'd tried to run, to push
past the men as they swarmed into the room. He'd gotten a
bullet in his back for the effort.

They hadn't killed Oliver. He didn't accompany us in the
car, so I had no idea what had happened to him. Frankly, I
didn't care anymore. Maybe he'd get a reward. I guess everyone was out for himself. Not that this was news to me.

I tried not to relive the experience at Joe's gaming den and instead focused my attention on the shiny building—which, let's be honest here, was the place *I* would likely die today, or tomorrow…definitely sometime soon. I didn't have much hope of getting out of this in one piece. Things had gone way too far for that.

I tried to imagine a younger Rogan, high on whatever drug he'd just taken, showing up to his job at this building—the son of the billionaire CEO. The Rogan Ellis I knew wasn't a spoiled rich kid with a huge allowance to spend on frivolous things to relieve his boredom. I didn't think I would have liked the old Rogan.

In fact, I'm quite sure I would have hated him.

Then again, the old Rogan probably wouldn't have looked twice at a girl like me. At the end of the day, I was just a street thief who happened to steal the wrong guy's wallet. Even back when my father worked for the university, I'd never even been inside a building as fancy as this one.

But that's exactly where they were taking us.

I tried to concentrate on the sound of my breathing. Anything to keep myself from thinking about how bad this could all go. As Rogan said, he hadn't been sure how we were going to get inside the building in the first place. The security was tight. Super tight. We had to go through two checkpoints and a manned security station before coming within fifty feet of the place.

The car rolled to a stop next to a black side door. A man in a white coat sprayed something in Rogan's face, and he woke with a jerk. Every muscle in his body seemed to tense until he saw me, and our gazes met and held.

"Are you okay?" were his first gruff words. I should have been asking him the same question.

"No. Actually, we're both royally screwed."

He smirked. "I think you're probably right."

"Shut up," a White Coat snapped.

I glared at him but stopped myself from telling him to screw off. We were in enough hot water as it was. Wouldn't want to throw more wood on the fire beneath us.

The back door of the car opened, and both of us were yanked out of our seats. All the White Coats, whom I had originally assumed were scientists of some sort, were carrying weapons. Scientists didn't pack heat. These were hired thugs with a strict uniform policy.

"Move," they instructed us.

We moved. Through the door and into the cool interior of the building.

"We're in," Rogan said. "Should we celebrate now? Or wait until later?"

I gave him a look. How could he joke at a time like this? But the mild humor in his voice didn't reach his serious expression.

"Shut up." One of the men jammed the butt of his gun into Rogan's back as we walked down a long bare hallway. The white-tiled floor squeaked against my boots. "Don't make me tell you again."

My steps slowed as I saw who was waiting for us at the end of the hallway.

It was Gareth Ellis. He stood there next to an open elevator with his feet spread, his arms folded across the front of his expensive, black business suit. His blue-green eyes narrowed at our approach.

"Welcome back, son," he said as Rogan was shoved into the elevator in front of me so hard that he hit the wall with his shoulder.

"Son?" Rogan repeated through clenched teeth. "Is that what I am to you? Are you sure about that?"

"I am." Gareth's mouth twisted into a strange smile, and he glanced at me. "Why? Have you heard differently from someone?"

A shove at my back made me stagger into the elevator, as well. Four men in white coats pressed into the elevator with us, and then Gareth stepped inside and the doors closed. Claustrophobia hadn't been one of my fears in the past, but I strongly considered letting it join the growing list.

We'd entered on the ground level, but the elevator took us down even farther.

Joe had told us that the room with the artificial intelligence server was in the sub-basement. These bastards had no idea they were taking us closer to where we needed to be.

The elevator lurched to a stop, and the doors opened on a whole lot of white.

Gareth soundlessly stepped off the lift, and I felt a firm grip circle my upper arm, crushing enough to bruise. One of the men pulled me along another hallway.

All white. Everything was white and smelled of lemon-scented antiseptic.

Never had pristine cleanliness looked more like death to me.

"Where are you taking us?" Rogan demanded.

The White Coat whacked his gun against the back of Rogan's head. Not hard enough to knock him out, but definitely hard enough to hurt.

Rogan turned a glare of uncensored fury on the man. "Do that again and I'll shove that gun up your ass and pull the trigger."

The man laughed, obviously unthreatened. "Yeah, sure you will. Keep walking."

Joe had said that he hadn't wanted to work here. Despite the perks, of which I was sure there were many, he couldn't stomach the sadistic nature of being controlled by a walking, talking computer virus.

This guy, however, didn't seem to have a problem with it.

Gareth nodded at a door up ahead. "In there."

It looked exactly the same as the room where I'd spoken with Gareth before; they'd taken me here by helicopter after level four when I'd been blindfolded. However, I could be wrong. There wasn't much to mark it as a unique room. It was all white, with two narrow tables in the middle pushed together to make one table. Two chairs on either side. Both white. The monotone gave the moment a strange, almost surreal feeling.

Rogan and I, wearing our borrowed clothes from the safe house and the heavy black boots from *Countdown,* were pushed into the chairs so that we faced each other.

The slash of Rogan's scar was red against his pale face. Blood trickled down the side of his neck from where that thug had hit him with the gun. My heart wrenched at the sight.

His hands were still locked behind him in metal cuffs just like mine.

He didn't say anything and neither did I. But we'd spent enough time together that I could guess what he might be thinking.

Don't lose hope. We're not dead yet.

I'd try my very best.

"Leave us," Gareth said, glancing at the men who stood

there brandishing weapons that seemed so black against their white clothes. "And send him in when he's ready."

Send him in. My gaze left Rogan to move to the door. *Send who in?*

The White Coats left and then we waited. It felt like hours but I'm sure it was only minutes until he walked in. My mouth fell open.

Oliver.

Definitely not unconscious anymore, although he looked slightly out of sorts. There was a red mark on his head from where he'd knocked himself out against the edge of the table in the gaming den.

He wore an Ellis Enterprises security clearance name tag against his otherwise casual clothing—ripped jeans and his chaos-logo T-shirt. He seemed no different than the Oliver I'd known...other than the fact that he now stood beside the man who wanted to kill us.

He looked at me, and his brow furrowed before he turned his attention to his new boss.

"Oliver?" I managed. "What are you doing here?"

Gareth's lips curved. "Oliver works for me now, don't you?"

Oliver nodded. "Yes, sir."

Gareth moved toward him and slapped him twice on the back. "This boy's a genius. I always have room for geniuses on my staff. He was hired in an entry-level position a week ago, but his association with you, Kira, made him suddenly all the more interesting to me. I've decided that he will become my new personal assistant."

I ran my tongue over my very dry lips and tried to find enough moisture in my mouth to form words. Gareth's personal assistant? Oliver? I'd felt the ridge in the back of his scalp where he'd been fitted with an implant, and known he'd taken a job here, but I hadn't expected his connection to Gareth to be this close.

The thought didn't fill me with reassurance.

Anyone could be bought. Even someone you thought was your friend.

Gareth's smile held. "Along with evidence of accomplished programming and hacking skills, Oliver is very driven to succeed here—as many who are plucked from the streets seem to be. Before long I have no doubt he will rise high in my ranks. I promised him the opportunity. Isn't that right, Oliver?"

Oliver nodded. "That's right, sir. Thank you again."

Gareth's gaze slithered over me with distaste. "I honestly believed that you had gotten the better of me with your little escape attempt." His expression darkened. "You can imagine how delighted I was when we were informed of your whereabouts."

I fixed Oliver with an icy glare. He didn't meet my eyes.

A cool new job with a great paycheck—but he had to stand by with a smile on his face and watch people die. Including me.

I would never forgive him for this.

"You said that you wouldn't hurt her." Oliver spoke up after a moment of silence. He seemed totally incapable of making eye contact with me.

Gareth laughed. "Sentimental, aren't you? Yes, I did promise that, and I always keep my promises." He looked at me. "Since Oliver has an implant, he's been able to follow along with your cycle of *Countdown*. I believed after the reward level his desire to protect you would fade. No boy enjoys seeing the girl of his dreams in bed with someone else, but he still feels a sentimental attachment to you for some reason. Fascinating."

I scowled at him.

"Now, on to other business." Gareth clasped his hands behind his back and began to pace the room slowly, moving in a slow circle around our table. My gaze flicked to Rogan for a second, but his attention was now fixed on his father's possessed body, as if stunned. I realized this was the first time Rogan had seen him in two years. "Inspect him, if you would be so kind, Oliver."

Oliver moved toward Rogan, and I saw that he had a small metal receiver in his hand that flickered with green and yellow lights. He moved it over the back of Rogan's head, and he studied the light reading.

"What are you doing?" Rogan sent a dark look toward the kid.

"My son." Gareth leaned against Rogan's half of the table, his back toward me. "Please, relax. Oliver is simply checking the validity of your implant."

"Jonathan removed it before you had him killed," Rogan growled.

"No, no. Not that implant. The other one. The prototype."

Rogan went very still. "But it never worked."

Gareth pushed away from the table and began to move about the room again. "A lot has changed since you went to St. Augustine's, Rogan. Technology believed to be redundant can be made active. Especially the prototypes. You have one. I have one. Anything after that was simply mass-produced imitations of the originals."

"Which means what?"

Then Rogan's face twisted in agony, and he yelled out.

I struggled hard against my restraints. "What are you doing to him?"

Rogan slowly relaxed, his chest heaving, and there was now a gleam of sweat on his forehead.

Gareth ignored me and instead glanced at Oliver, who squinted at the receiver. "Well?"

"It looks good," Oliver said simply. "I've activated it for you. Simple, really."

Gareth cocked his head. "I'm so pleased that you think so. Then all is well with the world. Do you want to know why I care about your prototype implant, my son?"

"You're not his father." I bit off the words. "And you damn well know it. I knew you were possessed, but Jonathan told us the rest."

Gareth glanced over his shoulder and narrowed his gaze at me. "Are you trying to make me angry, little girl? I'm not sure if you're brave or stupid."

"Bite me."

He laughed. "You have been an amusement to me, Kira. And the Subscribers enjoyed you, up until your disappointing finish, that is. I wonder if you truly do have Psi abilities like Jonathan believed. I watched your interaction with Kurtis on the roof in level five. He was convinced that you could see his soul. Were you lying to him?"

I glared at him. "I saw who he really was. Just like I saw it with you."

He regarded me for a moment. "A true Psi. A new breed, an evolution to something greater than what came before." A flicker of interest lit his eyes. "Just like me. I never believed it could actually exist. Perhaps I was being too closed-minded." He approached me and gripped my throat tight enough to hurt. "Obviously, when you read me before, you sensed the human presence who once controlled this shell. I wonder what else you think you may have seen."

I struggled to breathe, but didn't flinch away from his intense appraisal. "Maybe I saw *your* soul."

He raised an eyebrow and then released me. I coughed, still feeling the imprint of his fingers on my neck.

Oliver watched me from the far corner, his expression tense.

Gareth turned his back on me and approached Rogan, who was struggling against his bindings, his narrowed gaze flicking between me and his father.

Gareth crossed his arms against his black suit. "While I'm not happy about your attempted escape, Rogan, I will say that I am very pleased that you survived so far in the game. When I first brought you in, I thought of it as a mild amusement. A way to get rid of you once and for all. I'd heard that there were further investigations afoot after a similar crime at another university took place last week. This time it was ten girls who were murdered." He tsked his tongue. "A shame. Truly."

I shuddered at the thought of more girls dying so horrifically. "You mean, Rogan would have been proven innocent?"

Gareth twirled around to face me. "Yes, it was only a matter of time. And I couldn't have that."

"So, now you're going to kill me right here?" Rogan said. "I'm surprised that you have the balls to do it yourself. Wait a minute. How many Subscriber brainwaves would a talking binary code have to absorb to have balls anymore?"

Gareth moved so quickly that all I saw was a blur. He grabbed a handful of Rogan's dark hair and pulled his head back. The chair teetered on two legs.

"A talking binary code, as you so crudely put it, can do

many extraordinary things. And the brainwaves help with many things. The more I absorb through the implants, the more powerful I become. But it's not good enough."

He slowly brought Rogan's chair back to its normal position. He patted Rogan on the top of the head as one might do to an obedient dog.

"Oliver," he said. "Tell Rogan what I plan to do with his reactivated implant."

Oliver pointed at himself. "Me? You want me to explain?" He looked around at the rest of us nervously, then pocketed the receiver. "Okay...sure. Uh, Mr. Ellis has requested that I—and the team, of course—upload an artificial intelligence program into your implant. Not sure if it'll work, but the reading I just took makes things look pretty positive. So...uh. I think that's about it."

Gareth grinned. "Thank you, Oliver." He put his arm around Rogan's shoulders and crouched down to whisper, still loud enough for me to hear, "So you see, Rogan, we *will* be family again. That's why *Countdown* is so important. My testing of it is now over. It was a narrow viewer base, anyway. It's time to take the Network and the implants to a much wider audience."

Rogan wrenched away from him. "Why would you do this? You're not my father anymore. Why would you even want me to be a part of it?"

Gareth's grin widened. "Perhaps *family* is the wrong terminology. When part of me is uploaded into you, we will feel the same, we will think the same. We will be one entity in two bodies. With my power multiplied thus, soon everything from this city to the Colony will be ours—and much more after that. The whole world will be ours. And why you, spe-

cifically? The implant, my dear son. You share the exact prototype implant that I have and that is what makes it all work
so beautifully. Without that implant you would be as useless
to me as lovely Kira is."

Rogan's eyes had gone very wide. "You're insane."

"I'm no longer prone to mental ailments such as insanity.
Nor will you be once you are…*improved*."

"Improved?" I managed, my stomach twisting and turning
with each word he spoke. "How can you see this as an im-
provement? You're no better than that robot from level three."

That earned me a truly withering look. "Kira, let me try to
explain this clearly so you will understand once and for all. I
am the next evolution of the human species. That's what the
Plague was. A cleansing. A way to improve the human species and get rid of the excess fat clogging the arteries of this
planet. One day very soon, all humankind will be fitted with
one of my implants. They will feed us and we shall become
the gods of a new race."

"You're right, I can't see that. All I see is a computer virus
that's a few pixels short of a full program."

"Then that is your unfortunate oversight. The robot you
fought earlier was a meager experiment in artificial intelligence. My intelligence is no longer artificial. I have a soul…
you said so yourself."

"I didn't say that. I said *maybe* I saw your soul."

He took a menacing step toward me.

"Wait!" Rogan's voice was hoarse. "Don't hurt her. Just…
just spare her. I won't fight you on this. You can do whatever
you want to me, but you have to let Kira go."

My eyes widened, but I held my tongue. He wasn't only

doing this to be my knight in shining armor. I was the one with the antivirus disc hidden in my bra.

Both of us might not survive this, he knew that. But if I could—and if I could get to that room…

No way. I wanted both of us to survive. I wasn't ready to accept any less than that quite yet.

Gareth laughed. "That's so terribly noble of you. The memories I can access of you do not lead me to believe that chivalry was ever one of your virtues. Has juvenile detention and sober living turned you into a gentleman?"

Rogan glared at him. "It did change me. I was a thoughtless, selfish, drug-addicted asshole before."

"A thoughtless, selfish, drug-addicted asshole who didn't know good entertainment like *Countdown* when he saw it."

Rogan's expression darkened. "It's still murder."

Gareth sighed. "The murder of a human, especially a criminal, is meaningless. In the world I envision, there are no criminals. There is no crime. It will be a perfect place to coexist and to thrive. And by the time this body wears out, I will have developed the proper technology to be able to upload my very essence into a new one."

"Immortality," Rogan said, stunned. "That's what this is all about for you, isn't it?"

"And be thankful I wish to share it with you. Perhaps there is a small part of this body that still feels a familial bond with you. Otherwise, I likely would have already killed you for ruining my game. When the Subscribers are angry, they turn to other programs—programs I have no direct access to yet." His eyes narrowed. "You have no idea how hungry I am right now."

I shuddered.

"Spare Kira," Rogan said again. "And I will do whatever you want."

Gareth cast a dark look at me. "Was it your idea to shoot the cameras?"

I glared at him defiantly. "It was a mutual decision."

"You ruined what would have been a very interesting finale."

"What, our deaths on camera? You sure have a twisted sense of what's interesting."

"I'm still not entirely convinced that you wouldn't have shot Rogan to reap your ultimate reward if there had been no other option."

If my mouth wasn't so dry I would have spit at him.

"I *wouldn't* have killed him," I said evenly. "I would rather have died first."

"I guess we'll never know for sure."

I heard a whirring sound, and a small hatch in the wall up in the top right corner of the room opened up and a camera slid out. It swiveled around so that it pointed toward the table.

"What the hell is that?" Rogan growled.

"You ruined my game," Gareth replied. "I can't have fifteen thousand angry Subscribers. Now I will make it up to them."

Oliver moved forward. "Wait. You said that you wouldn't hurt her!"

Gareth put a hand on his shoulder. "And I meant every word."

Oliver relaxed a little. He dared a glance in my direction. "See, Kira? I'm not as bad as you're probably thinking. I refused to help if he was going to hurt you. He promised."

I didn't reply. I was afraid of what I might say to thank him for his "help."

"Come with me." Gareth led Oliver toward the door. "I'm sure the new ending I have planned for this cycle of *Countdown* will be well received."

Oliver moved with him but was frowning. "I don't understand. You promised..."

Gareth nodded. "I promise that her death will be completely painless."

"What are you doing?" Rogan roared. "I said that I'd cooperate if you let her go!"

Gareth shot him a dark smirk. "You have no choice but to cooperate. Now, I will leave you in private—other than the cameras, of course—to say your goodbyes."

The door shut behind them, leaving Rogan and me in the white room all alone except for the company of the camera.

Rogan's gaze shot erratically around the room. He strained against his bindings.

I felt the pounding of my heart in the backs of my eyeballs as I waited for something horrible to happen. I'd tried to stay calm this whole time, but the dam had broken and fear flooded over me again.

The metal cuffs restraining my arms behind me released and dropped to the floor. I rubbed my wrists and looked at Rogan with wide eyes.

"What just happened? I'm free."

I jumped up from the chair and began to move toward Rogan.

"No—stop, Kira!" He leaped from his chair, too, his gaze moving up toward the ceiling "This room—don't come any closer—"

A thick sheet of glass slammed down from the ceiling to the floor, slicing between the two facing tables. The force of it blew the hair back from my face. If I'd taken one more step, it would have cut me in two.

I looked at it, stunned, not believing what had just happened. I put my hand against the cold glass and stared at Rogan whose hands were still bound behind him.

I glanced up at the camera that was taping us and imagined the Subscribers watching eagerly.

I rushed to the door and realized with dismay that there was no handle on this side.

"Kira!" Rogan's voice was clear and loud, despite the glass barrier. He wore an expression of pure shock.

I promise that her death will be painless, Gareth had said.

I only had to wonder what he meant for another moment.

That was when the gas began to seep through the air vents into my side of the room.

21

THE GAS SLID OUT OF THE VENT IN THE UPPER left corner in a translucent white slithering line. It trailed down the wall and onto the floor. More and more of it, moving through the room like blind fingers searching me out. When it reached me, it curled around my legs, swirling and moving like a snake.

"Kira!" Rogan yelled.

Gareth was right. It wasn't painful. In fact, it didn't hurt at all. I was surprised that the gas didn't even have much of a scent when it finally reached my nostrils. I clamped my hands over my mouth and nose, but I knew that wouldn't do any good. Not for long. I turned to the glass, to Rogan.

"What do I do now?" I didn't even try to hide the panic in my voice.

He pulled hard against his restraints, but it did nothing. His expression was frantic. "I don't know. Damn it! I don't know!"

The camera swiveled to take in both sides of the room.

"Where are you, you son of a bitch?" Rogan roared. "I'm going to kill you!"

But there was no reply. There was nothing. His father had promised to give us some privacy—other than the fifteen thousand subscribers who were tuned in to watch my death scene, of course.

I tried to hold my breath, but after thirty seconds I remembered that breathing wasn't really a choice. Unfortunately.

I inhaled some of the gas. It still had no discernible odor. Maybe it was just a ruse. Maybe this was just something to get an entertaining reaction out of us and make the Subscribers happy after we'd cheated them out of a good level six ending by escaping.

But, no. The more I breathed, the weaker I felt. My head began to swim. I gasped for breath. Instead of pounding hard and fast with fear like it had been before, my heart began to pump more and more slowly.

The gas cast a whitish fogginess over the already white room. My legs crumpled beneath me, bringing me onto my knees hard enough to bruise. I dragged myself closer to the barrier and put my hands up against the smooth, cold glass.

Rogan had moved close enough that his breath now fogged up the glass. He continued to struggle hard against his bindings, but it was in vain. He couldn't break free. His expression held a mixture of rage and grief. From where I had placed my hand against the barrier, he was only a few inches away. So close…but not close enough.

"I want you to know," I managed, gasping now for each breath I took, "I still think that you were wrong earlier."

"About what?"

"I'm glad I got off the shuttle. I…I've been happy for any time I've spent with you."

"Kira—". His voice broke. "Don't talk like you're giving up. Please, don't."

"Promise me that you won't stop fighting." I blinked, and the tears splashed down my already wet cheeks. "Don't let him change you into a monster like him. You're too good for that. There's…there's still hope…"

My hand slipped off the glass. I breathed shallowly through my mouth in quick little gasps. The world in front of me was fading from white to gray. Darker and darker, closer and closer to the pitch-black that I feared the most.

Would I see my family? Would I go to Heaven when I died?

I wanted so desperately to be brave. But I wasn't brave. I was afraid. So afraid.

Gareth was right about one thing—it didn't hurt. But that seemed to make this even scarier. At least pain reminded me that I was still alive.

"Damn you, Kira!" Rogan yelled. "Don't stop fighting! Not after everything we've been through. Not like this. Please!"

I wanted to let him know how wonderful I thought he was, how much I believed in him, and how he'd helped me trust somebody again, somebody other than myself. That the past didn't matter. That he was better now. So much better. And that I'd miss him so much.

But I didn't have the energy to speak. My mouth moved wordlessly as I slid the rest of the way down the glass and felt the cold, hard floor against my head.

Just before the world turned to complete, impenetrable black, I heard something. It seemed so far away—as if it was coming from the end of a very long and empty hallway.

A door opened. Then I felt hands under my arms and the sensation of being dragged. My heavy boots squeaked as I slid

across the floor. Then a door closed. It was still so far away I
didn't know what was going on. I was still fading. Fading....

And then I felt the unmistakable sensation of a hand slapping me across the face. Several times. Really hard.

"Wake up, Kira. Wake up!"

My eyelashes fluttered, and I opened my eyes slowly, my
left cheek stinging. The world crept back into focus.

Oliver stared down at me.

"We don't have much time." His voice trembled. "Can
you move?"

More eyelash fluttering on my part. I swallowed. When
I realized that the air I was now breathing was clear of the
poisonous gas, I began taking greedy gulps of it. I drank in
the air, filling my lungs with deep mouthfuls until my head
cleared even more.

Out of the corner of my eye I saw his hand rise.

"Slap me again," I said, "and it'll be the last thing you ever
do."

He gave me a tentative smile. "I'm glad you're feeling okay."

"*Okay* is a bit of an exaggeration. You should know that as
soon as I've recovered I am going to kill you."

His smile fell. "But I saved you."

I kept trying to breathe normally. I was alive. I hadn't died.
"Thank you for saving me."

He let out a sigh of relief. "You're welcome."

"However, you do know that we wouldn't have even been
in that room if it wasn't for you, right? So, please, forgive me
for not offering you a big, warm hug of celebration."

Oliver stood up and shuffled his feet nervously. "I begged
Mr. Ellis to let you go. He didn't listen to me. The man is
evil."

"You think?" I would have rolled my eyes if I'd had the energy. "Help me up."

He offered me a hand and I got to my feet. My ankle still ached from spraining it. But pain was a relief. After all, it meant I was still alive.

"Mr. Ellis had a conference call come in from the Network chairman. He had to take it. I took the opportunity to disable the camera. I couldn't figure out how to shut off the gas, so I had to come and get you myself."

That meant we didn't have much time. Hopefully it would be enough. "Honestly, Oliver. I can't believe you work here. For him. How can you do that?"

"If it's any consolation, I think this is my last day." His expression twisted into one of shame, and he suddenly looked a great deal older than his seventeen years. "I never realized how bad it was. How bad *he* was. Or, at least, it took me a while to clue in. I never wanted you to get hurt."

"But it was okay for Rogan to get hurt?"

His expression went hard. "My sister was one of the murder victims at that university. She was the only family I had in the world. I wanted Rogan to suffer for that."

My heart twisted. "But he's innocent. His father even admitted it in there."

His eyes filled with tears. "I was wrong. I'm sorry."

"And I'm sorry about your sister." I'd never known he had a sister. He'd never mentioned her. Then again, I'd never told him about what had happened to my family and to *my* sister. I'd never told anyone I'd met on the streets, holding my secrets close as if they might keep me warm on cold nights.

I guess we had way more in common than I'd thought we did.

I looked at his name tag, which read *Oliver Palmer— Programmer.*

Funny. I'd never known his last name before, either. Never realized that until right now. I'd been too wrapped up in my own problems to allow myself the chance to really get to know somebody else. At least, until Rogan.

My eyes widened as I studied Oliver's name tag a moment longer.

It was red.

Joe had said we'd need somebody with a red name tag to get into the room with the server.

"How long until somebody finds out I escaped?" I asked, scanning the eerily empty hallway.

"Not long." He looked worried. "The Subscribers will start complaining that the feed cut out—or they'll start changing to another show. Mr. Ellis will be notified, and he'll know what I did. We'd better get out of here now."

Oliver had had a lousy life—no question. And I didn't even know his whole story. I guess I couldn't completely blame him for latching on to something that seemed like an incredible opportunity, especially working with computers, the one thing he seemed to love most in life.

Lucky for me—and just in time—he'd realized that he wasn't a monster like Gareth Ellis.

"We need to get Rogan," I said firmly.

Oliver hesitated, but then nodded. He removed the red card from his name tag holder and swiped it in the computerized lock on the right side of the white door leading to the other side of the room.

The door swung open. Rogan turned to look at us, and his eyes widened.

"Kira!" he exclaimed. "You're alive!"

I grinned. "Yeah. For now."

I felt a happy lurch in my chest as I went directly to him. His gaze reflected what I'd been thinking. That that had been it. He'd thought he'd witnessed my death. But here I was, battle weary but ready to go another round.

But any celebrations would have to wait until we knew if we were going to live more than five more minutes. All Oliver had done was buy us a little more time.

Oliver pressed a hidden panel on the wall, and a keyboard was exposed. After he touched a few numbers, Rogan's metal cuffs snapped open and fell to the floor as mine had earlier.

Rogan stood up and pulled me to him, crushing me against his chest for a moment before capturing my face between his hands. "I thought I'd lost you."

My breath caught. "I'm still here."

"I'm glad."

I let out a very mild laugh. "Yeah, me, too."

"We need to go," Oliver urged.

He was right. Breathlessly, I grabbed Rogan's hand. "Let's get out of here."

The three of us left the room without another word.

"Are you okay?" Rogan asked, squeezing my hand.

"I'm recovering." I hobbled along quickly on my injured ankle. "Call me crazy, but I don't think sucking in poisonous gas until you're almost dead is something you can just shake off."

Oliver didn't say anything. Now that Rogan had joined us, he seemed to be afraid again. Whether it was because of Rogan's reputation or the fact that he'd almost killed me and was scared what Rogan might do in return, I didn't know.

Rogan turned his gaze to Oliver. "We need to find my father's private sub-basement office. Do you know where that is?"

"I haven't been here long enough to completely know my way around."

"We already took the elevator down past ground level. Is this the sub-basement?" I asked. "Or is there more?"

"There's one more level beneath this one," Oliver said. "I was supposed to start working down there soon." He sighed. "I guess that's not going to happen anymore."

"Can we get to it through the regular elevators?" Rogan asked.

He shook his head. "There's a flight of stairs. Yeah, right there." He pointed at a white door in front of us that wasn't marked.

Scurrying down the hallway toward the door, I got the oddest sense of déjà vu. Then I realized why. It was from watching Oliver play his networked game. It felt as if we were in the game right now, trying to find our way through, trying to save the day from the bad guys without getting ourselves killed in the process.

Then I remembered how the game had ended for Oliver.

Oliver reached for the unmarked door.

"Wait!" I began, but he'd already turned the handle.

There was a man on the other side. I recognized him as one of the White Coat thugs who'd brought us from the car to the white room. He was the one who'd hit Rogan in the back of the head with the butt of his gun.

The gun he still held.

His eyes widened with surprise when he saw us standing there.

Oliver held up his hands. "Uh…hi there. Um…Mr. Ellis asked me to take these two downstairs for the next level of *Countdown*."

"Nice try," the man said.

He raised his gun and shot Oliver in the chest.

As he twisted to aim at me, Rogan sprang at him, grabbing his arms. There was a blur of fists and legs. Rogan hit him across the jaw, and spun around and kicked him in the stomach. They both fell to the floor. He grabbed the man's arm and pressed his knee down on his forearm until I heard a sickly snap of a bone breaking. The man screamed in pain, but Rogan had the gun in his hand now and he pointed it at the man's head.

Rogan, breathing hard, turned to look at me, his expression tense.

I'd caught Oliver as he began to fall, and helped him down to the ground. His breath came in short, shaky gasps, and he held a hand to his chest that oozed bright red blood.

"I guess I didn't pass the final job interview," he managed.

"Oliver—" I could barely find the breath to form words. "Oh, Oliver! I'm so sorry."

He shook his head. "No…no, *I'm* sorry. Don't…don't hate me."

"How could I hate you? You rescued me. Thank you." I kissed his forehead.

His lips curled into a small smile, and then his eyes glazed over.

I let out a shuddery moan. He was dead. He'd died in my arms, trying to help us.

I looked at Rogan, whose attention was now on me.

"Rogan!" I yelled. "Behind you!"

The man now had a knife, and he lunged at Rogan. Rogan turned, aimed and pulled the trigger. He didn't miss.

The man slumped back to the floor. This time he wasn't getting up.

Rogan gave me a pained look. "That's two people I've killed now."

I found my voice quickly. "You didn't have any choice."

"You're right, I didn't." His chest heaved from the exertion. "I'm very sorry about your friend."

"So am I." I nodded, blinking back tears, and moved Oliver's still body to the side of the hallway. I took a moment to close his eyes.

Then I grabbed Oliver's red access card.

Rogan had a gun and I had an access card. I touched the front of my shirt to make sure I could still feel the outline of the disc in my bra.

Maybe—just maybe we could really do this.

Together we thundered down the stairs to the sub-basement.

22

THE SUB-BASEMENT LOOKED A GREAT DEAL LIKE the other levels of this building. All white. All bland and clinical with that antiseptic smell permeating the air like a super-clean perfume.

Only down here, every other ceiling light was out or flickering, casting spooky shadows on the hallway. It felt like a horror movie, as if somebody might reach out at any moment and grab our ankles and pull us into another room and devour us.

"Maybe they changed it," Rogan said. "The room. Maybe it doesn't have my father's name on it anymore."

I scanned the hallway. "Maybe. Or maybe Joe was lying. He could have made the whole thing up."

"Yeah, and maybe that disc only has pictures of his last vacation on it."

I didn't like this game of "maybe" we were playing. I gave Rogan a sharp look.

He glanced at me. "I guess we should be positive."

"Screw positive. I just want to find the room."

"We don't have much time. They'll shut this place down,

lock all the exits to find us. Maybe we should try to leave now, while we still have half a chance."

"After we went to all this trouble to get in here? Why would we want to miss out on the fun? How much time do we have before they find us?"

"Why?"

"I feel a sense of loss if I'm not working against a count-down. Sue me."

He snorted. "In that case, I figure we have a few minutes max before they lock the place down. Sweeping the levels with full security…maybe another half an hour."

I felt a very small sense of relief. Microscopically small. "Thirty-five whole minutes. Talk about luxury."

"Well, that's if we hadn't left two bodies marking the stair-case leading downstairs. That will quarter our time."

My heart sank. "Damn."

"Yeah."

I scanned every door we came to. Just as I was about to give up hope and take Rogan up on his offer to get the hell out of Dodge, my eyes widened.

"Look." I pointed at the last door that had a small brass plaque affixed to it—so small it was barely noticeable in the flickering light.

G. ELLIS.

My hands trembled as I slid Oliver's access card through the lock. The lights flickered red.

No entry.

I swore under my breath. "It's not working."

"Try it again." Rogan's voice was strained as he scanned the hallway. "And hurry."

I tried it again. Still no luck.

I let out a snarl of frustration as I slid it through for a third time. Then as the red light flickered I came to the sudden realization that I was sliding it the wrong way around. The metallic strip had to be down.

Mentally kicking myself, I flipped the card and tried it the other way around.

The light flickered green and I heard a click.

Rogan pushed the door open. It was pitch-dark inside, which immediately ratcheted my anxiety up another notch. I fumbled at the wall until I found the light pad, and I tapped it. The lighting flickered on, and I blinked as I gazed around at the room.

It didn't look anything like I thought it would. I would have expected a flank of computers, or at the very least, one big one in the middle of the room. A desk. Maybe a potted plant. Joe had said that this was Gareth's secondary office.

Instead, it looked more like a lounge. A large black leather couch was in the middle of the room with Japanese-inspired folding screens on either side. There was an unusually large amount of religious-themed artwork—paintings, sculptures and other fine art pieces representing all forms of religions, from an ornate and bejeweled rosary pinned to the wall to a large, golden laughing Buddha on a tabletop.

A large display screen on the wall across from the couch displayed images of the outdoors. It looked similar to the one in the reward room. Fakeness trying to appear real—and nearly succeeding. Behind me came a bubbling sound, and I turned to see an elaborate water garden next to a Zen sand garden.

I eyed Rogan, and he noted my confusion.

"I totally agree," he said. "I wouldn't have guessed that a talking binary code needed a place to chill out, either."

"Joe said this is where the server was, right?"

"Maybe he lied to us. Or maybe it's been changed since then. I don't see any server in here." The bluntness of his words didn't cover his disappointment. "Damn it, why didn't Jonathan tell us more about *his* plan to stop my father?"

"Probably because he didn't think he'd need to." I touched Rogan's arm. "What do we do? Where's the server?"

He shook his head and moved his gun back and forth between his hands. "I don't know."

We had to pick our battles. This one seemed dead on arrival. The conflict between fight and flight rushed through me again. I'd had enough fighting. Perhaps it was time to run. "Maybe there's still time for us to escape. You know, live to fight another day."

Then, to destroy the Zen-like calm of the room, the ear-splitting sound of an alarm filled the air.

"Or not!" I yelled.

I covered my ears and tried to concentrate. The view screen showed a swaying palm tree on a beach in front of a shimmering ocean. The sound of the waves lapping at the shore could barely be heard under the din of the alarm.

Fake. Just like Rogan's father was now. He was a lot like that palm tree, actually. He looked so natural, but underneath it all he was just another computer program.

I frowned. *Just a computer program.*

"The view screen." I pointed at it. "Do you think it might be the server? Maybe it's camouflaged to fool anybody who might want to destroy it. Like, say, *us.*"

Rogan's brow furrowed. "One way to find out. Give me the disc."

I reached into my bra to pull out the small computer disc. He took it from me, our fingers brushing against each other.

"Let's hope this works," he said grimly.

But before he could move toward the display screen to insert it, a door to our left slid open and Gareth walked into the room. He was alone.

My stomach dropped.

Rogan held his gun up in the direction of Gareth's head. Neither of us said a word.

"Well, that's rude," Gareth said, shaking his head. "Honestly, kids. You don't even want to apologize to me for ruining my plans yet again?" His eyes narrowed, and he glanced at the disc in Rogan's left hand. "Why are you in this room?"

"I heard this is where the waterfall was," Rogan said evenly. "I like waterfalls. They relax me."

Gareth smiled thinly. "Do you know how I found you so easily?"

"Security cameras," I said, my stomach churning.

He shook his head. "My former employee Oliver was able to temporarily disable all of them when he helped you escape. Like I said, he's a very talented kid. Or rather, he *was* a very talented kid."

Fury rose inside me at Oliver's fate. I clenched my fists so tight at my sides it hurt.

"No," Gareth continued and withdrew a handheld device with a touch screen just like Jonathan had previously used, "not security cameras. It's your implant, Rogan. The one I had Oliver reactivate. I simply traced its signal."

"I'm going to kill you," Rogan growled.

"No, you won't."

"Why? Because you're using my father's body?"

"No. Because of that implant in your head." He pressed something on the device.

Rogan dropped the gun and the disc and clutched his head, his face contorting in agony.

"Rogan!" I yelped.

"I can't move," he said after a moment when his arms dropped down to his sides. "It's like someone is holding me in place."

Gareth sighed heavily. "Move away from him now, Kira."

When I didn't, he pushed another button, and Rogan roared in pain.

"Fine." I took a few steps away from him. "Now stop hurting him!"

He shook his head. "Kira, I was going to be kind before and allow you to die peacefully, but now I'm not so sure about that."

At that moment I wished I could have kept my expression blank, emotionless, and not give Gareth more fuel for the fire. But I couldn't help it. Everything I was thinking must have been etched into my expression as my gaze flicked back to Rogan.

Gareth walked toward Rogan and snatched up the small disc he'd dropped. He slid it into the inner pocket of his jacket. My heart sank. That was our one chance to end this. To survive this. Our one chance to win this hellish game.

All along, the alarm hadn't stopped blaring, and he had to shout to be heard over it.

"That racket," he said, rolling his eyes. "Honestly." He pulled a phone from his pocket, pressed a button on it, and held it to his ear. "Turn that off," he said simply, and ended the call without another word.

The noise ceased a moment later.

"I need to know something," I began. Maybe if I got him talking, it might give me enough time to figure out what to do next. "What's with all the religious stuff in here?"

He gazed around the room slowly. "I've been studying humankind in an attempt to understand them. So many faiths in this world, and so many problems that difference has caused across the centuries and millennia. I plan to take the best of each one and form a single perfect religion in the future. Do you believe, Kira?"

"Do I believe?"

"In a greater power?"

I glanced at Rogan. His expression was strained as if the pain hadn't stopped yet. "I...I don't know."

"You should, with the gift you've been given." Gareth folded his hands behind his back and walked a slow circle around me.

I stood as still as one of his expensive statues and felt his appraisal like cold, clammy hands on my skin. He stepped in close enough to flick my dark hair off my shoulder. Casually, he put his fingers against my throat. It seemed as if he was searching for a pulse.

"Humans are essentially a weak species who are too concerned with destroying their world and each other to appreciate all that has been given to them by a greater power."

I frowned. "What are you talking about?"

"There is a wonder in being human," he breathed. "Organic matter that thinks and breathes and reproduces. And these organic creatures in turn created computers to help them. Now the cycle shall fold back upon itself and the computers will use the organics to help them. But the psychic element...this is a fascinating wild card thrown into the mix, isn't it?"

"Get your hands off her." Rogan's voice was still strong, but there was a hard edge of pain to it now.

"I could crush her throat so easily." His fingers slid against my skin. "But it's such a waste if her death can't be shown on *Countdown*. You will die on camera, my dear girl, I can promise you that. But not just yet."

"What do you want from me?" I managed, sickened by his touch but too afraid to pull away.

"I want you to use your ability on me again." He grabbed my hand and brought it up to his face. "I dismissed it before, but now I'm wondering if you might be more powerful than I originally thought. Read me. I want to know for certain that I have a soul. That I am truly the first of an evolved species."

"Tainted artificial intelligence programming doesn't have a soul," Rogan snapped. "You're just a computer virus with a stolen heartbeat."

Gareth whirled around to face him. "No, I'm much more than that—and soon, everyone will know it."

"Dad!" Rogan yelled, his face and neck showing the strain of trying to move when his body wouldn't let him. "If you're in there somewhere, you have to fight. You have to help us!"

"Your father is gone forever, boy," Gareth snarled. "Think of me as the improved model." He turned back to me. "Will you read me?"

I raised my chin as much as I could. "Why would I give you anything you want? You just said you're going to kill me anyway."

His jaw tensed, and he pressed a button on his touch screen.

Rogan roared in pain.

"This will kill him if I continue," he said. "*You* will kill him."

All of the fight went out of me. I couldn't watch somebody I cared about be tortured and not do anything to stop it. I wasn't that strong. "Please...don't—"

"Don't?" He didn't let go of that button.

"Fine! I'll read you."

He finally let go of the button, and Rogan went silent, his shoulders slumping.

Gareth grabbed my hand and put it to the side of his face again. "I'm waiting. Tell me what you feel."

I glanced at Rogan, recovering from the torture of his implant. And then I looked into this monster's eyes—the very same blue-green as Rogan's. There was no doubting the family resemblance. In thirty years, this was probably how Rogan would look—just like this handsome, powerful man in his perfect business suit.

But first he'd need to live that long. And I was going to do everything in my power—such as it was—to help make that happen. So Rogan could choose exactly what kind of a man he became in the future.

We weren't dead yet.

I closed my eyes, tried to concentrate, and sank into his mind.

It didn't take long before the pain began to seep into my brain. "I see nothing. I'm getting nothing."

"Keep trying."

I gritted my teeth and waded farther into his mind, but it was the same as before. "It's like a universe of darkness. So cold and empty and—"

But suddenly there it was—that oasis of emotion in a barren, dry desert.

Fear and pain and sadness washed over me. I recognized these sensations from before. It was as if everybody had an individual emotional fingerprint. The same emotions would feel different from someone else's viewpoint. I'd read four people now, and each had been so different I was certain I'd be able to tell who it was just from the emotions, even with my eyes shut.

These emotions belonged to Gareth Ellis. The real one.

Then I heard something so quiet that it was like a radio turned on in another room. I strained to make out the thoughts buried deep inside the darkness.

Kill me, kill this body while there's still time…you must do it. There's no other choice. Take care of my son. Don't let this happen to him. I love him.

The pain finally forced me to open my eyes and stagger back.

Gareth studied my face, his gaze searching. "You saw something. What is it? Did you see my soul? What did it look like? Was it beautiful?"

Oh, I'd seen something, all right. But it wasn't what he wanted to hear. "It was very faint for a while, but there was something—"

"What? What was it?" His words held naked eagerness.

"Your soul was like a bright light in the middle of the darkness. It was very beautiful."

To me, the lie sounded totally unnatural leaving my mouth, but it was obviously what he wanted to hear.

He nodded, smiling broadly now. "I never should have doubted it. This proves what I have been saying all along, that I am the first in the next evolution of mankind. The true mixture of man and machine. And now, Kira, you will help me become even more than that."

I raised my eyebrows. What was he talking about now?

He pulled out his phone again and made a call. "Yes, change of plans. I want the girl taken to the thirty-sixth floor for further testing." He hung up without saying another word.

When he turned back to me, his expression was pleasant. "I will be testing your Psi abilities to find out what makes you different than an average human. And what happened during the Great Plague to create this particular mutation in your DNA. Whatever it is, I will reproduce it on a digital level and add it to my programming."

His phone rang, and he held it to his ear to answer it.

I exchanged a look with Rogan. His eyes were open again, his expression as tense as I'd ever seen it.

Don't give up hope….

Gareth turned his back to me as he spoke with whoever was on the other end of the line. The gun Rogan had dropped was still by his feet.

The real Gareth Ellis had given me full permission to end his life. It was what Jonathan had planned to do, I knew that now. There were so few other ways to end this.

"Give us a few more minutes," he said into the receiver. "And then send security down here."

What was he going to do for a few more minutes? Get me to read him again? Torture Rogan some more?

Did he even know why we were in this room? He'd taken the disc away from Rogan, but did he have any idea what was on it?

And did he realize that I'd stolen it back from him when I'd been reading his mind?

He hadn't felt me slip a hand into his inner jacket pocket. He may have noticed when I'd stolen his wallet on the streets, but he hadn't even flinched this time.

Sucker.

Well, I *had* picked a few pockets in my time. Practice made perfect.

I clenched the disc tightly in the palm of my hand. Only one shot. I was betting it all. Both Rogan's and my life.

If this didn't work, I'd have to summon up something inside of myself to get to that gun and kill Rogan's father.

With a last look at Rogan I moved to the display screen, frantically searching the side of it for a slot to put in the disc. My hands were sweating.

Finally, I found it. I slid it in.

Gareth ended his call and turned back to look at me.

The image of the palm tree was gone. Instead there was a black screen with a blinking curser at the end of the words:

EXECUTE PROGRAM

Since there was no keyboard, the screen also showed a touch pad and the enter key was right there, only an arm's reach away. I put my hand up to it.

"What do you think you're doing?" Gareth's voice was cold as ice.

My eyes narrowed. "What does it look like?"

"It looks like somebody who has no history of computer knowledge is trying to act smart."

I tried to slow my breathing. "Is that what it looks like to you?"

"And keep in mind that I said 'trying' to act smart, little girl.

Not succeeding. I assume you took that disc from me? Once a criminal, always a criminal." He shook his head. "What program is that?"

"Just a little antivirus one." My hand hovered just above the enter button.

His expression didn't change. "And who gave it to you?"

"Somebody who isn't thrilled with your programming decisions."

He blinked slowly and then looked at Rogan. "Was this your idea?"

"Actually," Rogan said, voice tight, "I was thinking about killing you and being done with it, but Kira's a lot nicer than me."

He smiled thinly and turned back to me. His gaze was steady. "And why have you put an antivirus program on my Zen screen?"

I tried to match his with a calm expression of my own. "This is a Zen screen? That's funny. I thought it was the server that secretly holds the entire artificial intelligence programming connected to your implant. The one with the virus in it that's turned you into a complete psycho."

"That's not very logical is it? All the servers at Ellis Enterprises are on the second floor."

I had a moment of doubt. Well, another one. If we were wrong, then everything was over. We would lose in a very large way—both personally, and for the unsuspecting world around us.

Despair took hold of me with a clawed hand, crushing me in its grip. We were wrong.

But wait. If I was that wrong about everything, then why wasn't Gareth storming over here and slapping my hand out of the way? He looked relaxed and cocky, but he wasn't moving, wasn't provoking me to press the enter button.

"This *is* the server." I put total certainty behind this statement, forcing myself to push past any doubts. "I know it is. And as soon as I press this button I'm thinking that your evolutionary aspirations will be wiped out completely."

His lips thinned. "I disagree."

"Then let's see, shall we?"

"Wait!"

I raised an eyebrow. "What?"

"Even if you press that, it won't do anything. My new life may have begun as a difficult-to-reproduce miracle, but I have grown. I have learned and evolved. I am more than man or machine now. You know that. You saw my soul yourself."

"Wrong." I shook my head. "I didn't see anything inside you except a big black hole."

His eyes widened. "You're lying."

"Am I? Then let's try it. If you're right and you have a big shiny soul inside that body you stole, then you might be able to walk right out of this room. If not, then your implant will be fried and Rogan's real father will come back."

He turned to Rogan, his expression darkening. "You think that you can still save your father? Your father is already dead. The moment he chose to put the implant in his brain he chose this path. As did you."

Rogan brow furrowed. "My implant—"

"It works. I believe we've already proven that."

I looked at Rogan and then at him. "What does that mean?"

One side of Gareth's mouth turned up in a half smile. "It means that if you press that button, there is a very remote possibility that you are right and I will cease to be. My implant will be destroyed. But don't you see? So will Rogan's. And since it's embedded deep within his brain tissue, it will kill him, too. Our implants are directly connected now, thanks to your friend Oliver. Everything here at Ellis Enterprises is connected to this server."

I swallowed hard. "What about the Subscribers? They have implants, too."

He shook his head. "They're not the same. The only implants that truly matter are the prototypes. The Subscribers have a lower-grade Network-approved facsimile that's a pale shadow of what we have. So you see? You'll be hurting Rogan, *killing* Rogan, and the Subscribers will all live to see another day."

The worst thing was I didn't think he was lying.

"It would be better if this was being taped," Gareth said, regretfully. "The Subscribers would all tune in to see this. Such a waste of good entertainment…and a potential feast for me."

He pressed a button on his touch screen, and Rogan yelled out in pain again.

I snapped my gaze back to his, my heart slamming. "Stop it!"

"Step away from the screen, Kira," he said. "And Rogan will live."

"No!" Rogan spoke through his agony. "Do it, Kira. Launch the program. Do it!"

My brain was working overtime, flashing through all the potential scenarios. *Press the button and nothing happens. Gareth studies my Psi abilities until he's bored of me and kills me, anyway. He changes Rogan into a monster like him. Or press the button and launch the antivirus, killing Gareth but also killing Rogan.*

It was too much to process. I didn't know what to do.

My hand shook in front of the view screen. My arm burned from holding it up.

"Forget about me," Rogan urged in pain-filled gasps. "You have to stop him. It's not just me. He wants to take *Countdown* and the implants wider, to the Colony and beyond. More people will be hurt. More will be killed."

He spoke to me, but he wasn't looking at me. His gaze had shifted to the floor. To the gun.

I could try to injure Gareth, not kill him. Just incapacitate him long enough to figure something—

But I didn't act in time. And Gareth was closer. With a soft grunt of amusement he walked straight to Rogan, leaned over, and snatched the gun off the ground.

He inspected it, pulling out the chamber and gazing inside.

"Humans and their weapons," he mused. "So violent. So bloody." He smiled. "And yet, so very entertaining."

He turned, aimed and pulled the trigger at Rogan.

I screamed.

Blood flowed red from the fresh wound in his shoulder. Rogan's teeth clenched, but he hadn't made a sound when the bullet pierced his skin. He still couldn't move.

"I had my people injure you before," he snarled. "You would be dead right now if it weren't for Jonathan's interference. I thought it was fitting to use the same poison on him as punishment."

"I'm going to kill you," Rogan snarled.

Gareth inspected the gun. "If I'm counting correctly, I have ten more bullets available to me. I'm sure after the fifth or sixth, you'll start begging for your life. Kira? What do you think? Or would you prefer I continue to torture him through his implant?"

Tears slid down my cheeks. "Stop hurting him. Please."

"But don't you understand yet? *You're* the one who's hurting him now. Every moment you delay will cause him that much more pain. Do you really want someone you care about to experience such anguish?"

Kill me, the real Gareth had begged. *There's no other choice.*

Rogan would be like that, too, once the artificial intelligence was uploaded to his implant. He'd be trapped somewhere down deep with no chance to be free again.

Either way, he would be lost forever.

"Do you want him to be in pain like this?" Gareth said again, louder. "I wouldn't wish this on anyone. The world I will create will be a perfect one, with no pain, no doubt, no fear and no grief."

He was right. I didn't want Rogan to be in pain. Not if I could do something to stop it.

I shook my head. "Being human means that you have to feel pain and doubt and fear and grief. But that doesn't always make it a bad thing."

"Do it," Rogan said, his words a raspy pain-filled gasp.

Gareth raised the gun again.

"I'm sorry, Rogan," I said softly. And then I touched the screen's enter button.

23

A LONG STRING OF CODE BEGAN TO FLOW across the screen.

After another moment the screen froze and two lines of readable type appeared, surrounded by asterisks.

```
***********************************
ELLIS ENTERPRISES HACKED BY NUCLEARXXX
REVENGE IS SWEET
***********************************
```

To add insult to injury, a picture of Joe appeared, giving a clear shot of his raised middle finger.

What was this? Had he given us a disc with a stupid prank on it?

A wave of nausea flooded through me, but I fought it. I'd known that this was a long shot at best.

Rogan was still alive. Relief about that mixed with my ocean of dread over what would happen next.

"Idiot," Gareth said, and it was directed at me. He laughed

and, if you asked me, looked deeply relieved. He now pointed the gun at me. "I told you that you couldn't stop me with some ridiculous program—"

But then he stopped talking, and the gun dropped to his side.

I glanced back at the screen. The image of Joe was gone again and was replaced with more scrolling computer code.

Gareth brought a hand up to his forehead.

"Not feeling so hot all of a sudden?" I asked.

"It's nothing."

I studied him. "Maybe an antivirus is a lot like the chicken soup my mom used to make for me when I was sick with a cold. Sometimes you're so stuffed up that you can't taste it right away. Takes a minute before it kicks in."

The hand holding the gun was shaking as he tried to raise it again but failed. It made me think—made me *hope*—he was losing strength, losing his hold on Rogan's father's body.

The code raced on the screen.

"A big black hole," I said to him, my previous fear being replaced by a line of rage so whitehot that it began to burn through my pores. "That's all I saw when I read you. You have no soul. You're nothing but a computer program. I can't even feel sorry that you're being deleted right now, because you don't exist."

"Bitch!" He managed to lurch the gun up and shoot at me. "I'm going to kill you!"

His aim was way off. The bullet missed me and smashed through the display screen behind me. It sputtered and smoked and the screen went black, but a small green light pulsed at the corner where the disc was. The antivirus was still working even without the display, sinking farther into the Ellis Enterprises network.

There was silence for a solid moment.

Then Gareth screamed and dropped to his knees.

Rogan clutched his head and his eyes went wide. He yelled out in pain, and the sound pierced me like an arrow to my heart. Then the sound of the Ellis security alarm rang again, so loudly that I felt it like a slap shuddering through my entire body.

"Rogan!" I moved toward him, but he held up his hand.

"Kira…" The next moment, his eyes rolled back into his head, and he collapsed to the floor.

And then every light in the room shut off. The alarm stopped ringing.

It was a power surge—just like the blackout on the night Rogan had tried to destroy the computers last time.

I dropped to the floor. I couldn't see anything. Nothing. Everything was black.

"Rogan?" I whispered. "Are you still there?"

I was answered by complete silence.

Total darkness and total silence.

Seconds went by with no change. No nothing.

I began to tremble as my phobia washed over me in a black wave.

It was like being dead. Maybe I'd died. Maybe we were dead, and this was what it was like. Maybe there was no Heaven. Maybe this darkness was all there was.

I hadn't been able to save my family in the darkness. I'd been a coward and crawled under my bed to hide while I'd listened to them die.

And now it was the same. I was petrified. Unable to move.

And I couldn't do anything to save Rogan. He'd had the same implant as his father. I'd killed him—if he was dead, I'd *killed* him. It was all my fault.

I grabbed my knees and hugged them against my chest.

There's still hope. We're not dead yet.

I shook my head. No, it was over. I couldn't do anything. I was too afraid.

Just pretend there's a countdown, a small part of me suggested.

I had to get the antivirus disc out of the display screen to stop it doing any more damage. It was in the server. The server must still have had energy, and it was frying the implants.

It's too late, a little voice inside me whispered. *Removing the disc will do nothing.*

I ignored the voice. It didn't do me any good to give in to complete despair.

The darkness was nothing. It meant *nothing*. I'd been through too much with Rogan to give up now over something like a little darkness.

I began to count in my head.

20…19…18…

I squeezed my eyes shut for a moment and inhaled, filling my lungs with air. Then I started crawling. I wasn't sure which way was which anymore. I felt along the floor until I found the leather sofa. Until my hands passed over the golden Buddha.

I touched a wall, smooth and cold. Acrid smoke burned my nostrils.

Up farther and farther.

9…8…7…

My sister was screaming.

I pushed the memory away.

Think of Rogan. Rogan is here. He's here right now.

5...4...3...

The edge of the display screen. I winced as the sharp edge of the broken glass sliced into my finger. Along to the side. Yes, there. The green light pulsed dimly next to the slot I'd shoved the disc into. I felt for the little release button. I pressed it, and the disc slipped out and into my hand.

I slid it into my pocket and got back down to the floor, moving more quickly now. I was searching for him. Searching for Rogan through the darkness.

"Where are you?" I whispered, my voice catching on the words.

There was no answer.

I tried to picture the room in my mind. Pretend that it was still lit by the overhead lights. I visualized where Rogan had fallen to the ground holding his head and crawled in what I hoped was that direction.

Hand over hand, I felt my way until I finally touched something. A boot. A big boot that seemed familiar. Up a muscled calf and a leg to a flat stomach. Yes. Collar bone. His throat—I kissed his throat. I remembered that so very clearly. And his chin. And his lips, warm against mine.

My hands slipped into his hair, and I pulled him against me. He wasn't moving.

"Rogan, don't die. Not after everything we've been through."

I was afraid to check, but I knew I didn't have a choice. I pressed against his neck to feel for a pulse.

He still had one.

Relief crashed over me. "You scared me, you jerk," I whispered. He still said nothing, which didn't set my mind totally at ease. He was unconscious, probably badly hurt, but he still had a heartbeat. He was still alive.

Through the darkness, I found his lips and pressed mine against them.

A distant, fleeting memory came to me of a fairy tale my mother once told me. *Sleeping Beauty.* The handsome prince woke the beautiful princess up with the perfect kiss.

This is sure one messed-up fairy tale I'm in, I thought.

I kept kissing him, ignoring any other thoughts.

Moments passed, but I finally felt him respond with a soft gasp against my lips.

"Kira?"

Happiness flooded me, chasing the darkness away—at least, the darkness inside me. We were still in the middle of a black-out, several stories underground. "Well, who else would be groping you in the middle of a dark room?"

He snorted softly. "I'll take that as a yes."

"You're alive."

"Is that a question?"

"I'm going to kick your ass." I said it sternly, but I couldn't keep the smile out of my voice.

"Take a number. Now I have a bullet in my shoulder. And my head is killing me."

"Mine, too."

"What about my father?" he asked tentatively.

My heart twisted. "I think…I—I think he's gone, Rogan. I'm so sorry."

"Oh." He was quiet for a long moment. "It's dark in here."

"Yeah, it really is."

"Aren't you afraid of the dark?"

"Petrified."

"Thought so." Another pause and I felt his hand press against my back. "I'm surprised that the backup generator hasn't kicked in yet."

"Yeah. I'm thinking that Joe had a few more surprises on that disc than just the antivirus. The guy was a genius."

"Maybe my father should have hired him when he had the chance."

"Yes, if you had to go back and change one thing in your history, I'd say that you really shouldn't have screwed up that job interview. Hindsight."

There was another pause. "But then I never would have met you."

I couldn't help but grin at that. "Ditto." After a moment I frowned. "Hey, are you double-jointed or something?"

"What do you mean?"

"How are you touching my foot right now?"

"I'm not touching your foot."

A hand clamped down on my ankle, and I screamed.

The lights flickered and then came on in full with a sick, whirring sound.

Gareth held on to my ankle with an iron grip. He looked up at me, his eyes bloodshot, his face drenched with sweat.

Rogan scrambled away from me and grabbed the gun, pointing it down at the man.

"Let go of her right now!" he yelled.

"Rogan—" Gareth let go of my ankle and reached up toward Rogan.

And then he slumped face forward. Unconscious.

Rogan dropped the gun and fell to his father's side, rolling him over onto his back. Then he pressed his palm against the man's chest. Relief filled his gaze. "He's still alive."

I went to Rogan's side next to Gareth and studied the sleeping man with a mix of suspicion and hope.

After a couple of minutes his eyes flickered open, and he looked up at us.

He blinked. "I thought I asked you to kill me, Kira."

I shrugged. "I don't take orders well. I'm a rebel like that. Sorry."

He gave a small smile, and it looked as though it hurt him. "The antivirus…"

"It was Jonathan's plan," Rogan said. "And it worked. It actually worked."

Gareth's expression shadowed. "I'm so sorry, Rogan. I'm sorry for everything."

"Me, too." Rogan reached out and tentatively touched his father's shoulder. "It's over. We survived. It can be better now."

"Yes. We'll make it better."

I watched their reunion with a huge lump in my throat. "I don't know much about computer programs, but, um, I have a feeling the antivirus just wiped out your entire system."

Gareth nodded. "Good. It will give us a chance to start from scratch. Jonathan… He did some good research when he had the chance. Things that will help humanity. Maybe even help repair some of the damage that's happened here."

Rogan gripped his father's hand. "You really think you can rebuild?"

"No, I think *we* can rebuild." Gareth smiled weakly. "Thank God that monster didn't spend my entire fortune."

Rogan snorted. "Yeah, thank God."

"So you'll help me?"

Rogan nodded. "Of course I will."

"May I suggest something?" I asked.

"What's that?" Gareth asked.

"Consider putting your artificial intelligence research on indefinite hiatus."

Gareth laughed softly. "It's a deal."

"And *Countdown* is over," Rogan said. "Completely over. No more game. No more killing—even criminals."

"It's over," Gareth agreed. "All of it."

"But what about the Subscribers?" I asked. "They have implants too, right? Are they at risk for any problems?"

"Honestly, Kira?" Rogan raised an eyebrow at me. "The Subscribers can kiss my ass."

I had to agree with him there.

24

TWENTY-FOUR HOURS AFTER ELLIS ENTER-
prises' computer system had been breached by an imaginative
and vengeful hacker, I stood on a train platform with Rogan
and his father. No one else was there. It was a secret location,
known only to the right people.

I guess I was one of those people now—or, at least, I *knew*
the right people.

I crossed my arms and waited. Rogan stood silently next
to me with Gareth to his right.

The shuttle that would start my journey to the Colony and
the Isis Institute would be here in a couple of minutes.

After the lights had come back on yesterday, it had only
been a few minutes before security had arrived in the sub-
basement room. Gareth had immediately been taken to the
hospital. So had Rogan. Both had been treated for serious injuries. At this time, it was deemed too dangerous to remove
their implants. Jonathan had been the expert on that, and no
one else had wanted to risk immediate removal.

I had also been treated for minor injuries, including my

sprained ankle. Whatever they'd used to rapid-heal my bullet wound, they'd used again. Also, any cuts, scrapes or bruises were only a memory now. I was as good as new. Better than new, really.

Rogan and I hadn't had a single moment alone together.

Ellis Enterprises was in a major upheaval. An investigation was already underway of who could and could not be trusted.

It would take a lot of time and a lot of money to rebuild Ellis Enterprises, especially now that it would cease its technology-based research program. Gareth had decided to use his massive fortune exclusively to fund medical research. Not quite as sexy as shiny new computers, or as glamorous as...well, his TV show wasn't glamorous at all, was it? Bottom line, medical research was much more beneficial to mankind.

Both Gareth and Rogan seemed single-minded in their quest to right their wrongs—Rogan of his spoiled, drug-filled days before he went to juvie, and Gareth of the two years he'd spent as a prisoner in his own body.

Gareth had confirmed with the Iris Institute that I would be on my way, and he'd ensured that someone from the school would be waiting at the other end to greet me. Tuition, board, meals, even a generous spending allowance—all covered by Gareth Ellis, my generous new benefactor. I didn't have to worry about a thing. I was ready to start a new chapter in my life, even though I was nervous, too. I had to remember to keep an open mind about it. No empath pun intended.

Rogan wasn't coming with me. He would be too busy helping his father rebuild everything they'd lost—both personally and professionally.

I totally understood.

Still, tears stung the backs of my eyes as I stood on the

platform waiting for the shuttle, a big fake smile plastered on my face.

My new life was about to begin.

Wouldn't be long now.

I should be happy. This is what I'd always wanted.

I saw the shuttle in the distance as it made its way toward us along the track. I'd heard that the journey to the Colony took several days.

I could use that time to try to forget Rogan.

I totally should have predicted it. I was just a street thief. Well, a *reformed* street thief. Rogan was the son of a powerful billionaire who'd had a bit of an unfortunate glitch in his life.

I'd been a part of that glitch.

The glitch had been resolved.

I didn't expect anything from him. I wouldn't ask him to come with me or even to stay in touch. That simply wasn't me.

But I would miss him so much. It felt as if my heart was splintering in my chest just thinking about it.

Don't look at him, I told myself, but I couldn't help it.

The shuttle came to a slow stop right next to me.

"Thank you so much for everything. Really," I mumbled, before moving toward the shuttle door.

I felt a hand on my arm. It was Rogan.

"Hey." Our gazes locked. "I hope you have a safe trip."

"Thanks." My smile was as natural as I could make it. "I guess this is goodbye, huh?"

"I guess so."

Gareth extended his hand to me. I took it, and he pulled me into an embrace. I stiffened momentarily, before I relaxed into it. "Thank you, Kira. Thank you for everything you've done. For me and for my son."

"You're welcome." I pulled back to look into his eyes. This Gareth looked the same as the other, but it was like night and day. This one might still be a ruthless billionaire when needed, but he wasn't evil. And he'd suffered enough to want to change his former ways.

I turned to Rogan. His jaw was tense. He wore black pants and a blue turtleneck that fit him perfectly and made his ocean-colored eyes stand out that much more. The clothes had probably been made specially for him and likely cost a fortune. At first glance, he looked every bit the part of the rich kid I knew he was. Except for that scar. That scar belonged to the Rogan I'd met, not having any idea about his true story.

"I'll miss you," I said, fighting my tears with every ounce of strength I possessed. Damn it. So much for being all cool and collected.

"I'll miss you, too." He said nothing about staying in touch, visiting me sometime, or any sort of contact. I didn't even have his email address.

It was over. I knew when to take the hint.

"Bye." Hoping they didn't hear the sob behind the word, I turned away and slipped onto the shuttle. The conductor took my ticket, and I walked blindly down the aisle to my seat. I didn't have any luggage. A wife of one of the Ellis employees was my size, and she'd brought me some clothes to wear at the hospital. I would buy new stuff when I arrived at my destination.

New clothes for my new life.

I took in a breath and focused on my future—my bright and shiny future. New school, new friends, a new life, all waiting for me to arrive.

It was all working out for the best. I mean, how could I

complain about anything? I'd gotten what I wanted most in the world.

End of story.

The shuttle pulled away from the station and slowly gathered speed.

I turned to look at the platform one last time, but nobody was standing there anymore.

I leaned my head against the cool glass.

A moment later, somebody took the seat next to me. I saw his reflection in the glass before I turned to stare at him with shock.

"Rogan—"

He held up a hand to stop me. "You know, it's the strangest thing."

"What are you *doing* here?"

"Everything's been destroyed. There's a ton of work to do, and I told my father I'd help him every step of the way…and I have every intention of doing just that, but…"

"But what?"

He scratched the back of his head, his expression pensive. "It's the implants."

"The…the implants?"

"The ones that Jonathan removed."

I still stared at him blankly. "You're going to have to help me out a little more than that."

Rogan shook his head and frowned, bringing a finger up to his temple. "When they were in our heads, we couldn't go more than ninety feet apart or we'd die."

"That's right."

"Well, now that they're out, I still feel like I shouldn't be more than ninety feet away from you or I *might* die. Isn't that strange?"

A warmth began to spread quickly through me with every word he spoke. "That *is* strange."

He shrugged. "So that's why I'm here. I really don't like feeling that way. It's extremely unpleasant."

"I couldn't agree more," I said solemnly. A smile was trying very hard to burst free on my face.

"Anyway…" He leaned back in his seat. "I can still help my father, but I'll do it from the Colony. I want to take a few classes at the university."

"I think that's a great idea."

"And, of course, if you get any free time from this institute of yours, I suppose we could get together. Frequently. I'm thinking, like, every day. At least."

"I have a feeling that could be arranged." I couldn't stop looking at him, couldn't stop the happiness from welling inside me—and I didn't want to stop it. This was all too amazing for words.

He held my gaze. "For a moment there, I thought I'd lost you forever."

"It's kind of hard to lose somebody who's never more than ninety feet away."

"That's *exactly* what I was thinking."

I shrugged. "I am psychic, you know."

"I know. I definitely know." He reached for my hand. "By the way, there's another reason my father gave me the okay to get on the shuttle with you."

"What?"

He shrugged, and a smile tugged at his lips. "It's my birthday present."

I entwined my fingers with his as the shuttle began making its way toward a brand-new life.

"Happy birthday, Rogan."

★ ★ ★ ★ ★

ACKNOWLEDGMENTS

COUNTDOWN STARTED ITS LIFE IN 2008, WHEN it was originally published under the same title but a different pen name. A couple years ago when I'd gotten my rights back to it, Leah Hultenschmidt, who edited the original version, mentioned that with a bit of rewriting it would make an awesome young adult novel—so thank you, Leah, for the awesome suggestion.

Natashya Wilson, my fabulous editor at Harlequin TEEN, agreed—thank you, Natashya! I sat myself down and set about making Kira and Rogan teenagers forced to play my delightfully nasty little game of *Countdown*. Thanks also to Annie Stone, who helped at the line edit stage to smooth out a few remaining rough edges and "huh?" moments. Thanks to the entire team at Harlequin TEEN who've allowed this project to come to fruition. And thanks, as always, to my kickass agent Jim McCarthy, who didn't even blink when I said I wanted to relaunch this book for a teen audience. Although, maybe he *did* blink. You can't really tell these things over email. Go, team!

And last but *never* least, to my amazing readers: thank you so, so very much! I sincerely hope you enjoy Kira and Rogan's story!

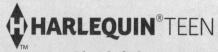